EL GRITO DEL BRONX
AND OTHER PLAYS

By

Migdalia Cruz

NoPassport Press
Dreaming the Americas Series

NoPassport Press Dreaming the Americas Series
First edition 2010 by NoPassport Press
PO Box 1786, South Gate, CA 90280 USA; -
NoPassportPress@aol.com

ISBN: 978-0-578-04992-2

No Passport is a Pan-American theatre alliance & press devoted to live, virtual and print action, advocacy, and change toward the fostering of cross-cultural diversity in the arts with an emphasis on the embrace of the hemispheric spirit in US Latina/o and Latin-American theatre-making.

NoPassport Press' Theatre & Performance PlayTexts Series and its Dreaming the Americas Series promotes new writing for the stage, texts on theory and practice, and theatrical translations.

More titles from NoPassport Press

Antigone Project: A Play in Five Parts
by Tanya Barfield, Karen Hartman, Chiori Miyagawa, Lynn Nottage and Caridad
Svich, with preface by Lisa Schlesinger, introduction by Marianne McDonald;
ISBN 978-0-578-03150-7

Amparo Garcia-Crow: The South Texas Plays
(*Cocks Have Claws and Wings to Fly, Under a Western Sky, The Faraway Nearby,
Esmeralda Blue*) **Preface by Octavio Solis; ISBN: 978-0-578-01913-0**

Anne Garcia-Romero: Collected Plays
(*Earthquake Chica, Santa Concepcion, Mary Peabody in Cuba*)
Preface by Juliette Carrillo; ISBN: 978-0-6151-8888-1

John Jesurun: Deep Sleep, White Water, Black Maria –
A Media Trilogy **Preface by Fiona Templeton; ISBN: 978-0-578-02602-2**

Lorca: Six Major Plays
(*Blood Wedding, Dona Rosita, The House of Bernarda Alba, The Public, The Shoemaker's
Prodigious Wife, Yerma*) **In new translations by Caridad Svich, Preface by James
Leverett, introduction by Amy Rogoway; ISBN: 978-0-578-00221-7**

Matthew Maguire: Three Plays
(*The Tower, Luscious Music, The Desert*) **Preface by Naomi Wallace; ISBN: 978-0-
578-00856-1**

Oliver Mayer: Collected Plays
(*Conjunto, Joe Louis Blues, Ragged Time*) **Preface by Luis Alfaro, Introduction by
Jon D. Rossini; ISBN: 978-0-6151-8370-1**

Alejandro Morales: Collected Plays
(*expat/inferno, marea, Sebastian*); **ISBN: 978-0-6151-8621-4**

12 Ophelias (a play with broken songs) by Caridad Svich
ISBN: 978-0-6152-4918-6

NoPassport is a sponsored project of Fractured Atlas, a non-profit arts service
organization. Contributions in behalf of [Caridad Svich & NoPassport] may be
made payable to Fractured Atlas and are tax-deductible to the extent permitted
by law. **For online donations go directly to**
https://www.fracturedatlas.org/donate/2623

Contents

Introduction:
"I don't consciously set out to write about blood"
Alberto Sandoval-Sánchez

4

The Plays:

Afterword
"My World Made Real"
Priscilla Page

479

Notes on Contributors
491

Endnotes
495

"I don't consciously set out to write about blood"[i]

Latina playwright Migdalia Cruz, a daughter of the Puerto Rican diaspora in New York City, has claimed that she is from another country, not Puerto Rico, nor the United States: "[M]y country is really the Bronx. I'm a Nuyorican, so my work always reflects that search for home. It's about not being at home on the island and not feeling at home in America. The people I write about are always in search of home."[ii] In her theatre world she makes her audiences dwell in the dangerous streets and humble apartments of the South Bronx. For American audiences, the infamous urban territory with the background of burnt out buildings is safe only at a distance in the movies. <u>Fort Apache, the Bronx</u> (1981), a crime drama film, can be seen as a primary stereotypical motion picture that perpetuates the dreadful visual imagery of the South Bronx—a war zone where gang violence, racism, and poverty rule and a wasteland where the American Dream spins downward into a nightmare. Cruz aims at deconstructing the dominant stereotypes that dehumanize the Puerto Rican and African American communities where she grew up. Her playwriting not only historicizes her birthplace and heritage but explores the humanity and emotions *de su gente*. Her characters are far from simply being a disenfranchised, unemployable, lumpen population in statistics. Play after play, Cruz tells everything about *el barrio*: the good, the bad, and *lo feo*. She takes audiences to the darkest places to unveil the anguish and dreams of lost souls in their heroic survival. In order to make sense of the "bad neighborhood," her characters embark on a mournful search for home. Cruz mourns the place of origin in the Caribbean where she was not born. She as well mourns the South Bronx as a community of survivors.

Cruz short circuits any notion of a home located in the realm of nostalgia. Her journey is the reverse of Dorothy's easy formula in <u>The Wizard of Oz</u> of clicking her ruby red shoes with the pronouncement of the magical formula "there is no place like home." Cruz complicates the return home because Nuyoricans, who were not born and raised on the island, nor speak Spanish fluently, are exiled from the colonized nation. On top of that, the continual awareness of not feeling at home in America haunts them. The issue here is belonging, as she says: "I think that all Puerto Ricans who live in the United States have to redefine home for themselves, particularly a cultural home because they don't have a country. I mean, their country is something that becomes foreign to them, and yet it's in the bones. So how do you reconcile that dichotomy?"[iii] If "home is where your heart is," then how can Cruz negotiate such a contradiction? She uses memory, which is the rightful maneuver to head home. As Tennessee Williams said in The Glass Menagerie, "for memory is seated predominantly in the heart."[iv]

Cruz rationalizes her journey out of the Bronx in affective terms: "So… You can take the girl out of the South Bronx – but you would have to cut my heart out to make me forget."[v] She refuses to forget the "tough place" where she came from. And, she is willing to die for those memories. The heart is the source of life and the site of heartbreaking memories as well. As long as Cruz is alive, she will write from the heart. And, through acts of sentimental re-membering, her theatre complies with what Tennessee Williams calls "memory play."(29) Finding a home for those diasporic memories requires to tell the truth and to speak from the heart. No matter how visceral and brutal, how bloody and abject life is, Cruz is doing what her teacher and mentor María Irene Fornés told her to do: "Until I met Irene and studied with her for five years, I couldn't tell the truth about who I was and where I came from. If it weren't for Irene, I would never have written because I never would have felt entitled to my voice."[vi] Re-touching, re-visiting, and re-covering the past in all its darkness entails a memory trip fuelled with blood and lived in the flesh that is deeply rooted in her childhood experiences of the South Bronx.

Not willing to forget, Cruz dares to write it all down. She stresses over and over again that the primal scene for her writing is the traumatic witnessing of the killing of her eight year-old friend who was raped, murdered, and thrown off the roof of her building. The horrific sight of the crime finds its way in her playwriting in the monologue entitled "Sand" in Telling Tales.[vii] The childhood traumatic scene of violence, liable to return as a corporeal symptom, comes back in her work through the imagery of blood. She clearly visualizes the body as a surface that registers given symbolic inscriptions and operates as a conduit for emotional discharge. Indeed, in Cruz's ars poetica the body figures prominently as the site of/for drama: "[I]f you strip a person of all their things, [t]he body is all you'll have. That's when you search for symbols. If you're looking at a naked body and you want to show mourning, you could cover the eyes or pull them out. It depends upon how much pain you're in. How do you make that theatrical? I think the greatest vehicle of an actor is their body: how they use it and what they do to symbolize what the words are saying."[viii] It is not by chance that Cruz chooses mourning as her primary example to elucidate the workings of her artistic praxis. Her theatre ritually showcases bodies in pain, mainly unruly bodies and bare lives. While the playwright exorcizes her own work of mourning bit by bit for what was left behind and for the beloved ones, each theatrical production allows for a letting go. Its bodily expression is the tears that wet her memories, involuntarily erupting in sobs and interrupting her public readings. Given that the characters work through their grief and pain, like the playwright herself, the actors perform on their material bodies the visceral effects of physical and spiritual wounds, pushing the limits of what audiences are accustomed to seeing in theatre: "My characters see only what is under the skin. Each must face the reality of their flesh before freeing their souls."[ix] As a result, Cruz's honesty of saying it all and her insistence on making the body speak in extremis situations have a tremendous impact on the audience both artistically and politically. These are naked bodies and souls in revolt that search for a spiritual healing that will show the path to a place called home: "My characters are in perpetual search for home which to them is a place where they are accepted and have history—a place for friends but also ancestors—and culturally, a search for a place where their soul lives beyond the stagnation of colonization and mainstream American life... I guess that journey which my characters take is inspired by a need for the validation of their cultural identity."[x]

In spite of Cruz's intention to chronicle the Puerto Rican migratory experience and revise the domestic colonial experience *en las entrañas del monstruo*, her work has been criticized for contributing to mobilize oppression and circulate racist stereotypes. From her perspective, Cruz has constantly emphasized that in her plays she explores the people she knows: "[In my work] the stereotype is no longer viewed as good or bad, but a reality with a spiritual journey."(78) She has to straightforwardly address the poverty, violence, criminality, drug trafficking, and homelessness to undo the hegemonic stereotypes; and in doing so, she validates the Nuyorican cultural identity with a dose of self-esteem, dignity, and pride. Cruz's class-consciousness informs her politics of representation, identity, and difference. To write about *su gente* constitutes an act of intervention in the cultural imaginary: "I don't find lawyers and doctors interesting. These are the people I find interesting and poetic, and these are the people I love... In writing about those things, I write hope... I believe in the power of people to heal themselves..."[xi] The Other has the right to cultural and social citizenship. The mastery of self at the hands of the Other is opened to unimaginable and unthinkable possibilities with the radical potential to take a position outside the hegemonic logic of reason and to destabilize the ideological binary constraints through which the Eurocentric Sovereign Self subjects the Other.

***

I first heard about Cruz's work in 1989 when Cuban American playwright Dolores Prida encouraged me to see Touch of an Angel at Duo Theater. She compared the production to a MTV video because of its superimposition of imagery, cinematic-

9

like mode of representation, and music component. <u>Touch of an Angel</u> is a dramatic opera that breaks the silence of incest in a devoted Catholic Latino family. A young woman survives her father's sexual abuse by convincing herself that an angel is the one who comes to her bed. The rape reaches its ultimate outcome when she gives birth to his child. Although I was shocked by Cruz's audacity to blatantly tackle the taboo subject, I was mesmerized with the stylish short fast paced scenes and the poetic dimension of the theatrical production. The refusal of a straightforward sequential development of the plot, the fragmentation of scenes, the intermittent dialogues, the gaps filling in for the unspeakable, the ambiguity of discourse, and the metaphorical modality, all played a part in the manifestation of an alternative way of doing theatre. It was totally different from what Latina/o theatre was all about at the time. It was not magical realism, nor surrealism. It was poetry in motion with a touch of realism that vociferated out loud the horror of incest. The young woman through her imagination managed to survive violence inside the home.

Likewise, in two other plays, Cruz empowers young women with imagination, the only tool to overcome the depraved parental misconduct at home and the neglect of the hegemonic "system" of power that looks away to their suffering and abandonment. In <u>The Have Little</u>, Cruz's first play, Lillian may be for some a stereotype of teenage pregnancy, but motherhood is her only way of survival. The love for her child highlights her innocence and purity in a world gone wrong. In <u>Miriam's Flowers</u>, Miriam carves flowers in her body with a razor blade after a train tragically kills her seven-year old brother. Left on her own, with unresolved trauma, Miriam finds all by herself a desperate way to mourn her brother through body scarification and promiscuity—-projecting in her own body, in this exasperating way, his bloody injuries and, at the same time, reproducing on her own skin acts of martyrdom learned in the reading of lives of saints.

Cruz points to the violence of poverty in the South Bronx with the hope that her characters, mostly young girls, clench to any possibility for survival in the infernal environment they bravely inhabit. These are bare lives that are left alone to survive in the fringe of America, among the detritus of the bodily and material waste under the forces of American domestic colonialism. Michi, Lillian's close friend, depicts the bleak condition of living in the South Bronx with revulsion. The only salvation is to find the way out of this landscape of total abjection: "It's this place. It's dirt. It's like a place where people die. I passed by my old building the other day and it was gone. Just like that. Like we never played there. There was a pile of broken stone and glass where my house used to be. And the schoolyard's now a monument-making factory. Row after row of tombstones for sale… Get the fuck out was my priority. And you should get out too."[xii] Michi's apocalyptic vision of the South Bronx registers not only the failure of the industrial capitalist project but makes visible the calamities of the Puerto Rican migration in such an inhospitable territory in the mainland. What's more surprising is that her description of the cataclysmic landscape evokes Walter Benjamin's allegory of the angel of history, inspired by Paul Klee' watercolor <u>Angelus Novus</u>. Benjamin's angel, blown by a storm against his will, prevents him from reconstructing the past and awakening the dead. The catastrophes and fatalities of humankind make a pile that grows skyward: "[The painting] shows an angel looking as though he is about to move away from something he is fixedly contemplating. His eyes are staring, his mouth is open, his wings are spread. This is how one pictures the angel of history. His face is turned toward the past. Where we perceive a chain of events, he sees one single catastrophe which keeps piling wreckage upon wreckage and hurls it in front of his feet. The angel would like to stay, awaken the dead, and make whole what has been smashed. But a storm is blowing in from Paradise; it has got caught in his wings with such violence that the angel can no longer close them. The storm irresistibly propels him into the future to which his back is turned, while the pile of debris before him grows skyward. This storm is what we call progress."[xiii] Does Cruz herself mirror the Benjamin's Angel of History in her dramaturgical practice? Why such an insistence on returning to the emotional wreckage and material debris left behind in the South Bronx? As an Angel of History, she takes upon herself the responsibility to revisit the South Bronx, to undo a diasporic past, and to redeem those who died and those who stayed behind in the rubble. However, in differentiation to Benjamin's angel at a standstill with immobile wings, Cruz has the agency to unearth the grief and pain and to recall them back in order to exalt on the stage their humanity and eulogize their bare lives. *Se hace historiadora de su gente* in the process, the South Bronx ceases to be the ghetto and becomes *el barrio de la familia* and loved ones.

Now, some may find it problematic to center stage the "ghetto." In <u>Out of the Fringe</u> Caridad Svich observes that a second wave of Latina/o playwrights, Cruz among them, "sought both a more realistic and more metaphorical kind of presentation, one that could exist outside the imposed 'ghetto' of 'Latino' theatre and sit in all its complexity at the 'American' table."[xiv] The blind spot here is the unintentional dismiss of the historical and political struggle of Latinas/os in the U.S. Svich's class rooted anxiety produces a counter-identification and disassociation from the "ghetto," the South Bronx that Cruz calls home. By fixing her gaze in the barrio, Cruz makes audiences to temporarily occupy the wreckage of the "ghetto." Her focalization on the South Bronx can be read in terms of anthropologist Kathleen Stewart's theoretical reflection that "[the] 'space on the side of the road' in the 'American' cultural landscape… is a space often crowded into the margins, and yet it haunts the centre and reminds it of something it cannot quite grasp."[xv] From this vantage point, Cruz's theatre materializes "a dwelling in and on a cultural poetics contingent on a place and a time and filled-in with palpable desire."(4) That "bounded local space on the margins"(5) with its specific poetic and historical *momentos de encuentros* allows for a "politics of 'othering' and the marking of difference"(5) which "could become an epistemological stance."(34) I propose that such a way of seeing is at the heart of Cruz's theatre: a practice of critical thinking translated into poetry that concedes to the Other its full humanity and spiritual faculty to survive in the most brutal conditions. This also explains Cruz's notion of redemption which grants her characters strategic agency: "I feel blessed by every character in every play I write, because for that short, ephemeral time when my characters are alive on a stage, I get to hear myself pray. Someone once told me that my plays had no redemption in them, which shocked me. Then I realized what they meant: that my plays didn't have patently happy endings. Redemption isn't about happiness, though—it's about beginning to heal the soul. This is the way you begin to feel the Divine inside you. This is hope. This is the place I call home."[xvi] Cruz juxtaposes "happiness" and "healing" to point out how her theatrical practice does not house the master narratives that promote the American Dream and the American Way of Life guaranteeing a happy ending. By questioning the hegemonic horizon of expectations, she puts forward her own way of doing theatre with a particular aesthetics.

Cruz has redefined Latina/o theatre's ars poetica and ideological framework in two crucial ways: first, once she distances herself from kitchen sink drama and the pedagogical dynamics of identity politics--what it means to be Latina/o, she concentrates on exploring the human dimension. And, second, without compromising her *conscientización política*, Cruz's ars poetica consists not in dogmatically telling the truth but on how she tells the truth: "I believe each character has its own poetry mined from a character's viscera to create a vocabulary of body that listens to the heart."[xvii] At work here is a feminist practice rooted on the body, one that vindicates that the personal is political. Cruz's feminist outlook allows her female characters the possibility of healing: "the ability to maintain hope in a hopeless situation"[xviii] can offer, if not salvation, survival. Her work may bring to light the ugly and corroborate that life is shit, but Cruz always insists that in the process there is the possibility of redemption. That makes a difference.

Of all of Cruz's works, who has authored at least forty plays, Miriam's Flowers and Fur are the most provocative and controversial. Both tease, seduce, shock, disturb, trouble, provoke, scandalize, and haunt spectators. Miriam's act of carving flowers on her skin as the only feasible way at hand to mourn her brother makes her body an open wound. Her abject practices inscribe the violence of poverty and register the fracture of the family after migration. In her desperate search to cope with the tragedy Miriam hopes to replicate the holy deeds of martyrdom in her appropriation of the cult of Catholic stigmata. Such a personal interpretation, on the one hand, shows how Catholicism has become a residual and a fragmented belief system in the diaspora; and, on the other hand, exposes how those ritualized acts offer her a subject position that enables her to reconstitute her relationship with her dead brother and the family in given Latino discursive formations and modes of identity articulation in social practices. Her agency consists of those bloody acts that bring some relief to her interminable pain. She bleeds abandonment. What emerges is an aesthetics of abjection that allows for the survival of the undead one day at a time in a culture of poverty and in a clash of cultures. Above all, her scarification gesticulates a scream, similar to a desperate graffiti, hoping to let the world know "I exist. I am alive."

The reincarnation of the figure of the subaltern in <u>Fur</u> happens to be a hirsute woman. Cruz employs discursive imagery of enfreakment to make a statement on practices of Othering and difference. The owner of a pet shop buys Citrona at a freak show and encages her in the basement. A beautiful woman notices him in the transaction and follows him. He ends up hiring her to feed the "love of his life." A love triangle emerges but it is not reciprocated given each other's fetish of love: the man wants to marry Citrona, the woman falls in love with the man, and Citrona wants to possess the woman. Cruz's intention is to push the limits: Citrona is both a lesbian and a cannibal. But what truly matters is her capability to love. Citrona's taste for the Beatles's songs accentuates her right to feel and express her emotions like any other human being. Citrona's aberrant desire gestures a search for freedom and pleasure through the breaking of taboos. Her inappropriate(d) body, like Miriam's, gives way to bringing into view disturbing images, forbidden desire, and instinctual impulses and sensations prohibited by the Law of the Father. Citrona and Miriam trespass into the outlawed territory of desire that displaces the disciplined and policed bodies of women in patriarchy. Miriam's Flowers and Fur makes room in the American cultural imaginary for violated and ailing bodies that dwell in "a space on the side of the road." For Cruz, Othering the stage means empowering those who inhabit the periphery, particularly Latina women trapped in a patriarchal order where the threat of violence looms. In a world of poverty they struggle to find their place, to find a home, to safeguard their cultural heritage, to stay alive in the most hostile environment at home and in the streets.

***

Having directed <u>Fur</u>, among other of Cruz's plays, Roberto Gutiérrez Varea in an essay entitled "The Poetry of the Oppressed" vividly depicts the uniqueness of her artistic practice in its poetic and aesthetic specificity: "She allows the most oppressed characters to speak, and when they talk to us, they sing their passions and their dreams, broken and imagined, like a beautiful aria... Migdalia Cruz has always given a voice to feelings often left unspoken, to people often left unheard. I can't help but marvel and listen. I am always moved and amazed by what they have to say."[xix] The plays compiled in this anthology speak to her talent and creativity. Her quest to open new worlds of sensibility and imagination gestures a new beginning in American theatre. Cruz imparts an aesthetic aura to the lives of the dispossessed: They speak poetry. These plays map out a journey from innocence to corruption, from solitude to solidarity, from oppression to liberation, from silence to a collective chant of poetry; all happening in the most minimal intervals of ordinary incidents.

A river of tears runs through Cruz's playwriting. The canyon of the playhouse echoes the silent and loud screams of the dispossessed. An ocean of blood pours out of a wound menacing to drown the survivors barely afloat. The power to heal and reach redemption resides in poetry and memory momentarily, in a split second, transformation can happen, as Papo says in <u>El grito del Bronx</u>. "I just must cover my ears and scream and when the sound comes back to me—that's like the ocean." Poetry can be found at the heart of horror and cruelty. The abject allows for the sublime experience to ephemerally take over. The poor are entitled to poetry. No matter how troubling, unnerving, and controversial those memories are, Cruz is not forgetting: "When I was growing up there were a lot of things that were unsaid, but felt. I want to get at that visceral thing— what no one talked about but was always there, etched in everyone's faces."xx She says it all in a poetic language of visual imagery ingrained in blood, screams, and tears. In her plays Cruz gives dignity to the poor, to those not having a homeland, and to those having to live dangerously on the wild side, among the wreckage and debris of capitalist imperialism. Each play in this anthology makes memorable a world rather not seen.

In <u>Yellow Eyes</u> a young woman walks the streets of the South Bronx at the risk of danger. Friendship does not so easily come in a social labyrinth where racial tension is accompanied with harassing and bodily assaults. The only safe space for Isabel is her great grandfather's home. At the age of 112, he teaches his great grandchild the colonial history of Puerto Rico from slavery to the migrant exodus of

Puerto Ricans from the countryside to the mainland. He possesses the knowledge and wisdom that makes her proud of her cultural heritage, one that the Anglo school system censors in favor of assimilation. After learning that she is the daughter of three races--Taíno, African, and Hispanic—-Isabel is empowered to articulate her diasporic identity and to wisely handle her racially mixed circle of friends. This is Cruz's only explicitly didactic play: She renders tribute to her great grandfather as she embarks on a journey to her Puerto Rican roots. Although <u>Yellow Eyes</u> is her most realist play, the stories José Maria tells about his adolescence, freedom, and unconditional love to his wife (who lost her mind) register a lyric flight and sensibility in sharp contrast to his harsh living conditions in a rundown apartment. The great grandfather's storytelling recovers what has been lost and forgotten after migration. Indeed, José Maria's untold stories constitute diasporic acts of intervention and resistance to salvage broken memories in the personal and collective spheres. At Isabel's coming of age, the recovery of ancestral voices, including the one of her great grandfather, are the necessary tools for self-respect and for the articulation of a transcultural identity always in the making. In view of the fact that Cruz's main objective is to pay homage to the sick old man and to stage the precious love relationship between Isabel and him, she leaves out overt sexual scenes and taboo breaking maneuvers that trademark her playwriting. However, the great grandmother's state of madness resulted from an attack in the streets when José Maria was beaten unconscious and she was raped. Her shame rendered the assault unspeakable, followed by insanity. The play at large points to the trauma of migration, the history of violence in the streets, the confinement of vulnerable older people to the periphery of society, and the here and now quotidian experiences of a diasporic young woman on a journey to a place called home as seen through her great grandfather's eyes.

Salt takes audiences to the darkest of places in urban America. Although the play takes place in the salt mounds reserved for winter road cleaning in the Southside of Chicago, it is just another "space on the side of the road" where life goes by unnoticed. In the living spaces carved in and around a salt mountain, a "tribe" of children endure pain and desolation due to social neglect and sexual exploitation. Innocent homeless children fall into the hands of a putative mother who snatches them to force them into prostitution. Belilah's acts of child abuse make visible the unspeakable atrocities that perpetuate a silenced history of violence. The enslavement that exposes them to harm and suffering, even death, re-actualizes the massacre of the innocent children whom Herod killed to prevent Jesus from being the King of the Jews. Cruz focuses on the human cost of neglect in order to hint to an overlooked history of "martyrdom" of the innocent from the past to the present. These are the violated, tortured, and scarred bodies of angelic victims who must fight against all odds for their survival and escape the viciousness of depraved pedophiles and corrupted politicians. In spite of it all, the children try to protect each other from all mistreatment and evil. They have the right to dream and imagine healing stories in a world gone wrong. In the children's worldview, there is even the possibility of turning garbage and "forgotten things" into beautiful objects--humble gifts of pure love.

Cruz opens the wounds of trauma entrenched in the spirit of destitute children to call attention to the national indifference of those in power in regard to the poor. In this way, by bringing to public consciousness the violence and poverty as lived on the streets, Cruz puts into question the national order of things. The bare lives of these children, who subsist among ordinary disposed things and who are subjected to extraordinary cruelty on a daily basis, show how some cannot escape a life of hurt. To reinforce her ironic criticism of the hypocrisy of the Catholic Church, she sets the play during the Christmas season and the coming of the Messiah; and, to put emphasis on society's apathy, she employs the hyper sensual rhythm and the sexual overtones of the lyrics of disco music. The message is loud and clear: These bodies are unaccounted for and dispensable in the real world. How can one forget Esperanza's opening statement in the film <u>Salt of the Earth </u>(1954): "This is our home. The house is not ours. But the flowers... the flowers are ours." <u>Salt,</u> for its capacity to move audiences from the most abject human condition to the supreme sublime feeling of communitas, stands out as one of Cruz's most poetic and allegorical achievements. At the end, hope and salvation may be found in death itself, the ultimate act of survival in the struggle for a dignified existence. Sadly, in a capitalist world of indifference and social iniquities, life goes on, or "such is life" some may say. Even so, the poor own the flowers—which is to say, they are entitled to *poesía*.

Unlike Lot's wife, who turned into a pillar of salt for her disobedience to the Lord in looking back to the destruction of Sodom and Gomorrah, Cruz refuses to look away from where she came. In her case, salt has a curative power: when applied to the open wound of memory, it has the potential to dry and heal the injuries. It may burn and hurt, and make you scream and cry. What we hear in <u>Salt</u> is Cruz's own hurt and cry, echoed in the torment and agony of the children. The South Bronx is that open wound. Her theatre is el grito del Bronx: a cry to let go of the pain, a cry to release the rage, a cry to heal.

<u>El Grito del Bronx</u> stages the collapse of a Puerto Rican family under the trials and tribulations of domestic abuse, incest, and crime. On her wedding day, in front of the dressing mirror, Lulu revisits her past to wash away the pain. As she traces a scar

imprinted on her leg, it allows for a series of flashbacks that make present the emotional anguish the family has gone through for years. After being fed up with his father molesting his sister, Papo kills him to stop Lulu's victimhood and to bring an end to the violent abuse at his hands. The history of violence that feeds Papo's rage at home and in the streets culminates in him becoming a serial killer. Lulu longs for the loving relationship she had in their childhood. With the hope to understand his actions, in her only and final visit to Papo she looks for answers. Her prison visit liberates Lulu from her guilt and restores the affective bond between the two. As if waiting to be executed is not enough of a death sentence, Papo tells his sister that he is also dying of AIDS. What matters here is his unconditional love for his sister not the act of patricide. Papo's visceral evidence of the love he feels for his sister are his damaged and scarred fingers. Showing his love for Puerto Rico, he tears his flesh to draw a map of the island, the flag, and tropical landscapes on the wall with his own blood. Making the audience's hearts break, Papo redeems himself once he confesses to her that sometimes he draws her under the trees looking at the moon. Redemption is possible despite all the hardships and rage in an urban culture of poverty and violence. They both let go of the ghosts that have haunted them through life. Papo hands Lulu her wedding dress and walks her back to the mirror. Then, he disappears in the dark. After feeling once again the scar on her leg, Lulu can finally move on, get married, and take residence in a place away from the South Bronx, once called home but still home in memory.

The poetic performance piece that closes this anthology "Da Bronx Rocks" (2005) encapsulates an epic vision of the South Bronx from the moment of its geological creation to becoming the contemporary global epicenter of migrancy. This is the ex-centric "space on the side of the road" that audiences inhabit over and over again in her theatrical productions. This is the cartography of memory where bare life translates into a poetics of survival. The poem, commissioned in collaboration with four other women by Mabou Mines, enacts a meditation on the history of each of the five boroughs from a female perspective. Cruz not only traces the European appropriation of the land from Native Americans and chronicles the arrival of migrants at different historical moments, but also offers a personal and intimate view of her family saga. The experimental theatrical project, like Cruz's theatre, was site-specific. Indeed, the poem reiterates and attests to the historical determined situatedness of the South Bronx as Cruz perseveres on her assertion that her unique experience of a sense of place makes the Bronx another country: the full title reads From the Country to the Country of the Bronx: Da Bronx Rocks: A Song." Not only that, each poem was set to music. This is significant because music plays an important role in her playwriting. The entanglement of music with space signals the double gesture of a politics of identity and a politics of location: "I always think characters have signature songs or music... The music seemed to always put me in that place, the way smell does."[xxi] Given Cruz's theatrical persistent employment of music to elaborate the psychology of her characters and to generate the ambiance of her plays (<u>Fur</u>, <u>Miriam's Flowers</u>, <u>Salt</u>), the piece constitutes an integral manifesto of her dramaturgical praxis: it is a poetics of place and identity in the making, well anchored in the topography of the South Bronx. At a political level, the piece bears witness to Cruz's unlearning and revision of history from the positionality of the subaltern. At a poetic level, it allegorizes the diasporic condition and the experiential process of decolonization. <u>Da Bronx Rocks</u> as an act of memory constitutes a lament: Cruz mourns the past in order to heal the wounds. The questions that she poses are the ideological matrix to what her playwriting is all about: "Where do the scars of history rest?" "Will my people leave treasures/buried in this new land? *"Patria, ¿dónde estás?"* *"¿Es esto lo que nos enseña la historia?"* Does anyone find home again?" "Can hope be born from disappearing?" "Where are we now?" Cruz's answer to these questions is her theater. It is not easy to be a Puerto Rican from the Bronx, neither can you get away from it: "I am a Puerto Rican from the Bronx... The Bronx is home." Both the Bronx accent and the Puerto Rican *"mancha de plátano"* mark her own body, a body that once inhabited a danger zone where "only the strong survive[d]."

In <u>Da Bronx Rocks</u> Cruz engages in a dialogue with Pedro Pietri's <u>Puerto Rican Obituary</u> (1973).[xxii] The poem furiously demythifies the "American Dream" from a Nuyorican perspective to condemn the colonization and exploitation of the Puerto Rican people. Pietri turns into poetry their trials and tribulations after migration. In a litany to honor the dead, he names the workers to break the silence imposed by anonymity and to impede the total oblivion *de su gente*. They will reach paradise, a place where they will finally realize that "PUERTO RICO IS A BEAUTIFUL PLACE" and "PUERTORRIQUEÑOS ARE A BEAUTIFUL RACE." If survival speaks to the memory of trauma, both Pietri's poetry and Cruz's theatre give *testimonio* to the history of violence and poverty of the Puerto Rican diaspora.

Migdalia Cruz *es la historia de su gente*. A lived in the flesh cultural poetics of resilience and a diasporic structure of feeling pulsates in each performance of her plays. The playwright has the last word to resist the hegemonic amnesia of the national imagined community, to intervene in the cultural landscape to voice the Other, and to embark on a poetics of remembrance to poetically document the existence of *los olvidados*: "… I'm sort of recording. Sometimes I feel more like I'm a historian than I am a playwright that I have a need to record and record honestly... I think of myself as someone who records history, and not any grand history necessarily... I do feel that I write about a world which is important."[xxiii] She chronicles the truth in a language of poetry, made out of blood, screams, and tears, which allows for hope at the heart of the most transitory hopeless instances.

Gracias Migdalia, Angel de la Historia de la comunidad puertorriqueña en la diáspora. Tu teatro es importante, aquí y en Puerto Rico.

Alberto Sandoval-Sánchez
Mount Holyoke College

YELLOW EYES

"There are only two lasting bequests we can hope to
give our children.
One of these is roots; the other, wings."
—Hodding Carter—

Yellow Eyes was commissioned as a one-act by Crossroads Theatre, Ricardo Khan, artistic director, for its Genesis Festival 1999, and subsequently re-commissioned as a full-length for its 1999-2000 season.

World Premiere: Crossroads Theatre (NJ), February 2000, directed by Talvin Wilks and performed by Pascale Armand, Elisa Bocanegra, Dyron Holmes, Jack Landron, Amarelys Perez, & Virginia Rambal.

Second Production: Tabia African-American Theater (CA), February 2002, directed by Velina Hasu-Houston.

Workshop: Hartford Stage (CT), October 2006, Brand:NEW Series, directed by Candido Tirado.

For my great-grandfather, José Maria Sotillo de la Paz y Cruz, who has inspired all the stories I have ever told...

Cast of Characters

DON JOSÉ MARIA SOTILLO—an Afro-Puerto Rican man of 112 who survived slavery and loves to tell stories. Born in 1859.

JOSÉLITO—DON JOSÉ at age 14, to be played by the actor playing IAN.

DOÑA ANA CECILIA SANDOVAL de SOTILLO—a Puerto Rican woman of 99 who sometimes forgets who she really is but is always sure of whom she likes.

ISABEL NIEVES—their 13 year old great-granddaughter; hungry for history; curious and precocious. Born in 1958.

IAN DURANT—Isabel's 14 year-old boyfriend, African-American, cool in that early 70s way, big afro and big attitude, wants to be an actor.

SHARON MCNAIR—Isabel's 13 year-old friend, African-American, sweet, straightforward, originally from North Carolina.

DOLORES(LULU) TIRADO—Isabel's 13 year-old friend, Puerto Rican, street-smart but recently converted to become a Jehovah's Witness, a pest.

MEDIANOCHE—José Maria's mother. A 13 year-old slave in 1859 Puerto Rico, to be played by the actor playing SHARON.

TIME:
One unusually snowy fall in 1971. There are also scenes from the past, in various years between 1859-1971.

PLACE:
Present: A rundown apartment in the Soundview section of the Bronx, New York, its front stoop, and a pizza parlor in the University Heights section of the Bronx. *Past:* Various locations such as a plaza in the Northwest corner of Puerto Rico, near Aguadilla, and on a ship in San Juan Harbor.

NOTE:
There is a bureau altar in ANA CECILIA's bedroom of the apartment, which can hold symbols for all the characters in the play. Maybe it can hold a piece of JOSELITO's ship's mast in the wood framing the mirror above the bureau or the mirror can be SHARON's mirror, etc.

In the native language of the Taino Indians of Puerto Rico, Jibaro means "one who escapes to be free". The jibaros are the mountain people of P.R. who are the offspring of escaped African slaves, Taino Indians,

& poor European farmers. They are considered the true people of Puerto Rico.

1845 — End of the slave trade in Puerto Rico.

1859 — José Maria is born into slavery on the island to his thirteen year old mother, Medianoche.

1872 — Ana Cecilia Sandoval is born.

1873 — Abolition of Slavery in Puerto Rico. José Maria is 14 years old.

1890 — José Maria(31) & Ana Cecilia Sandoval(18) marry.

1947 — José Maria & Ana Cecilia move to the U.S. to join their children

1958 — Isabel is born to the grandson of José Maria and Ana Cecilia.

1963 — JFK is assassinated

1968 — Martin Luther King, Jr. and Robert Kennedy are assassinated

1971 — Isabel enters 7th grade in Junior High School

PROLOGUE

"South Wind"
In the dark, we hear the recorded voices of ISABEL and
JOSÉ MARIA who play a game.

ISABEL: Where'd you get yellow eyes like that?

JOSÉ MARIA: I was born with them.

ISABEL: I was born with these eyes too.

JOSÉ MARIA: And these feet.

ISABEL: And these arms.

JOSÉ MARIA: And this head.

ISABEL: And this heart.

JOSÉ MARIA: And these words...

(We hear the sound of the wind, as the lights come up on
ISABEL, who is discovered behind the scrim-like sail of a
19th Century merchant ship.
SHE is holding a small box with a lid.
In front of the sail sits JOSÉLITO, a young JOSÉ MARIA,
with one arm and one leg strapped to the mast of a merchant

ship in San Juan Harbor, 1872. HE speaks to the wind which is
flapping the sails all around him.
As ISABEL lifts the lid off the box, JOSÉLITO begins to
speak—it is as if by opening the box, ISABEL is able to
release his voice into the air. As JOSÉLITO continues to
speak, ISABEL holds the box up to the sky and slowly fades
from view.)

JOSÉLITO: If I promise to introduce you to the South wind, will you loosen my ropes? I hear she's very beautiful. Women from the south of anywhere always are.

(Pause)

What's the use of being the wind, if you can't undo things? You can push large ships across great oceans, and yet, you can't untie me. At least, Don Pemplin, only ties half of me now. He says soon I'll be a freeman. He asked me, "Josélito, what will you do with your freedom? Will you drink and lay with women of your choice? That's what I would do, "he said. And I said "No, Don Pemplin, I will try to find my mother." He tells me she is dead, but I don't believe it. I feel her still. I can smell her sometimes in the cool breeze that pulls the sweat away from my eyes. She keeps me from growing blind with my own salt. She keeps my eyes open so I can keep watch for her. Maybe I can buy this boat from the master one

day. And I'll sail until I find her. Sail to Cuba, where
they say she was taken.

Do you know how to sail a ship, wind? It takes only
three stars to find your way. Every star has a mate
here on Earth. If you chart each star and then set your
direction by the North Star which never changes, you
know where on Earth you are. But your place in the
world?

If you're like me, you may never find it. But still, you
keep looking...

> *(A breeze comes across his face and*
> *HE revels in it, inhaling deeply.)*

Aaahhh, there she is...

(HE sighs again as lights cross to the Sotillo apartment, his
sigh overlapping
the sighs of the present.)

ACT ONE
SCENE 1

"Water. Boil."
In a shabby apartment, decorated with too much brown,
ANA CECILIA & JOSÉ MARIA sit side by side on the edge
of the bathtub, soaking their feet and calves. ANA CECILIA
pours a pot of hot water into the tub over their feet.

ANA CECILIA & JOSÉ MARIA: Aaahhh...

JOSÉ MARIA: *(Closing his eyes and breathing in a memory)* There she is!

ANA CECILIA: What?

JOSÉ MARIA: *(Pointing at his feet, trying to cover his embarrassment at being caught in a memory)* There it is...feeling better.

ANA CECILIA
Yes.
          (Pause as THEY both enjoy feeling
            the heat on their cold limbs)
When do you think we'll get hot water this time?

JOSÉ MARIA: I don't know, Ana.

ANA CECILIA: It's almost November, José.

JOSÉ MARIA: Yes.

ANA CECILIA: This is your fault, José.

JOSÉ MARIA: Of course.

ANA CECILIA: Don't humor me, Josélito.

JOSÉ MARIA: You haven't called me that in a long time.

ANA CECILIA: Did you call that lazy super?

JOSÉ MARIA: I call everyday.

ANA CECILIA: Call every hour. I'm going to stop paying the rent.

JOSÉ MARIA: You don't pay the rent.

ANA CECILIA: I won't let you pay any more rent for this icebox.

JOSÉ MARIA: Our grandson pays the rent.

ANA CECILIA: It doesn't matter who pays! Why don't you ever listen?! And why can't you even get the heat turned on?? I want a divorce.

JOSÉ MARIA: I know. But we've been married for eighty-one years.

ANA CECILIA: That's eighty years too long.

JOSÉ MARIA: Ah hah! So we did have one good year!

ANA CECILIA: *(Smiling in spite of herself)*
At the most.

JOSÉ MARIA: It must have been a really good year...I mean, you stayed for eighty more.

ANA CECILIA: I can barely remember that long ago.

JOSÉ MARIA: I remember every minute, Anita.

ANA CECILIA: *(A softer tone)* That's because you had nothing until you met me. It's easy to remember the only good thing in your miserable life.

> *(JOSÉ MARIA scoots a little
> closer to ANA CECILIA.)*

JOSÉ MARIA: I could make you warmer.

ANA CECILIA: How? You got a book of matches in your pants?

JOSÉ MARIA: You tell me.

ANA CECILIA: Ay, viejo!! <u>You</u> are too old for that. That thing of yours broke a long time ago—like a watch with no hands—
          (Acting it out with her hands)
you hear the ticking but it's not sticking.

JOSÉ MARIA: That's just the diabetes. If I take my medicine, I'm like a tree trunk—

ANA CECILIA: Ay, the water got cold already. It's your turn to boil, José.

(JOSÉ MARIA steps out of the tub and with the help of his cane begins to make his way to the kitchen stove, pot in hand.)

JOSÉ MARIA: Will you give me a little kiss when I come back?

ANA CECILIA: No.

JOSÉ MARIA: You know, I love you very much.

ANA CECILIA: Mmhmm.

JOSÉ MARIA: Tell me.

ANA CECILIA: I'm still undecided.

JOSÉ MARIA: How much longer do you need?

ANA CECILIA: How much time do you have?

JOSÉ MARIA: Ay, Ana Cecilia!

ANA CECILIA: The water??

JOSÉ MARIA: I'll call the super too.

ANA CECILIA: Good.

JOSÉ MARIA: And I'll make us some coffee.

ANA CECILIA: There is no coffee. Can't you move any faster? You walked better before.

JOSÉ MARIA: A lot of things were better before.

ANA CECILIA: (*Mumbling as JOSÉ MARIA speaks.*) Water. Boil. Water. Boil. Water. Boil.

JOSÉ MARIA: Sometimes I feel like my bones are just turning into dust.

ANA CECILIA: *(Suddenly getting out of the tub)* I'm going to the store.

JOSÉ MARIA: I'll go with you.

(ANA CECILIA sighs in frustration.)

ANA CECILIA: I can go faster alone.

JOSÉ MARIA: What are you going to buy?

ANA CECILIA: A gun.

JOSÉ MARIA: We don't need any food. Carmen and Candido dropped off some platanos and yuca. And some rice. And some bistec.

ANA CECILIA: I hate yuca. I want batatas. And coffee. I'm going to the store.

JOSÉ MARIA: It's cold out. It's getting dark so early now. You better wear your coat.

ANA CECILIA: If I wear a coat, is the Sun going to come out?

JOSÉ MARIA: *(Losing his temper for a moment)* What?! Please! Just put on your coat. And I <u>am</u> coming with you.

(*THEY put on their socks and shoes in silence.*)

ANA CECILIA: Of course, I'm going to wear a coat. I'm not crazy, José.
    (*A slight sigh from JOSÉ MARIA*)
I know when it's cold inside, it must be cold outside.

JOSÉ MARIA: *(Taking her hand and putting it over his heart)* But sometimes it's cold outside, but inside, it's warm.

ANA CECILIA: (Rubbing her hand across his chest) Your skin feels like leather. I think I once had a pair of shoes that were just...Do you remember my aunt Eusebia? She gave me a pair of brown leather shoes with ribbons to tie them closed. I loved those shoes. They were good for dancing. I wore them until the leather came apart in my hands. Then I saved the ribbon and tied it around my neck with a seashell hanging from it like a diamond.

JOSÉ MARIA: You were wearing that ribbon the day I met you.

ANA CECILIA: I never took it off. But one day when I was walking on the beach, the ribbon tore and my shell fell into the sand. I didn't notice it until it was high tide and I saw the waves cover over where I had walked earlier that day. I cupped my hand, scooped up a piece of the sea and placed my lips on it—so I could say good-bye finally to those old ribbons and those old shoes. It's easier to say good-bye when you do it through water. When your lips are moist with the taste of salt. That's why people cry I think. I think it's because they need to fill their senses with the taste of sadness. It's not enough to feel a tear roll down your face. You have to taste it and swallow it down so your insides know your sadness too.

JOSÉ MARIA: I won't ever leave you like those shoes.

ANA CECILIA: *(Smacking him in the chest)*
People leave you worse than shoes. They leave you to fill holes you didn't know you had. Shoes just leave your feet.
> *(SHE looks at him in silence for a moment.)*
You used to be taller.
> *(SHE walks toward the front door,*
> *stopping at* its threshold.)*

JOSÉ MARIA: *(With ironic sadness; SHE doesn't hear him.)* And you used to look up to me.

(*JOSÉ MARIA brings ANA CECILIA her coat and places it over her shoulders. SHE shudders slightly when HE touches her. THEY both stare at the door for a moment in silence. Then THEY turn back around, sit down, and begin to remove their shoes as lights cross to the Pizza Parlor.*)

SCENE 2

"Blood Sisters"
The Pizza Parlor.
Halloween, 1971.
The jukebox plays the Jackson Five's
"Never Can Say Good-bye."
SHARON & ISABEL are in identical vampire costumes.
They wear cheesy vampire wigs.
THEY eat slices of pizza as they discuss boys.

SHARON: How come he got a Puerto Rican name?

ISABEL: How come you got a Scottish name? You don't look like no McNair to me.

SHARON: 'Cause I'm from North Carolina. We all had names wit "Mack" in dem.

ISABEL: Tito ain't no Puerto Rican name.

SHARON: It's Spanish though, ain't it?

ISABEL: It ain't even a real name. It's a nickname.

SHARON: Well, he uses it like it's his name.

ISABEL: But it ain't though. Couldn't be.

SHARON: Why not? Tito's a good name. You just mad 'cause he never wrote you back. And I got a picture. To my greatest fan. Love, Tito Jackson. You wanna come over to my house and see the picture again? I got it hung up over my bureau mirror so I can see myself and him at the same time. And man do we look good together, girl.

ISABEL: Oh, really? I'm surprised he's not over your bed.

SHARON: You really are mad. You turning all red and raising your voice...

ISABEL: Shut up! I ain't mad. I'm just tired of the Tito talk. Every day that's all you talk about. Tito, Tito, Tito. You must have his name carved into your butt by now. There's four other brothers in that family, you know!? Talk about one a them.

SHARON: The other ones are too young for me.

ISABEL: Jackie's the oldest—not Tito.

SHARON: I mean—
(Pointing to her head)
—up here. I like a mature guy. Tito's got his head screwed on just right.

ISABEL: I like the Temptations better.

SHARON: Yeah? But you could never date a Temptation. But now with Tito, you might have a chance. I heard his girlfriend was Puerto Rican.

ISABEL: Yeah? He has good taste anyways.

SHARON: And what is that supposed to mean?

ISABEL: It's a joke, Sharon.

SHARON: So if he liked me, he would be having bad taste? Is that it?

ISABEL: Nooo, that's not it. You got the sense of humor of a short ugly stick today.

SHARON: Now you're calling me ugly?! Who stood up for you when those girls tried to steal your buspass??

ISABEL: You did.

SHARON: And who showed you how to walk home so you wouldn't get beat up again?

ISABEL: You did. But I've done things for you too.
    (Putting her hand gently over SHARON's)
Remember? That's what friends do. And I did not call you ugly. I think you're beautiful.

SHARON: You do?

ISABEL: Yeah. But I'm a bad friend so what does it matter what I think?

SHARON: I never said you were a bad friend. You just say hurtful things sometimes.

ISABEL: I don't mean to. Things just come out of my mouth wrong.

SHARON: You try too hard to make jokes all the time.

ISABEL: Alright, alright! I'm sorry. I'll never make another joke again. Jesus!

(DOLORES enters.)

DOLORES: Don't say his name like that! You'll regret it when you start tumbling down to you-know-where. You wanna go stop the trick-or-treaters?

ISABEL: I liked you better before you became a Jehovah's Witness, Lulu.

SHARON: We're having a private conversation here.

DOLORES: So? Don't boss me around. You're not my mother or my husband. You don't own me.

SHARON: If I was your mother, Dolores, I woulda drunk Draino and had a miscarriage. Problem solved.

ISABEL: Sharon! I never heard you talk like that. Who do you think you are? Me??

DOLORES: You're just jealous. Because you're too dumb to be in the same class as us. So I'm her best friend now.

ISABEL: Stop it, Lulu.

DOLORES: Well, it's true. What class are you in, Sharon? Seven-twenty-six? We're in Seven-two. That's a big ole difference—like twenty-four down from us.

SHARON: You can't say anything to hurt me, girl, so why don't you move on? There's little kids out there that need your help. You gotta stop them before they trick or treat too much and go to hell.

DOLORES: You better be careful. Even just wearing a costume is bad too.
Isa, I saw Ñeca and Flaca yesterday and they said it's okay to kiss Black boys, but you should stop hanging around with Black girls because if they touch your hair it gets nappy like theirs is. And you start to smell funny too.
ISABEL: You're too old to be so ignorant.

SHARON: So you can have a Black boyfriend, but you can't play with Black girls?

ISABEL: And you can get pregnant and have a Black baby, but if it's a girl, you can't comb her hair?

DOLORES: Did I say that?! What does being pregnant have to do with anything anyways? Come on, Isa! I gotta stop at least ten kids before I go home or my Mom will—

SHARON: Beat you?

DOLORES: Nooo. She don't beat me. She'll just be upset is all...

SHARON: Uh huh. She still drinking??

ISABEL: I don't wanna go. Not when you're acting all stupid.

DOLORES: Alright. But don't sit near me on Judgment Day. I don't wanna get caught by your blast and get all sucked down into—

SHARON: Just go.
> *(DOLORES exits smugly.)*
I hate that girl.

ISABEL: She doesn't mean to be that stupid...I think.

SHARON: You know they told me the same thing— Sondae, Clara and Nina and all a them came to me during auditorium and said I should stop being your friend.

ISABEL: There's a lot of stupid people around trying to tell other people what to do.

SHARON: Is it stupid?

ISABEL: You don't think they're right, do you?

SHARON: No. But it did get harder to be outside together. Maybe you could come to my house after school—

ISABEL: Are you scared of them?!

SHARON: It's not me they're gonna come after.

ISABEL: But they already beat me up last month. I hit that Nina right smack in the head with my clarinet case. They aren't gonna bother me any more.

SHARON: That's what you think. You're smart about school, Isabel, but you're a fool about everything else.

ISABEL: C'mon, Sharon. Nothing's gonna happen to me.

SHARON: We'll see.
> *(Pause; looking back and forth*
> *between herself and Isabel.)*
Do you think maybe we're too old for costumes?

ISABEL: Maybe.
> *(Pulling off her own wig)*
I never liked trick-or-treating anyway. But I do like the costumes.

SHARON: That's because you're gonna be an actress—
(*Breaking out into a song from Lerner & Lowe's My Fair Lady.*)
"You'll be broke and I'll have money, Ah, ha, ha, won't that be funny! Just you wait 'enry 'iggins, just you wait!"

ISABEL: Girl, that is strange coming out of a vampire.

SHARON: You're gonna be good in that play. I watched you practice this morning. I'm gonna bring my Ma to see it on Friday.

ISABEL: I hope I can't see you. You'll make me laugh.

SHARON: No I won't. I promise.

(*ISABEL looks at SHARON skeptically.*)

ISABEL: Uh, huh.

(*THEY put their wigs back on, helping each other tuck in the stray hairs. Then SHARON & ISABEL survey each other and hiss like vampires in unison, throwing their heads back and showing their fangs.*)

SHARON: *(In a Dracula-type accent)* Vant to come over to my house later and play Parcheesi?

ISABEL: *(Also in a Transylvanian accent)* Ve haven't done that in a long time.

> *(ISABEL & SHARON laugh.*
> *SHARON is the first to sober up.)*

SHARON: It won't be the same. Junie used to whup us at Parcheesi.

ISABEL: Yep. He just loved jumping people.

SHARON: He was a pain in the butt, but I miss him now.
> *(ISABEL squeezes her hand again.)*
I hated going to that hospital and seeing him lay there, disappearing into those hard, white sheets. He got so small when he got sick.

ISABEL: Can you catch what he had?

SHARON
Nah, sickle cell don't work like that. But you do gotta be Black to get it. That's what my mother tole me that the doctor tole her. That's weird ain't it? That there's diseases that I can get and you can't.

ISABEL: *(Teasing)* Yeah. Especially since we're best friends.

> *(SHARON smacks her playfully on the head.*
> *IAN enters in a Lincoln Hayes-Mod Squad*
> *style costume. HE greets ISABEL despite SHARON's*
> *disapproval.)*

IAN: Hey, Isabel.

ISABEL: Hi, Ian.

(IAN puts some money in the jukebox. The girls watch him.
HE knows he's being watched. HE plays the Fifth
Dimension's "Age of Aquarius" and begins to dance
psychedelically. The girls laugh. HE cajoles ISABEL into
dancing with him while SHARON glares.)

IAN: *(To SHARON)* Don't you dance?

SHARON: Not with no Mister "jacked-up-big- butt-hair-wannabe-somebody-on-TV-but-really-nobody-I-even-want-to-know" guy.

ISABEL: There's only one guy for her.

IAN: How about for you?

SHARON: *(SHARON pulls ISABEL away from IAN.)*
C'mon, Isabel.
>*(So only ISABEL can hear)*

You're not going out with that stanky skank, are you?
>*(ISABEL looks at SHARON guiltily and smiles.)*

ISABEL: Well...Since we started working on the play together—

SHARON: Oh, man! I don't believe it!

>*(SHARON stalks off leaving ISABEL with IAN. It goes from day to night.*
>*The lights cross to the Sotillo apartment.)*

SCENE 3

>*"Sailing Dreams"*
>*Late night.*
>*In the apartment, ANA CECILIA sleeps as JOSÉ MARIA watches her in silence for a moment—*
>*then HE speaks.*

JOSÉ MARIA: If I stare at you while you sleep, will you dream of me?
>*(Pause)*

You look so peaceful. Women are like the sails of a great ship, they can bring you to amazing places you would never find otherwise. Otherwise, you could only travel as far as your arms could take you. And you can't row to the really important places. No, to get to those places you must sail. And a good sail is tightly woven, with no rips or tears, but tightened onto the mast by years of feeling the heat of the sun and the mist of the sea.

(Pause)

I wonder if you can feel my eyes on you, and if you do, if they make you feel safe...

(Tying one of his arms to one of hers)

Now I can sleep too.

(As JOSÉ MARIA closes his eyes, ANA CECILIA gently puts her arms around him and THEY both sleep.
SHARON enters the street as if SHE is lost and searching for a way home. We see her cross the stage as the lights go from night to day. Lights cross to ISABEL & IAN outside the apartment.)

SCENE 4

"Pick and Pick and Pick"
ISABEL & IAN stand on the stoop of the apartment. IAN picks at his afro as HE speaks.

IAN: Why does it bother you so much?

ISABEL: I don't know—men aren't supposed to be so concerned with their hair. But you pick and pick and pick. It makes me forget what I was saying. You hypnotize me with all that picking.

IAN: I gotta take care of my hair. It gets too nappy if I don't and then I don't look good. I need to look good for my baby, don't I?
> *(Pulling ISABEL to him affectionately)*
Don't I?

ISABEL: Yeah. You look good. Hey, Ian, do you wanna come in and meet my great-grandparents?

IAN: No. I got grandparents of my own.

ISABEL: Not just grandparents—<u>great</u>-grandparents. I bet you don't got any of those.

IAN: Oooh, I bet they smell like shoes in an old trunk. Are they still walking around?

ISABEL: Yeah—slowly, but surely.

IAN: I don't wanna ever be that old. My grandpa is in a wheelchair—and he lost all his hair except this white ring that goes all around his little ole pea head. Man, does he look nasty.

ISABEL: I can't wait to get that old. Then you can stop worrying about everything. So what if you have a ring around your head?! I have daydreams about being that free.

IAN: Oh, yeah? Well, I have nightmares. Just last night, I had a dream that I was real old like that and I couldn't find my way back to my house. I just kept wandering and wandering around asking people if they knew who I was, and nobody knew me. At first, I thought I must be dead, but then I remembered that being lost just felt like being dead—like you disappear for a while until you find your way. I just kept telling myself that if I kept moving forward I would find my way back home because the Earth is a circle. Then I woke up and I had wrapped my sheets all around my body in a knot—like I had tied myself to the bed. What do you think that means?

ISABEL: I think it means you can't escape from yourself. Like you were searching all over but only to come back to the same place.

IAN: Hmmm...I think it just means that I'm going to lose my hair one day.

ISABEL: Ay! You and your hair! Dag!
(*Looking up at the Sotillo's apartment window*)

I hope I get old the way Papabuelo did. He doesn't tell the same story over and over like most boring old people. Every time I see him, he has something new to say. I like that. But Mamabuela...I don't know. She's so mean. She gets worse every time I see her.

IAN: And you want me to meet her? Forget it. I'll wait out here. I need to learn my lines. I keep forgetting that one scene where you run away.

ISABEL: I don't run, I leave, so you can come find me. Will you come up later?

IAN: Maybe.

ISABEL: Hey, Ian! How come you got a Scottish name?

IAN: It was my father's name, stupid. Go see your people.

(Lights cross to SHARON talking to
a framed photo of Tito Jackson.)

SCENE 5

"No More Tissues"
SHARON is standing in front of her bureau mirror,
speaking to a framed photo of Tito Jackson, of the Jackson

Five, whose image is reflected in the mirror too. SHARON
looks like
she's been in a fight that she won.

SHARON: You shoulda been there, Tito. Man, did I get that Flaca good. She won't go around talking about me anymore. I bet she won't say nut'ing to nobody for a long time. I hit her right in the mouth.
(Playing out the scene into the mirror)
My fists were like bop, bop, bop. I bonked her like a car horn.
(Responding to her mother's voice —
which only SHE can hear)
What??! I'm not doing nut'ing. I don't wanna come in there and cry with you. There ain't no more tissues. I will but—can I just—can I—Wait up.
(Turning back to Tito in the mirror)
Don't worry, Tito. She won't live with us after we're married.
(Hearing her Mom's voice again.)
I said I don't wanna. That's not—Stop it already! Is Jesus gonna bring Junie back, Ma? Is he? Then shut up calling for him. It's been a year already, Ma. Leave me alone!
(Turning back to Tito in the mirror)
Sometimes she's so loud I want to scream so I can hear my own thoughts for once. Inside is where you're supposed to cry. My stomach fills up with tears

sometimes and makes me feel like throwing up—but I don't tell Ma because she would start thinking I'm dying or something. She watches me all the time now like I might.

(Pause)

She makes me want to disappear sometimes. I can't stand her eyes on me all the time. Most days I stay out until I know she's asleep. So I don't have to see her eyes looking at me, but really looking for Junie. I won't ever be him.

(SHE gets on tiptoes to kiss the image of Tito. As SHE does so, a small snapshot of her brother, Junie, falls out of the back of the frame. SHE picks it up and looks at it in silence for a moment.)

I forgot I put you back there, Junie. My two favorite boys together forever.

(Kisses the photo of Junie and hides it back in the frame.)

If nobody finds you, nobody can take you away from me. Not again.

(From the fire escape outside SHARON's window, we see ISABEL pounding on the window.)

ISABEL: SHARON! SHARONI?! Are you okay?
(no response)
SHARON! I know you're in there. I see you. Talk to me.

SHARON: *(To herself)* I don'wanna see nobody no more.

(The lights cross to the Sotillos' front door.)

SCENE 6

"My Fair Couple"
ISABEL knocks on the door and JOSÉ MARIA answers it too quickly like HE has been waiting by the door. It startles her.

ISABEL: Wow! That's service.

JOSÉ MARIA: It took you a long time to get here. Your mother called to say you'd be here an hour ago.

ISABEL: Oh. Did she? I guess she was wrong. I'm here now anyway. Dag! She watches me like a hawk. She gets on my last nerve.

JOSÉ MARIA: You can say that only because you have a mother who loves you and watches out for you. I would give anything to have had a mother to watch over me.

ISABEL: Why didn't you? What happened to her?

JOSÉ MARIA: When I was just a little baby, my mother was forced to leave me in Puerto Rico and go to work on a sugar plantation in Cuba.

ISABEL: Do you remember her?

JOSÉ MARIA: I only really remember her smell, I think. Like the loose dirt around a newly dug garden—sort of like flowers but more like the earth. And I remember who I imagined she was. I heard many stories about her.
ISABEL: What was her name?

JOSÉ MARIA: She was called Medianoche, because she was so Black that she looked like the middle of the night. Nothing could be better than to be so dark that you became a part of the night...that's what I thought when I was a young boy anyway.

ISABEL: Sounds like an insult to me.

JOSÉ MARIA: You're smarter about those things than I was, Isabel. I didn't know you could use a name to show evil thoughts. Though I knew that the blacker you were the harder they hit you or made you work or laughed at you. Maybe it was because it was my mother's name that I couldn't imagine anything bad about it.

ISABEL: I have the opposite problem. I only think of bad things people might be trying to do to me. I don't trust nobody.

JOSÉ MARIA: Even me?

ISABEL: You know what I mean. Other people. Them. People who call us things.

JOSÉ MARIA
People call you things? Like what?

ISABEL: Like—I dunno—spick—dirty spick—dirty P.R.—Rican Wench—Spanish bitch—

JOSÉ MARIA: Who calls you this?

ISABEL: Girls. At school. And the man who used to run the grocery store. And the bus driver on the bus going to school.

JOSÉ MARIA: Those aren't good people.

ISABEL: Of course not. But it's no big deal. Everybody hates somebody.

JOSÉ MARIA: Some things don't change.

ISABEL: Oh, I don't know...Things just change slowly—like there are some nice people around here too.

JOSÉ MARIA: Are there? Is your boyfriend nice?

ISABEL: Who told you I had a boyfriend? Ma? She bothers me about everything.

JOSÉ MARIA: I saw him walk you over here.

ISABEL: You could tell just from his walk?

JOSÉ MARIA: I could tell from how he watched you walk—into the building. Men's eyes linger on the women they love.

ISABEL: Dad doesn't look at Ma like that.

JOSÉ MARIA: Hmmm...he just doesn't do it when he knows you're watching.

ISABEL: Sharon says I stare too much. Makes people uncomfortable. But how else can you learn about people, except by staring and recording it in your brain.
JOSÉ MARIA: You could listen too, Isabel.

ISABEL: I listen—most of the time.

JOSÉ MARIA: Sharon's a wise young lady. How come you don't bring her by anymore?

ISABEL: She's never around when I come over here—always out walking around and thinking too much. She even passes by me sometimes—looking into the air like she's reading it.

JOSÉ MARIA: She uses her eyes like a blind person uses his fingers.

ISABEL: Yeah. I'm worried she'll bust a vein someday from all that thinking.
                    (Pause)
Ian wants to meet you.
JOSÉ MARIA: Oh, yes? I want to meet him too. He better be treating you with respect.

ISABEL: Ay, Papabuelo! Of course. I'm not a sinvergüenza like Lulu.

JOSÉ MARIA: What does Lulu do?

ISABEL: Nothing anymore, now that she's got religion. But before, forgedaboutit!

JOSÉ MARIA: Oh...well don't—don't you do—that.

ISABEL: I won't. Should I ask him to come in?

JOSÉ MARIA: Of course.
(ISABEL runs to bring IAN inside to meet JOSÉ MARIA
& ANA CECILIA. DOLORES is flirting with IAN as
ISABEL approaches.)

DOLORES: You know, Papi, I think you're fine. I
know Isa complains about your hair, but I love it. It's
so...I don't know—round. Historical. Round things
always make me think of history or geography.

IAN: I love geography.

DOLORES: *(Pretending not to already know this)* You
do??

IAN: Yeah. I have a globe my Uncle Nathan brought
me from Korea, when he was fighting over there.

DOLORES: Oooh! I bet it's beautiful—with all those
countries...and all those oceans. Will you show it to
me sometime?

IAN: Maybe. I'm not going to stay in the Bronx
forever. I wanna go around the world one day—like
my Uncle did. He's been everywhere. Places where
they never even seen Black folks before. He told me
that was the best, 'cause then nobody tried to tell him

how to act because they wasn't afraid of him. It was more like he was special than different. You know what I mean?

DOLORES: I know exactly what you mean.

(ISABEL strides up to them. IAN nervously pulls at his afro with a pick when HE sees her.)

ISABEL: So what is going on here??

DOLORES: Oh, Isa! Don't be a boba ! I was just telling Ian about my church and stuff.

ISABEL: Right. And stuff. C'mon. My Papabuelo's waiting.

DOLORES: Can I come too?

ISABEL: No.

DOLORES: Call me, if you wanna go to church, Ian.

IAN: Okay. Alright. So long.

(DOLORES exits.)

ISABEL: That girl wants everything I got. Bitch. C'mon.

(IAN & ISABEL go to stand outside her great-grandparents front door.)

Can you hurry up! He's waiting.

IAN: Cool it! I don't get along with old dudes.

ISABEL: He's not no old dude—he's my great-grandfather—and you gotta get along wif him.

IAN: Or what?

ISABEL: I din't say or nuffin. I'm just saying. It's important.

IAN: The things you gotta do for a chick, man.

ISABEL: You watch too much Mod Squad. Talk regular in front of them, okay?

IAN: Yes, Ma'am.

(IAN kisses ISABEL. ISABEL pushes him away.)

ISABEL: Are you crazy?! They'll see us.

IAN: Through the door? What?! They got x-ray vision or something?

ISABEL: Just—just act normal okay?

IAN: I'll try.

*(ISABEL knocks on the door.
ANA CECILIA answers.)*

ANA CECILIA: Yes? What do you want?

ISABEL: This is Ian Durant, Mamabuela. He wanted to meet you.

ANA CECILIA: Are you a nurse?

ISABEL: No. I'm Isabel.

ANA CECILIA: Then go away.

(ANA CECILIA tries to close the door but ISABEL puts her foot in it preventing it from closing.)

ISABEL: Mamabuela! Don't you recognize me?!

ANA CECILIA: Hmmm...You look a little like the lady who comes to clean the house every week.

ISABEL: That's my mother—Carmen. The wife of Candido, your son's son.

ANA CECILIA: Son Son. What's that? Chinese? Go away, ChinChon.

(JOSE MARIA appears behind ANA CECILIA.)

JOSÉ MARIA
Let the children in, Ana Cecilia!

ANA CECILIA
Why? They didn't bring my medicine, did they?
                (Throwing the door wide open)
Alright! Come in! Everybody! Just come to my door and knock and I'll let you in like you're family and you'll rob me blind.

ISABEL: I am family, Mamabuela.

ANA CECILIA: Humph!

(ANA CECILIA goes to a chair and sits in it deliberately closing her eyes tight. SHE moves her lips, silently mocking IAN & JOSÉ MARIA.)

JOSÉ MARIA: Come on in, children.

IAN: (Approaching JOSÉ MARIA with hand extended) Happy to meet you, sir.

JOSÉ MARIA: *(Imitating IAN's serious manly tone, as HE shakes IAN's hand)* And I to meet you, young man. Sit.

> *(ISABEL & IAN sit on the floor at JOSÉ*
> *MARIA's feet. There is no other place to sit*
> *since ANA CECILIA is blocking as much of the sitting area*
> *as possible. Long, awkward silence*
> *as JOSÉ MARIA surveys IAN.)*

So...Isabel told me that you two are in a play together.

IAN: Uhm, yeah. "My Fair Lady." It's a musical.

JOSÉ MARIA: Oh, that's nice. Are you the star?

ISABEL: I'm the star.

IAN: I thought it was more like we both were the star.

ISABEL: Really? It's not called My Fair People is it? Or My Fair Couple?

IAN: *(With a laugh)* No, I guess not. Anyway, we both have pretty big roles—hers is the biggest, of course.

JOSÉ MARIA: Isabelita, how come you didn't tell me that you were THE My Fair Lady?

ISABEL: I don't know. You didn't ask me.

JOSÉ MARIA: I'm asking now. You know it's hard for me to get out of the house these days, so why don't you do a piece of it for me now? I would love to hear you.

ISABEL: Really? Well, okay, I mean, what do you think, Ian?

IAN: I think it would be fun. Let's do it.

ISABEL: The part you keep forgetting would be good.

IAN: *(Embarrassed)* Yeah...it would.

(IAN & ISABEL act out a scene from MY FAIR LADY, the middle of Act 2, Sc. 1, for JOSÉ MARIA & ANA CECILIA. ANA CECILIA gets increasingly agitated as SHE listens. IAN plays Henry Higgins and ISABEL plays Eliza Doolittle. ELIZA/ISABEL mimes throwing slippers at HIGGINS/IAN.)

ELIZA/ISABEL: There are your slippers! And there! Take your slippers, Professor Higgins, and may you never have a day's luck with them!

HIGGINS/IAN: *(Astounded)* What on earth?
                    (HE comes to her.)

What's the matter? Is anything wrong?

ANA CECILIA: *(To JOSÉ MARIA)* Are they Koo-Koo?? I don't see any slippers.

JOSÉ MARIA: Ssssh! Ana, please.

ELIZA/ISABEL: *(Seething)* Nothing wrong—with you. I've won your bet for you, haven't I? That's enough for you. I don't matter, I suppose?

HIGGINS/IAN: You won my bet! You! Presumptuous insect. I won it!
What did you throw those slippers at me for?

ELIZA/ISABEL: Because I wanted to smash your face. I'd like to kill you, you selfish brute. Why didn't you leave me where you picked me out of—the gutter? You thank God it's all over, and that now you can throw me back again there, do you?

ANA CECILIA: *(To JOSÉ MARIA)* That's where I'd like to throw you—Pracatan! Back to the gutter. Did you write this story?

HIGGINS/IAN: *(Trying to stay calm)*
So the creature is nervous, after all?

(ELIZA/ISABEL gives a suffocated scream of fury and instinctively darts her nails in his face. HIGGINS/IAN catches her wrists.)
Ah! Claws in you, you cat! How dare you show your temper to me?

ANA CECILIA: *(Over IAN's following action)*
¡Ah, Hah! ¡Eso! ¡Poohn! ¡Poohng! ¡Así!

HIGGINS/IAN: *(HE throws her roughly onto the sofa, where SHE falls into ANA CECILIA's lap.)*
Sit down and be quiet.

(ANA CECILIA pushes IAN to the floor.)

ISABEL: Mamabuela!

(ISABEL rushes to help him up. IAN immediately checks his hair then takes out his pick and starts picking.)

IAN: Did I get flat in the back?? It feels all flat now. Dag!

ISABEL: You look fine.
ANA CECILIA: Don't push any woman around in this house, Higgins.

ISABEL: It wasn't for real, Mamabuela.

ANA CECILIA: *(Pushing ISABEL back down on the couch)* I know—I know what's real!

ISABEL: So you were trying to protect me?

ANA CECILIA: Ay! I don't know! Stop asking questions and get rid of this—

JOSÉ MARIA: He's a nice boy, Ana. Don't get yourself so excited.

ANA CECILIA: They were the ones screaming about stupid things. Screaming! ¡ME CAGO EN LA LECHE DE "THOSE SLIPPERS!"
JOSÉ MARIA: You better go children. I think Doña Ana is tired.

ANA CECILIA: Bring my medicine next time.

JOSÉ MARIA: *(As IAN and ISABEL move to the door.)* Maybe you can come back later.

ANA CECILIA: No, they can't. We still have to do our shopping that we didn't do yesterday. Hurry up and put on your shoes old man.

JOSÉ MARIA: *(As ISABEL rushes IAN out the door)*
Nice meeting you. I liked your play.

ANA CECILIA: It was caca. That play was caca. You hear me? Like big fat mohones, floating in the toilet. Just like that. Oooey! !Que porquería!
(Watching him)
Well? Aren't you going to get dressed? It's fascinating how slow you are. You move like you're underwater.

JOSÉ MARIA: Sometimes I feel like I am.

(THEY look at their front door as it goes from day to night. Lights cross to SHARON sitting alone at the Pizza Parlor.)

SCENE 7

"Messed-up Girl"
SHARON, dressed in her Sunday best, waits at the Pizza Parlor for ISABEL to arrive. SHE puts money in the jukebox and plays "Just My Imagination" by The Temptations. As SHE moves away from the jukebox, DOLORES enters.

DOLORES: Who you waiting for, Sharoni?

SHARON: Don't call me that.

DOLORES: Ooh, chile! I like your hair. Who straightens it for you? Doña Paca does mine, but she always burns my scalp. She says I got such bad hair that she has to burn it to make it better.

SHARON: You need to go away.

DOLORES: It's a free country. I can eat pizza, if I want to.
>   (*DOLORES eats her pizza in silence,*
>   *as SHARON watches the door.*)
So...how's your brother. He's a fine looking boy. If I was younger, ooh, chile, watch out! I'd be right there—

SHARON: He's dead, Dolores. He died like a year ago. I'm on my way to the church now for a memorial service.

DOLORES: Oh, girl, I'm sorry. I thought he was still in the hospital. That's a shame. How old was he?

SHARON: Eleven.
>   (*DOLORES continues to eat in silence,*
>   *SHARON gets up.*)
I guess it's time to go. I thought maybe I'd see Isabel.

DOLORES: Why didn't you call her?

SHARON: They cut off our phone because Ma keeps forgetting to pay. She forgets everything now.

DOLORES: You don't have a lot of money, huh? I could ask my stepdad to give you some. If I don't tell my mom—he gives me stuff. And his job is paying good now after the strike.

SHARON: We got enough.

DOLORES: You looking so skinny too. Why don't you have some pizza? I'll buy you a slice.

SHARON: I'm not hungry.

DOLORES: Then why did you come to a pizza parlor?

SHARON: Have you seen Isabel or not?!

DOLORES: I saw her after school. She went over to her grandpa's house—with Ian, of course. Those two are getting disgusting. You want me to go with you?

SHARON: No.

DOLORES: I wanna go. Pay my respects and all.

SHARON: You didn't even know he was dead.

(DOLORES suddenly runs over to SHARON and hugs her. SHARON lets herself be hugged, fighting tears.)

DOLORES: Please, can I go?

SHARON: *(Pushing her away)* Get off me. Why would you want to go anyway? You're not my friend.

DOLORES: Yeah...that's true.
         (Pause; Pondering this)
I don't know. I like churches. They always got a good smell to them. And I like to pray. Like when I feel that pressure on my knees and I think I can't stay that way any longer? That's when I feel God inside me. My Ma taught me that—that when it starts to hurt like that—ooh, chile, that's a good feeling.

SHARON: That's messed up, girl.
   (DOLORES hugs her again, even tighter. SHARON
          pushes her away—
       more gently this time.)
Okay. But don't hug me anymore. It's hard enough, okay?

(THEY exit together. DOLORES moves to take SHARON's arm, but thinks better of it, keeping a respectful distance instead.)

DOLORES: Okay.
> *(Pause)*

I like when people hug me—when I'm sad I mean.
There's nothing wrong with touching people.
> *(Pause; SHARON sighs)*

I guess it depends though—how they touch you.
> *(SHARON starts to run.)*

Hey, wait up.
> *(SHARON falls to her knees)*

Hey, your dress. You'll get all dirty. Get up. Don't do that!

(DOLORES tries to get SHARON up as the lights cross to JOSÉLITO on the deck of a ship.)

SCENE 8

"Blood Runs"
1873. Dawn.
JOSÉLITO on his knees on the deck of a ship, which HE is cleaning with a cloth and a bucket of water. HE is ranting at the wind.
As HE speaks, a light slowly comes up on JOSÉ MARIA looking out his kitchen window recalling this memory.

JOSÉLITO: Don't do that! Don't make me think so much. Every time you come to me before a storm, I have this memory of my mother. On her knees.

Begging to take me with her. But I don't know if it's real. It's a memory that's like a dream now. I used to dream of my father until I understood that a Spaniard had forced himself on her. That's how I came into this world. I have two souls. The gentle one my mother gave me and the one an animal forced on us both. My father is someone I think of when I see animals get slaughtered. When blood runs from warm flesh into the soil under it, I think of him.
Sometimes I cut into my skin with seashells just to see that blood and remember. It always surprises me too—that I still have blood. "Hasn't it been drained out yet?" I wonder.

> *(Pause)*

How could any man do that?

> *(Pause)*

JOSÉLITO & JOSÉ MARIA: *(In unison)*
And what does that make me?

> *(Lights on the past fade as the Sotillo*
> *apartment is filled with morning light.)*

SCENE 9

"Que Triste Pasas"
Morning.
ANA CECILIA & JOSÉ MARIA try to have breakfast.
JOSÉ MARIA sits at the kitchen table, his right leg up on a

83

chair. ANA CECILIA sits with her head down, staring at the plate but not seeing it.

JOSÉ MARIA: Nothing? You have to eat something, my love.
(ANA CECILIA does not look up; Playfully)
If I feed you, like the queen that you are, will you eat then?

ANA CECILIA: If you try to put a spoon near my mouth, I will bite your hand through to the bone and I will not let go until the police come to tear me off you.

JOSÉ MARIA: Maybe you're just not hungry. Today is just one of your bad days. You'll feel better soon. Soon the dreams will go away, Ana.

ANA CECILIA: I woke up with the taste of his dirty fingers on my tongue, in the moist corners of my eyes. I woke up breathing him. Did you see my sheets?? Soiled. Because of him. It doesn't go away, José.

JOSÉ MARIA: You have to let me take you to the doctor. You're making yourself sick with—

ANA CECILIA: Why can't you stop talking? Most people need some silence, but not you. You will talk all night if I let you. Even if I never say one word back. Blah, blah, blah. On and on. Do you really have

anything important to say, old man? I can't believe
you do. I, on the other hand, have so much to say.
And I choose to keep it to myself. Do you know why?
Because I appreciate silence. That's a sign of good
breeding. I was raised to be a lady. Not like you,
Señorito. No. When you were a boy, you were tied to
a piece of iron. That's what my father said. You had a
piece of iron tied around your neck and you carried it
where ever you went so you couldn't get anywhere
fast and you couldn't swim away. Do you remember
that piece of metal?
I wish I had one for your tongue so that I could lock
your mouth so you would only speak when I let you.
And I would only let you, if I thought you had
something to say. And you would only have
something to say if you
were quiet for a very long time. That's the only way to
learn to value speech. You see, these are things only I
can understand—not you. Not ever.

(Pause)

Your food makes me sick. I can't eat what makes me
sick. It makes me sick because you cooked it—your
hands touched that. Your hands aren't human.
They're like his hands. You are not a man to me,
señorito. You are this.

(Spitting into the bowl of food in front of her.)

Like nothing. Like my dusty-smelling mouth. This
desert you made when you didn't save me. You even
turned my spit into sand.

(JOSÉ MARIA begins to cry quietly.)
Look at that! Did I make you feel something? You can never feel as much as me.
(ANA CECILIA gets up and goes to the bedroom. From the bedroom, we hear her sing "Noche de Ronda" by Agustin Lara.)
"Noche de ronda que triste pasas, que triste cruzas, por mi balcón.
Noche de ronda cómo me hieres cómo lastimas mi corazón.
Luna que se quiebra, Sobre la tiniebla de mi soledad, ¿A dónde vas?
Dime si esta noche tú te vas de ronda como ella se fue, ¿Con quién estás?"

*(JOSÉ MARIA joins in making the
song an oddly tragic duet.)*

JOSÉ MARIA & ANA CECILIA:
"Dile que la quiero, dile que me muero de tanto esperar que vuelva ya,
que las rondas no son buenas, que hacen daño, que dan penas
y que acaban por llorar."

ANA CECILIA: *(A different, gentler person; a transformation; all is forgotten for a moment)*

That is such a beautiful song. People don't sing songs like that anymore.

(Crosses over to her place at the table and begins to eat. JOSÉ MARIA begins to eat too, cautiously watching her for signs of an explosion that do not come.)

This soup needs more pepper.

(JOSÉ MARIA hands her the pepper-shaker in silence.)

You'll have to get more pepper. We're almost out.

(JOSÉ puts his spoon down and moves gingerly away from the table. It is difficult for him so we can tell HE is in physical pain.)

You better put something on that leg before it gets more swollen—then you won't be able to stop it from hurting.

JOSÉ MARIA: It's too late for that, I think.

(The lights on ANA CECILIA dim, while a shimmer of light remains on JOSÉ MARIA, as lights come up on MEDIANOCHE kneeling under a palm tree. SHE's dressed in a raggedy, torn dress. It is 1859. Her legs and dress are matted with blood. SHE is barefoot. SHE speaks to the baby SHE has just given birth to. SHE is gathering palm tree leaves and swaddling her newborn baby in them.)

MEDIANOCHE: *(singing a song SHE made up for her baby)* Chee-re-poh. Chee-chee-re-poh.
Chee-re-poh. Chee-chee-re-poh.

(speaking to the baby)

They told me you would never live—My son…I'll call you Obatalá. A strong spirit. You bring me light, Obalito. Your eyes are light.

These palms will protect you. Nature protects us. I don't remember the name my mother gave me—but every morning I feel that name inside me. The only home I know is that place between my mother's legs—swimming through her blood, I swam to you.
I crossed oceans to have you.

(Pause)

Over that dark water, I lost your grandmother.

(Pause)

I remember the warm kisses her wet eyes rained on me…her sweet lashes pouring over my face.

(Pause)

Feel me always in the water that moistens your lips, Obatalá. And I'll listen to the air of my breath for you.

*(Lights cross to the Pizza Parlor
later that afternoon.)*

SCENE 10

"The Serious Answer"

Late afternoon.
ISABEL & IAN slow dance in the pizza parlor to the song
playing on the jukebox. It is "Thin Line Between Love and
Hate" by The Persuaders. THEY wear their My Fair Lady
costumes. ISABEL looks bloodied and bruised. IAN looks
slightly ruffled, while ISABEL's shirt is badly torn.

ISABEL: I tried to get all the blood off but I couldn't.
      (THEY continue to dance in silence.)
I love dancing with you.

IAN: Yeah? Me too.

ISABEL: Do you love me?

IAN: Maybe.

ISABEL: If you, me and your mother was in a boat
and it started to sink, who would you save?

IAN: Myself. How about you?

ISABEL: My mother.

IAN: Oh. You wanted the serious answer.

ISABEL: I guess I did. Don't I always?
      (Pause)

How many more times do you think they'll beat me up?

IAN: It won't happen again. I'm going to talk to them.

ISABEL: Well that should do it.

IAN: Don't take an attitude with me.
                    (Silence)
Are you okay?

ISABEL: Yeah.

IAN: If I'da gotten there sooner, this wouldn't have happened.

ISABEL: Yeah. You woulda probably gotten us killed with your bad temper.

IAN: *(With a mischievous smile)* That's not all I got that's bad.

ISABEL: Man, you are so stupid.

> *(IAN holds her a little closer as
> THEY continue to dance in silence.)*

ISABEL: I tell you what was bad—us—in that play tonight.

IAN: I thought we were good.

ISABEL: No, uhuhn. Forgot almost all the lines. I think between us we wrote a whole new thing.

IAN : Made it better, probably.

ISABEL: And these costumes—I wanted to show my Papabuelo.
(Pause)
What am I gonna do? If I tell my dad I got beat up again, he's gonna send me to Puerto Rico for sure. He already said he wants me to go there over Christmas.

IAN: I bet it's beautiful there.

ISABEL: You want me to go?

IAN: I didn't say that.

ISABEL: Are you going out with Dolores now?

IAN: No.

ISABEL: I just got beat up for you.

IAN: I know. I'm sorry.

ISABEL: What am I gonna tell my mother? Will you come wif me?

IAN: Uhnuhh. I met enough of your family. I gotta go.

ISABEL: Aren't you even gonna walk me home? What—are you embarrassed now to be wif me? You think we'll get beat up? Scared it might muss up your hair?

IAN: Don't be stupid, Isabel. Of course, I'll walk you home—if you want. I could use the exercise.

ISABEL: Oh, man. Don't do me any favors. Maybe you should go find Dolores and she can exercise her mouth on you.
IAN: Maybe so. Don't say things you can't take back.
> (ISABEL tries to run off. IAN grabs her
> by the arm.)

Don't run away from me like that!
> (ISABEL pulls herself free and exits.)

Why are you doing this, Isabel? That's it. I'm gonna start dating Black chicks. Like Linc says "Never put too much cream in your coffee, sons of Africa, or pretty soon you'll be having milk. 'Nuff said, all done."

(Lights cross to Scene 11 in various locations.)

SCENE 11

"Aleluya"
A snowstorm. Night.
ISABEL tries to rinse the blood off her dress in a sink.
DOLORES sits on the stoop watching for rats. SHARON
walks along the street kicking up snow as SHE goes. JOSÉ
MARIA sits at the kitchen window, looking out.
JOSÉLITO paces on the dock. ANA CECILIA tries on
various pieces of clothing, checking herself out in the mirror.
Each person is caught in a pool of light
as he or she speaks.
At times, the ensemble may react physically to what another
character is saying, i.e. If a character mentions their hands,
perhaps the other characters will find a reason to touch their
own hands—a subliminal suggestion to link all the
characters psychically. This scene should feel like a dance.

ISABEL: *(As SHE tries to wash the blood off her clothes)* I
don't mind the blood, but it's when they spit on me
that I wanned to throw up. You can scrub and scrub
and never get those stains out. If you get hit hard
enough, you bleed. But when someone hates you

enough to spit at you, it burns into your skin—like a mark you can't ever erase. Papabuelo has marks like that.

(Pause)

This blood's not coming off.

(Lights cross to DOLORES, who is trying to kill rats with a piece of wood from a broken old shelf. The rats are running back and forth from the garbage to the stoop of the Sotillo apartment. Her mouth is bleeding.)

DOLORES: Come back here! I wanna kill you! You dirty, juicy things. Why do you have such big ole fat juicy tails? They look like my fingers. Chasing around in the garbage. 'Cept, I ain't no garbage-picker. Nuhuhh.

(Hitting a big rat, smashing it, then talking to it)

Got you, chubby!

(SHE scrapes the rat into a shoebox and looks into it like it is a coffin. SHE crosses herself.)

(Lights cross to the Sotillo apartment.

JOSÉ MARIA sits by the kitchen window, with a blanket draped around his shoulders, as ANA CECILIA speaks from her bedroom.)

ANA CECILIA: *(Beginning to undress; watching herself in the mirror)* Hepa! Looking pretty good—pero ese viejo. ¡Olvidaté! I forget how old he is he's so old.
  (Conjuring a courtship scene from 1889 in her head, SHE sees JOSÉ MARIA tying ropes into nautical knots and arranging them neatly on the ground on a dock in San Juan.)
Look who's here. I expect to see rats hiding by the boats—but it's Señorito José.

  (Lights cross to a dock in San Juan Harbor. 1873. JOSÉLITO is looking at his hands. HE stands on the dock, looking at the ship HE was once a slave on. JOSÉ MARIA looks out the window as JOSÉLITO speaks.)

JOSÉLITO: I don't know why I came back. If I'm free now, I could go anywhere. But instead...
                              (Pause)
All I know is this boat...And the stars to guide her with.

  (Lights cross back to DOLORES. Unable to contain her excitement, DOLORES looks up at the Sotillo window, sees Papabuelo there and holds the rat up so he can see.)

DOLORES: There he is! They say he's old—like people in the bible used to be. What's he doing in the window? He's gonna catch a cold that way—but maybe he don't catch colds 'cause he don't go nowheres no more. Now they say he used to love picking in the garbage—jus' like you. That's where they got all they furniture. Mmmhmm. I hate old people. What are they still here for? Somebody needs to jus' put 'em in a box and close the top.

(Lights cross to JOSÉ MARIA & ANA CECILIA in ANA's memory from 1889.)

JOSÉ MARIA: Señorita Ana, what are you doing out in this heat? Aren't you afraid of burning that beautiful skin?

ANA CECILIA: I don't burn, I simmer.

JOSÉ MARIA: *(Slightly shocked by her blatant flirtation)* Señorita! I'm sure I don't know what you mean.

ANA CECILIA: Are you turning red for me, Señorito?

JOSÉ MARIA: I have to get back to work.

ANA CECILIA: *(Lifting up her skirt to above her ankles)* Do you know how to recognize a snakebite? I think one bit me as I walked over here through the sugar...cane.

JOSÉ MARIA: That's quite a walk. There's not a lot of sugar cane in San Juan.
(Taking a quick, shy glance)
Looks like a mosquito. Make a paste with a little salt and water. That'll bring down the swelling.

ANA CECILIA: *(Trying to be innocent but not really succeeding)* Oh...is that how you bring it down?

(Lights cross to DOLORES.)

DOLORES: And he's always going around telling all those dumb stories. And then Isabel thinks she's slick with all them stories. I got stories too. But she won't listen to mine. Maybe I'll tell one to you, chubby...

(Lights cross back to JOSÉ MARIA &
ANA CECILIA.)

JOSÉ MARIA: So what do you really want, Señorita Ana?

ANA CECILIA: I want you to kiss me.

JOSÉ MARIA: Do you? Why? I know your father warned you about men—like me.

ANA CECILIA: He says many things I don't hear.

JOSÉ MARIA: There are some who would like to see me dead for kissing a young girl like you.

ANA CECILIA: Yes. Exciting, isn't it? But I think I would be in trouble too.

(Lights cross to JOSÉLITO in 1873.)

JOSÉLITO: You can see the sky best from the deck of a ship as it cuts through the darkest part of the night.

(Lights cross back to JOSÉ MARIA &
ANA CECILIA in 1889.)

JOSÉ MARIA: And you think a kiss from me is—

ANA CECILIA: Worth it. I'm sure of that.

JOSÉ MARIA: Don't you think I'm a little old for you?

ANA CECILIA: I don't like boys my age. They are so immature.

JOSÉ MARIA: *(Holds out his arm, stroking his skin back and forth with two fingers indicating his skin.)* And this?

(Lights cross to ISABEL still trying
to get the bloodstains out.)

ISABEL: Why do people have so much blood anyway? If I didn't have blood, would those girls still wanna hit me? If they couldn't see how much they were hurting me, maybe they would just go away. People like them like seeing all that red. Then they feel like they're better than you, because they kept their own stuff inside. Papabuelo once told me that it's good to bleed sometimes, because it lets the air in—so you remember to breathe.

(Pause)

Maybe he can help me remember.

(Lights cross back to JOSÉ MARIA and ANA CECILIA, still in ANA CECILIA's memory from 1889.)

ANA CECILIA: *(Touching his fingertips with hers)* You have the most beautiful hands I've ever seen. Each finger so strong and straight. I thought you would have calluses on your hands from pulling on so many ropes, but—

JOSÉ MARIA: You've been watching me work on the ship?

ANA CECILIA: No...Only a few—maybe five times...I happened by.

(Lights cross back to DOLORES.)

DOLORES: My stepfather doesn't let me tell any stories. He says I lie. And then he tells Mami so she won't let me go out—but I don't lie. I don't ever lie. I don't ever, ever lie.

(Lights cross back to JOSÉLITO in 1873.)

JOSÉLITO: Even when the air is still, the feeling of that stillness on your face lifts your eyes toward the starlight.

(Lights cross back to JOSÉ MARIA & ANA CECILIA still in ANA CECILIA's memory from 1889.)

ANA CECILIA: Kiss me.

JOSÉ MARIA: No. Not until you know what you're doing.

ANA CECILIA: I know.
            (SHE suddenly jumps up and kisses him quickly on the lips.)
You see?

JOSÉ MARIA: *(Gently pushing her away)* That only proves that you know nothing about me. To me a kiss

is a serious thing. I like my kisses to mean something.
And I like them to last a very long time.

ANA CECILIA: *(Raising her chin and closing her eyes in anticipation of a kiss)* I'm ready.

JOSÉ MARIA: Good day, señorita.

> *(HE walks away. ANA CECILIA sighs
> as SHE watches him exit.)*

ANA CECILIA: He makes me feel like I'm flying.

> *(Lights cross back to JOSÉLITO.)*

JOSÉLITO: I often dreamed of changing places with a
star. Then I could guide others. And maybe someone
who loves me would look up and see that I'll be with
her always in that part of the sky. And that would
make her happy, I hope. And I would finally have my
wings made of stardust.
> *(A rainstorm begins; smiling at
> the thought of his bad luck)*
But then, of course, it would rain.

> *(Lights cross to ISABEL.)*

ISABEL: I wish I had raindrops flowing through me, or snowflakes, or even tears. They don't leave any stains—on the outside anyways.

(Lights cross back to DOLORES.)

DOLORES: Once upon a time, there was a beautiful girl named Dolores, who lived in a shoebox, in a closet, and nobody ever let her out because they couldn't see she was beautiful because they couldn't hear her screaming—because she was in a box. So, one day, she cut a hole in the box with her teeth and ran out of that house. Because her stepfather—because...And then she didn't know where to go because she couldn't find her grandmother's house, because it was in P.R., so she went to the church instead.

(Lights cross to ANA CECILIA.
Her memory fades as SHE speaks.)

ANA CECILIA: He was so shy. Shy men are like jewels, their value only increases with time. No one ever treated me so much like a lady. No matter how hard I tried to tease him, he never once lost respect.

(Lights cross to JOSÉLITO in 1873. As JOSELITO
speaks, JOSÉ MARIA, in the present, finishes his
sentences, lost in his own memories.)

JOSÉLITO: And my wings would fill with water and I would fall back down to the earth—

JOSÉ MARIA: —in shiny drops that she would drink.

JOSÉLITO: And when she took me inside her—

JOSÉ MARIA: I would clean the dirt from her heart that someone else put there.

JOSÉLITO: If I could remove that darkness, she could start on a new road that no one could follow.

JOSÉ MARIA: Her own road.
                    (Pause)
It's snowing so hard now—

JOSÉLITO & JOSÉ MARIA: —like it won't ever stop.

(JOSÉ MARIA watches his memory of JOSÉLITO fade as ANA CECILIA speaks.)

ANA CECILIA: *(Her face darkens as SHE speaks.)* But that viejo, out there...I don't know who he is. I want to ask him, "What did you do with my José?" You buried him somewhere so deep that I can't find him with my eyes or my fingertips...or my lips, but still I search. I'm covered with the sadness of searching. I can taste my José when I swallow my own tears. "Ah, there he is, " I tell myself, "welcome home."

(ANA CECILIA begins to pray.
Lights cross to DOLORES who is putting the top on the shoebox, covering the rat.)

DOLORES: There. That's better. You gotta rest now.
(Kneeling down and slowly singing
a hymn over the dead rat.)
"Aleluya, Aah-aah-leluya-aah, ah-le-eh-lu--ooh-ooh-ooh-ooh-ya!."

(Lights cross to SHARON, who walks through the snow, kicking up snow as SHE walks in the dark. Finally, SHE tosses herself down and makes snow angels. JOSÉ MARIA sees SHARON from his window and calls out to her.)

JOSÉ MARIA: Sharon!

(SHE doesn't hear him because of the wind and because SHE is so intent on making her snow angels. JOSÉ MARIA continues to watch SHARON as a light comes up on JOSÉLITO
who surveys the scene around him, searching.)

JOSÉLITO: I think I'll be able to tell when I have found my family. Not by the way they look, but how they will make me feel.

(Pause)

Even if they have passed into Heaven, I can see them in the velvet petals of a flower or in the fierce waves of a storm at sea.

SHARON: *(Speaking to Junie in heaven)* There. That's better than writing letters to heaven.

(Pause)

You know what I want to say anyways.

(Pause)

When you look down from heaven and see these angels waiting for you, I know you'll find your way home.

(SHE continues to make snowangels as the lights grow to softly include JOSÉLITO, JOSÉ MARIA, ANA CECILIA, DOLORES, and finally ISABEL. THEY all look up at the sky for a moment. Then ISABEL exits with the sound of the wind.)

END OF ACT ONE

ACT TWO
SCENE 1

"¡Feliz Cumpleaños!"
In the dark, the sound of wind begins.
A snowstorm. JOSÉ MARIA's birthday.
ISABEL stands on the outside of the front door, listening to
her great-grandparents argue. SHE is holding a gift-
wrapped package. On the inside, ANA CECILIA throws a
set rat trap at JOSÉ MARIA, who stands at the kitchen sink
washing his face. It snaps as it hits the wall,
barely missing him.

JOSÉ MARIA: Coño, mujer! What are you doing??
Are you trying to cut my nose off with that thing?!

ANA CECILIA: I wasn't aiming for your nose, you
dirty man! I'm going to cut it off one day and you
won't be able to bother me any more. I'll snip it off
with scissors one night and chop it into my morning
eggs. That's the way I want to wake up! You should
know better. Servants should never go after the lady
of the house.

JOSÉ MARIA: But I'm your husband.

ANA CECILIA: In your dreams, old man! In your
dreams!

Go cook me dinner! And don't put too much onions this time. If I get gas, I cannot sing. If I cannot sing— the people suffer from not hearing me.

JOSÉ MARIA: Of course they do. We all suffer.

ANA CECILIA: If you were really my husband, you would have protected me.

(ANA CECILIA goes into the bedroom as ISABEL knocks on the door. JOSÉ MARIA answers.)

JOSÉ MARIA: Isabelita! You walked all the way here in this snow? You must be frozen.

ISABEL: Naah. I like walking around in bad weather. It's safer wif nobody hanging around in the street.
(Pause)
Why does she think you're her servant?

JOSÉ MARIA: So you were listening?!
(ISABEL looks embarrassed.)
She thinks everybody's her servant.

ISABEL: Mami says she's crazy.

JOSÉ MARIA: You don't get to be as old as your great-grandmother without being a little crazy.

ISABEL: How old is she?

JOSÉ MARIA: Ninety-nine.

ISABEL: Wow! She is old.

JOSÉ MARIA: I'm even older than that.

ISABEL: But you look better than her. You got pretty eyes, Papabuelo. Different from other eyes—but not crazy like hers. Papi says your eyes are green but they look yellow to me. Like pieces of gold smack in the middle of your face.
    (Handing him the wrapped package)
Happy birthday, Papabuelo.

JOSÉ MARIA: (Unwraps the gift; it contains cherry-flavored chewing tobacco) ¡Que cheveré! They let you buy tobacco?

ISABEL: Yeah. I tole the man at the drugstore that it was for you. I had to hide it from Mami though. She thinks your eyes are yellow from too much of it. She doesn't see what I see. Your eyes tell me things I couldn't figure out by myself. How'd you get yellow eyes like that?

JOSÉ MARIA: I was born with them.

ISABEL: I was born with these eyes too.

JOSÉ MARIA: And these feet.

ISABEL: And these arms.

JOSÉ MARIA: And this head.

ISABEL: And this heart.

ANA CECILIA: *(Slapping JOSÉ MARIA playfully on the butt)* And that fondillo.
> *(ISABEL laughs.)*
And you? I know why you're here. I made a fresh batch this afternoon.
> *(Taking out what appears to be candies on a tray.)*
Eat one.
> *(ISABEL hesitates. ANA CECILIA*
> *slaps her across the head.)*
Go ahead! They won't last forever.

JOSÉ MARIA: Leave the girl alone, Ana Cecilia.

ANA CECILIA: I said take one!
> *(ISABEL takes one and holds it in her hand.)*
Eat it! You people always enjoy my chocolates.

ISABEL: *(Reluctantly putting the candy-like substance in her mouth—it's really pieces of soap dipped in Hershey's chocolate.)* Oooey!
> *(Her mouth foaming up from the soap)*

That stuff's nasty.
> *(SHE tries to spit it out, but sees her*
> *great-grandmother is still watching,*
> *so SHE forces herself to finish the piece.)*

ANA CECILIA: You want another one?
> *(ISABEL vigorously nods "No.")*

You'll want some later. Good chocolates, huh? Poor people have their minds in the sugar all the time. You're like dogs for it. Hungry for it. I never liked sweets myself. They weaken your heart. People fall in love when they eat too much candy. Always with the wrong person. That's why so many children have children. They don't know. Their minds are in the sweets, covered with sugar. No sense.

> *(ANA CECILIA exits as ISABEL wipes*
> *the inside of her mouth on her sleeve.)*

JOSÉ MARIA: She never gives me any of her chocolates.

ISABEL: You can have all of mine. Dag! She did that to me the last time. Doesn't she know that people aren't supposed to eat soap?? And the way she carves them up to look like chocolates—that's sick, papabuelo. Why did you marry her?

JOSÉ MARIA: She was the first person who didn't stare at my scars like I was a criminal.

(From inside JOSÉ's head a scene from the past is conjured. It is 1889, ANA CECILIA & JOSÉ MARIA each dance with imaginary partners in a plaza in Puerto Rico. THEY dance near each other—perhaps back to back—talking so that no one else at the dance will know that they are talking to each other. ISABEL freezes during this exchange.)

ANA CECILIA: What's that on your neck? Did you try to kill yourself?

JOSÉ MARIA: No. It's just a mark...from before.

ANA CECILIA: What kind of mark?

JOSÉ MARIA: They tell me I was put in chains the day I could walk. I don't remember that day. Even though I'm a free man now, I still remember the chains. Why did you ask if I tried to kill myself?

ANA CECILIA: I could never marry a suicidal man. Too much drama.

111

JOSÉ MARIA: You want to marry me?

ANA CECILIA: Not today.

JOSÉ MARIA: And if I told you that I've been watching you dance all night, waiting for you to look at me—And thought the only way I would become a slave again, would be to your heart—would that be too much drama?

ANA CECILIA: More like melodrama. ¡Sangano! I'm near-sighted. I couldn't see you anyway—until you stood right in front of me.

> (THEY stop dancing and speak with their
> backs to one another, barely touching.)

JOSÉ MARIA: I see you even when my eyes are closed—when I'm asleep and dreaming.

ANA CECILIA: Are you falling in love with me, Josélito?

JOSÉ MARIA: Oh, yes. And you?

ANA CECILIA: I'm undecided.

JOSÉ MARIA: Really? I'll have to work harder then— I'll set a new course for your heart every day until I reach it. If there's one thing a sailor knows, it's that there's always more than one route to the important places.

ANA CECILIA: But that doesn't mean the port is open when you get there, señorito.

JOSÉ MARIA: No. But I'm very patient, señorita.

(THEY allow themselves to touch for a moment, each taking in the essence of the other.)

*(ISABEL interrupts JOSÉ MARIA's reverie.
The memory fades as ISABEL speaks.)*

ISABEL: So you fell in love with her? Because she din't think you were a thief or a killer or somefin?

JOSÉ MARIA: Isabel! I fell in love with her because she didn't care that I was a slave.
In my nightmares, I see men putting pieces of iron around my neck, my wrists, my ankles. Then I can no longer feel the air—like God's breath—against my skin. With metal on me like that again, I would stop being free. When I wake from those nightmares— she's the one who holds me till I can fall asleep again.

ISABEL: You don't still worry about that, do you? Nobody's gonna take you from the Bronx and chain you up again.

JOSÉ MARIA: There's different ways of being chained, Isabel. You like this place?

ISABEL: I did like it. But now I can't even walk home with my friend Sharon without somebody saying something about it. It don't make no sense. The Black girls say we can't be friends no more because I'm Puerto Rican. And the Puerto Rican girls say I shouldn't be hanging around with no Black girls. I remember when nobody cared who was friends with who. Then Martin Luther King got shot and I got beat up the next day. I didn't kill him, why were they picking on me? And anyway, wasn't he was ours too. That was three years ago, but the fighting still hasn't stopped.
JOSÉ MARIA: I told your father he should send you to Puerto Rico. It's safer there.

ISABEL: Oooey, no! My stupid cousin Evelyn will be there and she's always so mean, just because I speak bad Spanish. I can't help it. I'm from here, Papabuelo.

JOSÉ MARIA: You're from there too, m'ija. It's in your blood—on your face. La mancha de platano siempre se te nota.

ISABEL: Great! I'm stained with bananas. That's supposed to make me proud? Sometimes I wish I was an orphan and then I could do anything I wanned because nobody'd be watching what I do all the time.

JOSÉ MARIA: You don't mean that.

ISABEL: Uhh huh! I do.

JOSÉ MARIA: Then we wouldn't be talking like this. I'd just be some old man you might or might not meet on the street. You'd see me and you'd think "why is that wrinkly thing still alive?"

ISABEL: I'd never think that, Papabuelo.
          (*Taking his hands in hers and kissing them*)
Do you miss P. R.? Maybe you can go with me over Christmas.

JOSÉ MARIA: There's parts of it I miss. I miss feeling the sand fill the spaces between my toes—letting the Sun pound on my back, turning my insides into a thick, hot soup that cures anything. I still think the Sun has the power to heal. Sometimes when I'm not feeling so good, I sit right over there by that window

and let the light caress my face. It always makes me feel better.
>   *(Looking out the window)*
Look at how hard it's snowing now. I guess I won't be able to go out.

ISABEL: Where were you gonna go?

JOSÉ MARIA: I don't know. Somewhere. I always hope I might go somewhere.
>   *(Pause; Noticing a big bruise on ISABEL's arm.)*
What happened to your arm? Did that sinvergüenza boyfriend do this to you?? Tell me, Isabel! Tell me the truth.

ISABEL: No, Papabuelo. Ian would only hit me if I tried to take away his stupid pick. That boy is so vain.

JOSÉ MARIA: So what happened?

ISABEL: I got beat up by some Black girls. They don't like me going out with Ian.

JOSÉ MARIA: Did you tell them you were Black too?

ISABEL: No.
>   *(Pause)*
I am?

JOSÉ MARIA: What do you think I am?

ISABEL: I don't know. You're just my Papabuelo.
                              (Pause)
So you can be both?

JOSÉ MARIA: You're three things, nena. You're
African, Spanish and Indian.

ISABEL: Indian?

JOSÉ MARIA: Taino. On your mother's side. You're
all mixed-up, nena.

ISABEL: You're telling me.

JOSÉ MARIA: You're a jibara, nena. That's a true
Puerto Rican. That's something to be proud of. I
know people think jibaros are fools from the
mountains—but that's not so. Jibaros are what will
keep our culture alive. They have all this blood from
everywhere and that makes them stronger than
everybody else. You are like a tree with strong roots
all connected to a different river. You can drink from
them all. That will keep you proud.

ISABEL: Proud? I just feel confused. If I told those
girls who beat me up that I was Black, they would say

I wasn't because I don't look like them and because I got a Spanish last name.

JOSÉ MARIA: Does it matter what they say?

ISABEL: No. But they would never believe me.

JOSÉ MARIA: You want me to come to school and play show and tell?

ISABEL: I don't think that would matter to them. They already got it in their heads what a Puerto Rican is. You would just be a Spanish guy with a tan.

JOSÉ MARIA: This "tan" made people think I wasn't human. Did I upset you?

ISABEL: I'm just upset that there's this disease that only Black people get and you might die because Sharon's brother—

JOSÉ MARIA: Mi'ja, I'm one hundred and twelve years old. I'm gonna die soon of something.

ISABEL: Don't say that.

JOSÉ MARIA: It's true. I'm not afraid of it anymore.
            (SHARON enters the street, slowly
               walking along it—like she's lost.)

I respect Death. That's why it stayed away for so long.
But it won't stay away forever. And you better learn
to respect where you came from or you'll never be
happy and that's the same as being dead—maybe
worse.

ISABEL: I'm trying, Papabuelo. But it's hard for me. I
don't like so many things...But I love you. Nothing
makes me happier than to be with you. And to have
the same blood as Sharon is so slick. She'll freak out.

JOSÉ MARIA: Freak out?

ISABEL: Yeah...because—I don't know. I always
thought I wanned her to be my sister instead of the
sisters I got because we got so much the same, and
now...I don't know. We got even more.

JOSÉ MARIA: There's a lot of important things to
fight for—like a sister, or a mother...or a wife. Make
sure you fight only for the good things, nena—the
things you can't live without. Those girls who hit you
are so blind by their bad fight that they can't even see
you. Like an angry blind man, trying to catch a bird
by swinging his arms. What a useless thing! That bird
is just going to fly off, into the sky, to a better place—
And if you can't even see it go, then you'll never be
able to catch it.

ISABEL: If I could fly, Papabuelo, I wouldn't have to run away from those wenches.

JOSÉ MARIA: Maybe you should stay home, nena.

ISABEL: I'm not afraid.

JOSÉ MARIA: There's no place that's safe for us.

ISABEL: Sure. If you just bring Mamabuela and she gives out her special chocolates, the bad people will be running away from you like poisoned rats.

JOSÉ MARIA: Don't disrespect your mamabuela, Isabel.

ISABEL: But she's an evil old wench—

JOSÉ MARIA: (Slapping ISABEL) Don't ever say that again!
> *(Silence, as JOSÉ MARIA takes*
> *in what just happened.)*

You don't understand nothing about her. You don't know everything, Isabel. Since we got attacked, we don't even leave the house.

ISABEL: What do you mean you got attacked?? Where?

JOSÉ MARIA: It doesn't matter.

ISABEL: What do you mean it doesn't matter?? Somebody attacked you, I wanna know about it!

JOSÉ MARIA: Why? So you can keep making fun of her? Of me?

ISABEL: I would never make fun of you.

JOSÉ MARIA: A few blocks from here. Some kids knocked me down onto the pavement so I passed out. But your poor grandma...They didn't just rob us, m'ija. Now she won't even let me kiss her.

ISABEL: How could they do that to an old lady?

JOSÉ MARIA: I don't know...How could I <u>let</u> them do that to her?

ISABEL: If you were passed out, there was nothing you <u>could</u> do.

JOSÉ MARIA: A man doesn't let—that wasn't supposed to happen.
                    (*Pause*)
I still can't believe it...How does a boy of fifteen lose respect for a woman over ninety years old?

(Lights cross to ANA CECILIA who speaks, watching the falling snow from her bedroom window.)

ANA CECILIA: *(Recalling the attack)*
One of them, the darkest one, put his fingers so deep inside me that I bled. I couldn't believe how much that disgusting little animal looked like my José. I kept looking into their eyes. Wasn't one of those boys going to see his own grandmother in my face? Wasn't one of them going to feel the shame of what they were doing and stop or at least run away? But no, all of them stayed and watched...I thought they had killed José. He lay on the ground looking like he was not even breathing. Both of us bleeding together. After a while they left—when I lost the energy to cry that seemed to bore them. When the ambulance came, I was too ashamed to tell them what happened. I thought they would never believe me. I didn't believe it. And this old man just got a cut on his head. The doctor kept asking me what did they do, but I wouldn't say. Nobody has to know that. I wish I could forget it.

JOSÉ MARIA: *(Overlapping with ANA CECILIA)* I wish I could forget it.

ISABEL: So that's why she's so cuckoo.
> *(A quick look at JOSÉ MARIA to make sure HE's not going to slap her again.)*

122

I mean, more even than she used to be. I feel bad now.
I'm so sorry, Papabuelo. I didn't know.

JOSÉ MARIA: There's a lot you don't know, Isabel.
You judge people too harshly.
Ven aca, nena.

(ISABEL goes to him and HE hugs her.)
(From the other room, ANA CECILIA begins to sing
"Bésame Mucho" by Consuelo Velazquez. ISABEL joins
in.)

ANA CECILIA: "Bésame, bésame mucho.

ANA CECILIA & ISABEL: Como si fuera esta noche la
última vez!

(ANA CECILIA comes out of her room dancing and
singing. SHE pulls ISABEL to her feet and dances with her
as all three sing.)

ANA CECILIA, JOSÉ MARIA & ISABEL:
Bésame, bésame mucho. Que tengo miedo a perderte
perderte después.
Quiero tenerte muy cerca, mirarme en tus ojos, verte
junto a mí.
Piensa que tal vez mañana yo ya estaré lejos muy lejos
de aquí."

*(ANA CECILIA hands ISABEL an awkwardly-wrapped
package. It is the same box
we saw in the PROLOGUE.)*

ANA CECILIA: ¡Feliz cumpleaños, Isabel!

*(ISABEL stares at the gift in amazement as ANA CECILIA
drifts back to her room,
dancing and singing softly.)*

ISABEL: She never remembers my birthday.

JOSÉ MARIA: She always remembered. She just
never got you a gift before. Go ahead and open it.
  *(ISABEL does so. The box is empty. It is the same box
    ISABEL opened in the PROLOGUE.)*

ISABEL: There's nuffin in here.

JOSÉ MARIA: Maybe you have to use your
imagination.

ISABEL: Yeah...then I can have anything I want and it
can last forever...
                (Pause)
If you could have anything in the world for your
birthday, what would it be?

JOSÉ MARIA: The tobacco's pretty good.

ISABEL: No—uhn uhh. I mean, anything! Like would you like to meet God?

JOSÉ MARIA: I can wait for that one. But if I could have anything...hmm...You know what I'd like? To hear your great-grandmother say she loves me.

ISABEL: She's never said it?

JOSÉ MARIA: No—not yet. What do you think I have to do to make her say it? I need some tools to help me, Belita.
ISABEL: Tools?

JOSÉ MARIA: Tools of love. Not made of metal or wood. The best tools smell like the ocean—and a Christmas dinner of arroz con gandules y lechon.

ISABEL: Oh...you mean like flowers? On TV, women always fall for flowers.

JOSÉ MARIA: Yes. Flowers would be nice. But how do you find flowers in a snow storm?

ISABEL: Leave it to me. There's a place over on Fordham Road that sells them. Except—

JOSÉ MARIA: What?

ISABEL: I don't have any money left. That tobacco
tapped me out. But I know where I can get some.

JOSÉ MARIA: Don't do anything crazy, Isabel.

ISABEL
I won't.
(Getting up and putting on her coat)
Wish me luck.

JOSÉ MARIA: Be careful, m'ija.

ISABEL: Always.

JOSÉ MARIA: Here. Take a key. I don't always hear
the door before Doña Ana. And I—I want to surprise
her, okay?

ISABEL: (Taking the key HE offers her) Okay. Oooh!
It's warm.

JOSÉ MARIA: (Kidding her) That's because I keep it
by my heart, nena.

(ISABEL puts the key down the front of her blouse, into her
bra. It does not fall out. SHE is very proud. ISABEL exits.
JOSÉ MARIA

watches her go from the kitchen window.)

JOSÉ MARIA: I hope she's alright. I put crazy ideas in her head. That's what Ana Cecilia always says. And maybe she's right. But what if Isabel can find the right flowers for my Ana? That's not so crazy. I need them soon.

(Lights cross to IAN sitting on the front stoop.)

SCENE 2

"I Must Confess"
IAN sits on the front stoop, watching ISABEL walk off. HE spins his globe and speaks to it.

IAN: Dag! She just walked right past me—like I wasn't even here.
(Pause)
I hope nobody saw that.
(Picking at his hair)
That's the last time I put myself out for a woman.
(Pause)
Lincoln Hayes never put himself on the line for Julie. Nuhuhh. He may be her partner in crime fighting, but he will not take a bullet for her—I mean, maybe he would—but not just because she's a woman. I mean,

he's a hero and heroes have to stand in the way of bullets, right?

(Pause)

Like my Uncle Nathan. He took a bullet for his country.

*(Spins the globe and stops it over
a hole in its surface)*

Here's where that bullet landed after slicing through the thick Asian air and entering my Uncle's right hand. He said he was spinning you at the time. Just like this.

(Spinning the globe again)

And out of nowhere a sniper fired one shot. "What was he trying to do?" he said. "Shoot the world? No wonder they lost. You can't get rid of the world that easy."

(Pause)

Unless your world's just one person.

(Pause)

I even wrote her a song...

*(Singing his song; a soulful ballad; SHARON enters in the
middle of IAN's song, unseen by him.)*

"My world is hell without my Isabel.

My life's so blue without you.

You bring me happiness—

and I must confess—

You're indeed—all the woman—I'll ever need.

If for any girl I fell, it's for you, my Isabel...

It's for you my Isabel..."

> *(Speaking)*

I guess I shoulda told her that.

> *(IAN sees SHARON glaring at him.)*

IAN: Don't give me that look!

SHARON: Wow! I didn't know shit could talk.

IAN: Don't start.

SHARON: I don't know what she sees in a selfish, stuck-up "dude" like you.

IAN: You don't know because you don't know me.

SHARON: I don't want to know you.

IAN: And I don't want you to know me.

SHARON: There ain't nothing to know.

IAN: Even if you knew you wouldn't know, because what do you know anyway?!

SHARON: If I wanted to know, I would know, but I don't so I don't. So what's that to you??

IAN: Nothing. You're nothing to me.

SHARON: That goes double for me.

IAN: Double nothing is twice nothing is beyond nothing, sister.

SHARON: Ooh, no you didn't. No, no, no. You do not call me sister. I only ever had one "bro" and he is not you.

IAN: Why do you hate me so much?

SHARON: I don't care about you enough to hate you.

IAN: If you gave me a chance, you might even like me.

SHARON: No. Uhnuhh.

IAN: I sing better than Tito.

SHARON: He plays the bass.

IAN: (*Sings and dances to the Jackson 5's "The Love You Save."*) "Stop, the love you save may be your own. Darling take it slow—or one day you'll be all alone. You better stop—"
  (*SHARON exits. HE stops singing.*)

I better stop. I wish I was somebody else right now.
Anybody else.

> (HE watches her go and then
> exits in the opposite direction.
> Lights cross back to the Sotillo apartment.)

SCENE 3

"Poets Respect Silence"
JOSÉ MARIA takes out some tobacco and begins to chew, as
we hear ANA CECILIA clearing her throat from the
bedroom. SHE makes loud, nasty phlegm-filled sounds.
ANA CECILIA enters.
SHE is wearing a strange outfit that only
SHE thinks is beautiful.

ANA CECILIA: I wrote you a poem, viejo. For your
birthday. Are you ready?

JOSÉ MARIA: Yes, I think so. Do I have to do
something?

ANA CECILIA: You just have to listen, cabron.

JOSÉ MARIA: I can do that.

(ANA CECILIA opens her mouth but no sound comes out of
it. JOSÉ MARIA watches her closely, waiting for

*something to come out. Finally, SHE closes her mouth, and
bows.)*

JOSÉ MARIA: That was—beautiful.

ANA CECILIA: I worked on it a long time. In my
room. My gooseness, you think I don't do nothing
back in there, but my mind is—
        (Making a spiraling gesture with her hand)
—like that! Going, going, all around. If you tried to
take a picture of my mind, forgedaboudit, you'd get
lost.
        *(ANA CECILIA exits. JOSÉ MARIA
        goes to the kitchen window.)*

JOSÉ MARIA: Her poems are getting better.
        (Pause)
I hope Isabel will be alright.
        (The lights cross to the street.)

SCENE 4

"Lost"
*IAN, SHARON & DOLORES each taking a different path
down the street, lost in thought. THEY speak their
thoughts. SHARON carries a board game tied with a red
ribbon. IAN carries a globe. DOLORES carries a rosary.*

SHARON: I keep getting lost on my way home.
You'd think I would remember the way, but this snow
makes it so I get all turned around.

IAN: I'm going to give this to Isabel. Then she'll love
me again.

DOLORES: Is the holy spirit a man or a woman? I
think she's a woman—because she's gotta have long
hair to hide behind.

SHARON: Do I go right or left here? Each time I leave
it takes longer to get back.

DOLORES: The holy spirit's gotta hide or somebody
will try to take her power away.
If somebody takes her power, then we got no hope left.

IAN: Or maybe she won't...Maybe she'll never
understand that we could go someplace that's not here
and everything would be better.
Even if I find her, I won't know what to say.

SHARON: Everything takes such a long time when
you're sad.

IAN: I waited too long. It won't work anymore.
Might as well not even try.

DOLORES: Without hope, you might as well be—you know—dead.

SHARON: I think it's right. I just keep walking until I smell my mother's cooking.

IAN: I miss her face. I could get lost there. I can't let myself get lost.

DOLORES: When you got the holy spirit, you're not lost anymore.

DOLORES, IAN & SHARON: I'm almost home.

(Lights cross to ISABEL.)

SCENE 5

"Parchessi For Love"
ISABEL is rushing to get the flowers.
SHE bumps into SHARON who carries the parchessi board
tied with a red ribbon.

SHARON: Hey!

ISABEL: Hey!

SHARON: You never came to my house for a game, so I thought I'd come find you.

ISABEL: I got a set just like that one.

SHARON: Oh...I was gonna give this to you for your birthday. It's tomorrow right?

ISABEL: Yeah. You usually forget.

SHARON: I know. You usually remind me. Where have you been?

ISABEL: Around. I can't play today.

SHARON: If you don't wanna be my friend anymore just say so. Don't be running away from me all the time. Sneaking off to kiss that stupid boyfriend of yours.

ISABEL: He's not my boyfriend. And anyway, what do you mean run? It's you who keeps disappearing. Where do you keep going? You walk around like a ghost, haunting the street. What are you looking for all the time?

SHARON: I just have to walk sometimes. And you have not been around, girl.

ISABEL: I'm around now. Look.
             (Putting out her hand)

Touch me and I won't go away.

    (SHARON takes her hand, then slaps it away.)

You see?

SHARON: See what?

ISABEL: *(ISABEL takes SHARON's hand and holds onto it tightly.)* We're the same you and me.

SHARON: Nuhuhh. I'm better looking.

                (THEY laugh together.)

ISABEL: No. Seriously. I'm Black.

SHARON: Since when?

ISABEL: Since always.

SHARON: You can't just be Puerto Rican one day and the next day be Black.

ISABEL: Oh, yes I can. My papabuelo told me.

SHARON: Being Black is more than that. What do you feel like inside?

ISABEL: I feel stupid. Like I shoulda known this my whole life—but I didn't.

SHARON: Yup. That is kinda stupid.

ISABEL: You'd think with all the beatings I got—
            (*Knocking on her own head*)
—some sense would get knocked in here.

ISABEL & SHARON: (*In unison*) But nooo.

SHARON: There's probably nothing that could do
that.

ISABEL: I've missed you, Sharon.

SHARON: I know. That's why I came looking for
you—one more time.

ISABEL: But you didn't know you were looking for a
Black girl, did you?

SHARON: You're crazy, Isabel. You can't just take on
being Black like it's an overcoat or something.

ISABEL: I'm not. I just think somewhere inside I
always knew it. It doesn't seem all freaky or anything.
                (*Pause*)
Remember when we was little kids in kindergarten—
and the teacher asked us to sit in separate parts of the
room because we talked too much?

SHARON: Yeah...She said she never knew two girls so different yet so the same. Like we had the same mother or something.

ISABEL: Right. And we used to play that we did. I was Isabelli McNieves. And you were Sharoni McNieves.

SHARON: We're too old to play that game again. And it's not a game anymore, Isabel. Who you are can get you killed these days.

ISABEL: I know that. Who knows that better than me? You gotta stop thinking that you're the only one who can figure out my problems.

SHARON: You don't take things serious like you need to, girl.

ISABEL: Sure I do. But I don't gotta walk around like I'm half-dead to do it. Listen, Sharon, it's not your fault that Junie died. Everything isn't your problem. I'm not your problem. When are you going to stop trying to protect me by avoiding me? Or only meeting me at the pizza parlor?

SHARON: I wasn't doing that.

ISABEL: Yes, you were.

SHARON: I came over here in a snowstorm with a stupid parchessi board. Is that avoiding you?

ISABEL: You don't need an excuse to see me.

SHARON: I do when you got that lame-ass boyfriend following you around.

ISABEL: He's gone.

SHARON: Did he take that trip around the world yet?

ISABEL: Not with me.

(THEY both smile at the sexual innuendo.)

SHARON: You wanna be friends again?

ISABEL: What have I been saying all this time, Sharon?!

SHARON: You really liked playing my sister?

ISABEL: Yeah. I really did. When my Papabuelo tole me, then I knew you was family. Not just in my heart—but in my blood.

(ISABEL begins to cry.)

SHARON: What are you crying for?

*(SHARON begins to cry as SHE
watches ISABEL cry.)*

ISABEL: I don't know. Maybe the same thing you're crying for.

SHARON: I really need a sister right now.

ISABEL: Me too.

SHARON: It can't be that easy.

ISABEL: I know. But between you and me—it always has been.

SHARON: There ain't nuttin easy about being your friend, Isabel. So what is it you are now? A Porto-Blacka-Rican?

ISABEL: Except when I'm talkin'. Then I'm a Porto-Blacka-Rican speakin'.

SHARON: You're just cracked, girl.

ISABEL: Don't look so worried, Sharon. At least we know we're okay—right?
I mean...aren't we?

(THEY embrace briefly and then pull away and push each other playfully on the head.)

ISABEL: Hey, I got an errand to run. Why don't you come?

SHARON: Okay.
                    (Awkward pause)
My Ma asked for you—the other day, at the church.

ISABEL: Oh, no! Junie's memorial. I can't believe I forgot. Nina and them came after me that night.

SHARON: I told you they was going to.

ISABEL: Who cares?! We gotta go find some flowers.

SHARON: Flowers? It's snowing.

ISABEL: I know. First, we gotta find some money and go to the florist on Fordham Road. They got the best flowers. My Papabuelo asked me to get flowers that Mamabuela could not forget. They have got to be something.

SHARON: Get something orange. That was Junie's favorite color.

ISABEL: Okay. Orange it is. For Junie.

SHARON: But where are we gonna get money?

ISABEL: Don't worry about it.

SHARON: It's not stealing, is it?

ISABEL: Not when it's for love.

(THEY exit arm in arm as the lights cross to IAN & DOLORES.)

SCENE 6

"Holy Spirit"
IAN & DOLORES on the way to church, walking arm in arm.

DOLORES: You're gonna like this. There's a lot of singing.

IAN: Oh, man.

DOLORES: And sometimes the holy spirit lifts you up and makes your eyes roll back in your head.

IAN: I thought Jehovah's Witnesses were quiet.

DOLORES: Oh, they are. We changed to Pentacostal last week. My Ma likes the minister better.

IAN: Dolores...I don't know —

DOLORES: It's beautiful. You'll see. I get the holy spirit almos' every time.

IAN: What's it look like?

DOLORES: It's like — it's like going around the world.

IAN: Oh...

DOLORES: And then coming back home.

(DOLORES grabs IAN's arm tightly, pulling him toward the church as IAN picks nervously at his afro. Lights cross to SHARON & ISABEL on the stoop and JOSÉ MARIA in the apartment.)

SCENE 7

"Tools Of Love"
JOSÉ MARIA sees ISABEL & SHARON outside, from the
kitchen window. ISABEL holds an amazing bouquet of
orange and white flowers. On the stoop, ISABEL &
SHARON speak.

ISABEL: Aren't you gonna come up?

SHARON: Naaah...I'll wait here. I like the snow. It
makes everything so quiet. Sounds like a church out
here now.

ISABEL: Okay. I'll be out soon.

(SHARON watches ISABEL enter the building, then her
eyes move up to JOSÉ MARIA's window for a moment.
SHE sees JOSÉ MARIA standing there, looking up at the
night sky, so SHE looks up too. SHE decides to follow in the
direction of one of the stars and exits, kicking snow in front
of her, while keeping her eyes on the sky. JOSÉ MARIA
hurries to sit in a chair like HE hasn't been watching for
ISABEL this whole time. We hear the key in the lock.
ISABEL enters brandishing the bouquet of flowers.)

ISABEL: Look, Papabuelo! I tole you I could get
them! Ain't they fine?!

JOSÉ MARIA: Beautiful.

(Smelling them)
They smell like papaya and sea grass.
(Getting dizzy)
Oooey! I better sit down. That smell is so strong...

ISABEL: You don't look so good. Maybe I should call my mother.

JOSÉ MARIA: Don't bother her. She just got home from work.

ISABEL: I know. She almost caught me.

JOSÉ MARIA: What do you mean?

ISABEL: I had to kinda—take some money from her stocking stash. She keeps it in her bureau, second drawer from the top.

JOSÉ MARIA: Isabel!

ISABEL: It's okay. It was the first time I ever did that. And it was important. I had to buy some tools of love.

ANA CECILIA: *(Eavesdropping on the previous conversation)* Tools of love?! My sister Patito's husband had one of those. He made it out of wood and kept it in his pants. And when the young girls would go by his house, he'd sit out there on the porch and lift it up like he was—well, you know. And the girls would scream. One night, he even tried to put it inside my sister, but that was that—she took it away from him and burned it. Took the ashes and spread them over her altar so that God would keep him away from her. It worked.

ISABEL: Aren't you gonna give them to her?

JOSÉ MARIA: Yes, sure...Don't you smell that?

ISABEL: What?

JOSÉ MARIA: It's so strong. It's giving me a headache. Just let me close my eyes for a minute, m'ija.

ISABEL: Okay. You want me to rub your feet with alcohol?

JOSÉ MARIA: That would be nice.

(ISABEL gets a bottle of Florida water and begins taking off JOSÉ MARIA's socks.)

ISABEL: But you have to tell me a story.

JOSÉ MARIA: I do? About what?

ISABEL: About when you was a little boy.

JOSÉ MARIA: You like those stories, huh?
Alright...Did I ever tell you about the first ghost I saw?

ISABEL: (Impressed) The first one? Dag! How many
you seen??

JOSÉ MARIA: Enough. Enough to recognize good
ones from bad ones. The one I'm thinking about now
came to me when I was about five years old. Don
Pemplin, the old master had taken me out to his ship.
He was showing me how to get places by looking at
the stars—letting them lead you to wherever you
needed to go. After my lesson, I begged him to let me
stay and sleep on the deck of his ship. It was so
beautiful there. He let me stay, but he shackled me to
the mast. I don't know where he thought I would run
to. But it didn't matter. I lay back against the sails of
that ship and watched the stars. They became alive in
my head. They began to talk to me, whispering,
"José...come to us. There's a space here we're saving
for you. Come, José. We know you want to fly with
us." And I did.
*(A light comes up on JOSÉLITO, as wings sprouting from
his back burst through the chains that tie him to the mast of
a ship.)*
I closed my eyes and imagined my chains turning into
dust at my feet, and great brown wings sprouting from

147

my spine, lifting me up, gently like the arms of my mother. I never knew my mother but I always thought being in her arms would feel like that.

ISABEL: It does feel like that. I mean when you're a baby.

(As JOSÉ MARIA continues to speak, we see JOSÉLITO pull MEDIANOCHE and the palm-swaddled baby from the water.)

JOSÉ MARIA: I knew it. Anyway, I was having this wonderful daydream, when I saw this piece of seaweed walking toward me. It was white though, not green or brown, so I closed my eyes again. I thought maybe something had gotten caught in my eye or that I was just seeing things from rocking around on the ship. All that rocking can go to your head they told me. But when I opened my eyes again, it was still there but closer.

(We see MEDIANOCHE squeezing JOSÉLITO's feathers and water gently drips from them onto the baby's face. MEDIANOCHE rubs the water over his lips and all three rock together.)

It smelled like the inside of a coconut—like its milk. Sweet, but slightly burned. And that smell came over me, inside me. Into my mouth, down my throat. I thought it would choke me, but once I realized it wasn't trying to hurt me, it just filled me up like a

delicious piece of roast pork—with the skin still on—
like I was never allowed to eat. We just got the fat to
eat, and pretended it was meat. This thing—whatever
it was—knew how hungry I was. And I thought to
myself, "Is this God feeding me? Is God a piece of lace
from the sea?" I didn't get an answer that day, but I
know each day I get closer to one.

ISABEL: What do you mean?

JOSÉ MARIA: When I close my eyes, I go to so many
places. I can see my mother—she looks so young—
like you Isabel—And I can see them take me away
from her. I can see her scream as they whip her on the
back of her knees. That's where I got whipped too. So
I couldn't walk without limping. I can see the doctor
who helped straighten out my legs. That was the
second time they had metal wrapped around them,
but this was good metal. I wasn't afraid of this metal.

ISABEL: Papabuelo, you're scaring me.

JOSÉ MARIA: There's nothing to be scared of
anymore. I see the stars now too. But how can I see
the stars when it's still snowing so hard? Or maybe it
stopped snowing. Look out the window, m'ija.

ISABEL: *(Moving to the window and looking out)* Yep. It's still snowing alright. Real hard. These are like the biggest snowflakes I ever seen.
> *(Opening the window and catching a snowflake on her hand)*

Look! Fits like almos' exactly in my hand. You see?
> *(No response)*

Papabuelo?
> *(ISABEL comes and takes JOSÉ MARIA's hand.)*

Papabuelo? You sleeping? You can't go to sleep now. Not before we give her the flowers.
> *(Pause)*

Papabuelo...Not yet. You don't gotta go yet. God couldn't want this—not after all you already been through—not after I brought you the tools of love.

> *(ISABEL begins to cry quietly. ANA CECILIA enters picking up the flowers and putting them in a pitcher with water.)*

ANA CECILIA: Finally—that viejo finally left me something that smells good.

ISABEL: Did you love him, Mamabuela?

ANA CECILIA: He was a good servant.

ISABEL: But did you love him?

ANA CECILIA: Sometimes.
> *(Long pause)*

Sometimes, I could not stop loving him.
> *(ANA CECILIA takes the blankets from the foot of*
> *JOSÉ MARIA's bed and gently covers JOSÉ*
> *MARIA. JOSÉ MARIA moves to join JOSÉLITO,*
> *MEDIANOCHE*
> *& the baby.)*

Let's sing him to sleep, Isabel.
"Arrorró mi niño, arrorró mi amor.
> (Hushabye my child, hushabye my love.

Arrorró pedazo de mi corazon.
> (Hushabye piece of my heart.

Ese niño bueno que quiere dormir,   (The
good child who wants to sleep,
cierra los ojitos después los vuelve abrir."   (closes
his eyes to later open them again.)

ISABEL: Did you see that?! Three tiny angels just
lifted him by his shoulders—lifted him to heaven.

ANA CECILIA: (With a wicked little laugh) How do
you know they weren't devils?

ISABEL: I know an angel when I smell one.

ANA CECILIA: Yes. It smells like sand and ocean
now. Open the window so his soul can go free.

ISABEL: Papabuelo is going home.

ANA CECILIA: (In a whisper) I love you, José Maria, I always loved you. I wanted to die first, so that no one would ever know how much I needed you. I never wanted anyone to know.

> *(ISABEL moves into an isolated*
> *pool of light on the front stoop.)*

EPILOGUE

"A Box of Air and Memory"
ISABEL leans against the stoop of the building, looking out
and talking to the wind, which SHE has released from inside
the box that ANA CECILIA gave her. SHARON sits on the
stoop with her eyes tightly closed.

ISABEL: Hello, wind. Papabuelo told me where to
find you. Do you know that that was the first time I
heard my great-grandfather's real name? Hearing his
name made him a man to me. Made him real.
Sometimes I thought I made him up. People look at
me and think I don't have any African blood. But it's
not on my skin—it's inside—
(Pointing to her heart)
—here. It's in the stories I tell. In the music that
makes me move. In the things that make me smile. Or
sometimes cry. My great-grandfather taught me that
to live life you had to remember to watch the stars and
be in awe of them. You have to be able to close your
eyes and see the earth melt from your eyelids into
your head. And from your head into all your lower
parts, until you're walking on the earth, connected to
it—not just by gravity, but by family. And because of
him, I know how to dance with the angels. That's a
dance that frees your soul.
(Both ISABEL & SHARON look up into

the sky, and see a shooting star.)
One day, I hope to look into my child's face, and see yellow eyes there too.
        (ISABEL closes the box and calls out to SHARON.)
Hey, Sharon, where'd you get eyes like that?

SHARON
I was born with them.

ISABEL
I was born with these eyes too.
  (SHARON gets up and takes ISABEL's hand. THEY look up and each try to catch a snowflake in their free hand as THEY both take a deep breath. For a moment, the only light is the twinkle of the stars with the sound of the wind.)

End of Play

SALT

inspired by Ford's *'Tis Pity She's A Whore'*

Salt was commissioned by Steppenwolf Theater
Company for their New Play Lab series, Anna Shapiro,
lab director.
First reading at Steppenwolf,Chicago, IL,
 June 1997, directed by Juan A. Ramirez.

Second reading at camposanto, San Francisco, CA,
May 1998

First workshop production at Iowa Playwrights
Laboratory, February 1998, directed by Juan A.
Ramirez.

Second workshop production,
Actors' Theater RAW Space, February 1998,
directed by Loretta Greco.

Third Workshop production at Stanford University,
May 2004,
directed by Micaela Diaz-Sanchez.

For Juan & Joel because they know why...

Cast of Characters

GUADALUPE—a man-boy of 13 who is darkly intense and beautiful, except for His right ear which is malformed and burned-looking. He sells himself for money to give to his sister, BELEN, and their surrogate mom/madame, BELILAH LOVE. HE is in love with BELEN.

BELEN—a woman-girl of 13, GUADALUPE's twin sister, just as intense as GUADALUPE, but thought less beautiful by some. SHE has a deformed right arm—like thalidomide children do.. SHE is afraid of the dark. SHE is in love with GUADALUPE.

LUCIA (LULU)—a castrated boy of 10 who wears girls' clothing. Small, fragile, white. HE plays with dolls made of trash which he finds outside a field house. Things left by other children. Forgotten things—like baseball cards and socks. HE collects the plastic rings from soda bottles and makes jewelry for himself and the others. Christmas bows and other holiday trash, is his favorite. His left hand is tattooed with the Immaculate Heart of Mary—a bleeding heart surrounded by thorns.

GRACE—BELILAH's daughter, a plain girl of 16, half-black, half-white who talks too much, and knows nothing but thinks she knows everything. Very quick to give advice.

BELILAH LOVE—a woman of 40, who looks 50. A chain-smoking, hard-drinking, childsnatching, former prostitute. SHE keeps an eye on the family she's made for herself who live on the salt mounds.

VASQUES—BELILAH's manservant and son, half-black, half-Mexican, 20, a dwarfish former prostitute who is obsessively in love with her. HE works in a cemetary now for money and is most comfortable with the dead.

FATHER JANUSZ CZEKAJ(pron.: Yan-nush Zeh-cash)—35, a Catholic priest who still believes in God, but the Church is a question mark.

ANGIE—a doll made of garbage who speaks to LUCIA; really GRACE pretending.

ROCKET (RODRIGO)—33, a black Puerto Rican park custodian who cleans churches in his spare time. Loves Disco and Soul music, and also Bullwinkle cartoons. Always wears a hat.

CUSTOMER ONE/DOM, a bartender—a man with a secret sexual appetite for children, but also serves drinks at the local tavern.

CUSTOMER TWO/ ALDERMAN MOROSH—a man who's in love with LUCIA, but is also the ALDERMAN for the tenth ward, in which the play takes place.

CUSTOMER THREE, & BISHOP HARRISON—A man who enjoys delivering bad news and dangerous gifts. In whatever form he takes, there is always a scaliness to him, and he has very long fingernails, and four-fingered, thumb-less hands.

TIME: From Christmas Eve to New Year's Day sometime in the near future.

PLACE: A Salt mountain for road clearing in the Southside of Chicago, IL, and its environs which includes a metal-grated bridge, a bus graveyard, a furnace, and industrial dockage; also, on the periphery of the main environment is a church, a tavern, a field house, a shabby apartment and a beach. The living spaces of the people in this play are carved in and around the salt mountain. BELILAH has the shabby apartment which SHE sometimes lets GRACE sleep in.

PROLOGUE

SPILL THE WINE
Christmas Eve, 3 a.m.
VASQUES sits in front of the furnace, carving a small makeshift cross, as HE speaks to a cloth-covered child-sized corpse. HE is covered in woodshavings and dirt. His face is covered in purple burn marks.

VASQUES: I believe there is a purpose to my life. I was made short so I could write on pieces of wood that are low to the ground. I write on them with a chisel, and when I finish that, I fill the spaces with blood. This helps the wood stay shiny—and then the blood don't go to waste. I'm thrifty by nature...and nature—
(HE indicates his size)
—was thrifty with me.
(Touching his face)
These are part of my nature too. Walking into fire. I get too close to the flames sometimes—during the cremations. I can't help but get in real close. I like seeing all those ashes flying up into the sky, and it's so warm then. That's the only time I feel my hands anymore—at a cremation. I chisel now from memory. I remember how each one of my fingers moved and sculpted beautiful things. Things that don't exist anymore. Things with brushed hair...but we're all matted now, aren't we, little one?

(HE gently strokes the corpse's head.)

Why do you suppose they killed you, Arlene? Maybe you weren't useful enough. When you're useful, they keep you around. Maybe you cried? Oh, no, no, no. Mustn't do that, little girl. There's no room for tears when everybody's dying. You don't know who to cry for anymore. Makes no sense to cry...especially if you're crying for yourself.

(HE begins to sing as HE gets ready
to place the corpse into the furnace.)

"Spill the wine, dig that girl. Spill the wine, dig that girl—

dig that girl! Yeah! Dig that girl! Oh. You got to spill that wine, spill that wine..."

(Stops singing)

That was my father's favorite song. Miss Belilah told me. You never got to hear that song, did you?

(HE examines the corpse more closely.)

Who cut you into so many pieces, child? Looks like he did it with a very small knife. Gracie said it made her sick to see you like this—but I'm not sick—just sad. Did you know him? One usually does... I should have been watching you. I have to watch everything more carefully now.

(Pulling out pieces of ARLENE.)

I should arrange them in the right order anyway. Left here. Right there. That's better. Don't want to wake in the afterlife on the wrong foot. I know no one believes in one anymore, but I do. I had a vision. I saw lotus blossoms coming out of my stomach and these flowers had hearts that were beating. That's how I know. When I put my hand over my heart, I smell flowers. Take care of her, daddy. I know you know about flames.

>   *(HE places the corpse in the furnace, followed*
>   *by the cross, and then reaches into the flames*
>   *and pulls out a child's hand.)*

A souvenir if you don't mind, child. Maybe there are memories written on your palm...

>   *(HE puts the hand over his eyes.*
>   *From offstage we hear GRACE call.)*

GRACE *(Offstage)*: VASQUES! Hurry it up! We got other things to do.

ACT ONE
SCENE 1

THE NUTCRACKER
Christmas Eve, mid-afternoon.
At the Slide Inn Tavern.
We hear John Lee Hooker's "Blues For Christmas" playing
on the jukebox.
ROCKET talks to DOM, the bartender.

DOM: Cro-magnonism is what it's all about.

ROCKET: Cronyism.

DOM: Hmm? Yeah. Same difference. I know what I'm saying here. Politics are pre-historic, you know what I mean? Who strokes who, and for how long. That's it in a nutcracker.

ROCKET: Nutshell.

DOM: Yeah. Same difference. It cracks your nuts to think about it.

ROCKET: At least you got it figured out. Some things aren't so clear.

DOM: Oh, yeah. I know. That's what I like about this place. You know there was a massacre not far from here.

ROCKET: You mean the one with all those nurses?

DOM: No. Was that by here too?

ROCKET: Yeah. Right over at 100th and Calumet.

DOM: Wow! That's really close. I was talking about the massacre at 114th and Avenue O.

ROCKET: You mean the Leopold/Loeb Wolf Lake thing?

DOM: No.

ROCKET: Oh, you're talking real long ago. The Pottawatomie--white man thing.

DOM: Uhmm, no. How many massacres have there been here anyway?! I was talking about the Republic Steel thing. You heard of it? The 1937 Memorial Day Massacre—when the cops came and fired on some workers who were on strike. Killed ten of them.

ROCKET: Woah! That was cold.

DOM: Tell me about it! My granddad was on that picket line.

ROCKET: He survived though. A miracle.

DOM: Yeah. That's what we always said.

A miracle...But what an evil mother-flower
son-of-a-gun, he was. I figured once
something like that becomes part of your
history, forget about it—you can't ever be
normal again. This was his tavern.

ROCKET: Nice place. How come it's so empty? I'd
expect it full of guys on a day like today.

DOM: The holidays are funny. It starts out
empty and then after all the family stuff is
over, the men come running to get away from
their children and the wives. That's why I like
working the holidays—starts slow, but in the
end, pow! You could make as much as you
made all week in three hours. So, you just
moved here?

ROCKET: Yeah. I go where the work is, know
what I mean? Follow the trade.

DOM: What do you do?

ROCKET: This and that.

DOM: Uh, huh. A lot of my clients are in that
line of work.

ROCKET: Really? Work's just work. And it

can happen anywhere. Business always picks
up this time of year. Whatever your business
is.

DOM: That's true. You think massacres are a
business? I had a cousin killed eighteen
people, so that was almost like a business.
Daily work. Daily bread. He robbed all of
them, before—
ROCKET: Sounds like he grew up around here.

DOM: Yeah. A dopey diddlewad of a guy.
But then he got famous, sort of.

ROCKET: But he's dead and you're mixing
cocktails. I think you won.

DOM: Yeah? Hey, how'd you know he was dead?

ROCKET: You can't kill that many people and not be.
I mean, even if the State hadn't caught him, inside he'd
be coal black, like burnt ashes. Can't call that living.

DOM: You're right about that.
                    (Extending his hand)
I'm Dom.

ROCKET: (Taking his hand and shaking it) Hey, Dom,
I'm Rocket.

DOM: That's a new one. You're the first rocket I ever had inside here.

ROCKET: Everybody needs a little rocket now and then.

DOM: So? Are you a dealer or what?

ROCKET: You could say that. This—
        (HE takes out a bottle filled with a clear liquid.)
is what I sell. Wanna try it?
DOM: Looks like water.

ROCKET: Tastes like wine.

DOM: This isn't like that Zooma stuff.
I hate that malt liquor crap.

ROCKET: Uhnuh. This stuff'll save your soul.

DOM: *(Nervous, but not sure why)* Nah. I'm trying to cut down.

ROCKET: Let me know when you're ready. It's out-of-this-world.

DOM: I'll do that.

ROCKET: *(Taking a big swig of the liquid)*
Tasty! Nothing else is as good as this.
> *(Puts the bottle away, moving to the jukebox)*

DOM: Bet you'll find what you're looking for. I got the best jukebox in town.

(ROCKET plays Donna Summers' "I Feel Love" as we hear, from the salt mounds, BELEN's prayer. ROCKET hears her, but DOM does not.)

BELEN: *(As SHE is being fingered from behind by a masked CUSTOMER THREE)* Does it hurt to be dead? Is it different from this? This hurts.

ROCKET: Can you crank this up?

DOM: What are you? Some kind of disco king or something? That's all right. I have my share of polyester days too.

> *(DOM turns up the music from behind the bar and then dances and lip synchs to the music, but it actually gets softer as BELEN continues.)*

BELEN: Sometimes they hurt me so much, I can't feel my legs no more—and then I think I might die. But I don't. Can you hear me? I guess you got a lot of

voices in your head. OW! Oh, I'm sorry, I wasn't "ouching" you, it's this man. He got way too long fingernails. I think I'm bleeding now. But you bleed too, don't you? Maybe you hear so many voices your ears start to bleed. I don'wanna make nobody bleed. But you know what surprises me? How warm blood is. I almos'don'got the heart to wash it off. When I seen you in my dreams—you've always got blood on your face. I like that we got something the same.
(The music gets loud as ROCKET gets up.)

DOM: Hey, where you off to? The good part is coming.

ROCKET: I know.

(ROCKET exits. DOM turns on a fan.)

DOM: Took all the air with him. What a dipsy-doodle!

(Lights cross to behind the salt mounds.)

SCENE 2

REAL ESTATE
Christmas Eve, mid-afternoon.

BELILAH behind the salt mounds, looking through real estate ads. As SHE talks, the sound of a child crying is heard in the distance.
VASQUES sits beside her in silence.

BELILAH: *(Looking at the real estate section of the Chicago Sun-Times)* I need at least three bedrooms. Near a park. Parks are good for kids. They need that freedom to run around without worrying about cars. Of course, there are other dangers.
(Pause; the crying gets more urgent)
Maybe we could do with two bedrooms. The kids all get along. Two big bedrooms. We could separate the boys from the girls with blankets. That would fun for them—just like playing indians.
(Pause; the crying gets unbearably loud)
SHUSH! You know that scares people away! *(The crying subsides.)*
How can they expect me to read my paper, if they don't stay quiet?
(Spotting something perfect in the ads)
Ooh! Now this one would be nice. Two bedrooms, by a park, washer and dryer included. Washer—and—dryer...Hard to imagine. And I've had to imagine all kinds of things.
(The crying begins again.)
Don't make me come over there!
(The crying gets softer.)

Yeah...the things I imagine are the things in everybody else's head—the things they don't want to think about. But they don't understand survival like I do. That's the danger of knowledge—forces you to act. That's why you're so lucky, Vasques. You don't ever think.

(The crying gets louder.)

I SAID SHUSH!! Don't be crying about that little ungrateful child anymore! I don't want her name mentioned around here again. Do you all understand?!

(VASQUES exits toward the sound of the crying. The crying stops.)

Thank goodness. A woman could go crazy with all the tears. Tears only bring more pain. My feet ache when they cry.

(Pause)

The soles of my feet are bleeding now...

(Lights cross to Calumet Beach.)

SCENE 3

RATS

Later that afternoon.
GRACE is lying on the beach looking at the sky.
VASQUES stands beside her holding up a blanket to cut the wind. GRACE directs him on how to hold it to best cut off the wind.

GRACE: More to the left. Now a little forward. Tilt the top of the blanket forward, but keep the bottom back. Yeah. That's good. I have very delicate skin, Vasques. Can't afford to get wind burn. My face is my fortune, like they say.

VASQUES: Who says?

GRACE: They! People. Everybody. Why do you always ask such dope-a-moe questions?! Don't you know nothing?!

VASQUES: I don't know who they is, Grace. That's all. And you don't either or you would tell me.

GRACE: Sssh! Don't talk. You spit too much. It's like a rain shower down here. Look at that!

VASQUES: What?

GRACE: That big-butt star. I didn't know you could see stars in the daylight.

VASQUES: It's almost night. It comes earlier every day. Have you noticed?

GRACE: Have I noticed?! Yes. It's called winter, Drooly Dripper. Shut up. Just listen. Learn something. I try and teach you things and you spoil it every time with the blah, blah, blah of your bean brain.

VASQUES: My arms are getting tired.

GRACE: Put it down then and go home.
(HE holds the blanket up with renewed strength.)
That's better. I don't know why people wait till the summer to go to the beach. Wintery beaches got more space. You can hear the water. And see things you can't see with so many people all crowded up together. I like being able to see. Look! Even the rats love it. See how they jump. Even a rat has more fun than you, Vasques. I never seen you jump like that. With freedom...and joy.

VASQUES: I jump sometimes.

GRACE: Yeah? Let's see.

VASQUES: Then I gotta put the blanket down.

GRACE: That proves it. If you had real joy, you could jump with anything.
(GRACE gets up and pulls the blanket out of VASQUES'
hands.)
Gimme that! I'm going back. You stay here and study those rats. A half-brother of mine has got to know something.

(GRACE exits in a huff. VASQUES watches her go, then turns to study the rats.)

VASQUES: *(Suddenly smiling)* Rats have large territories. They walk the earth trying to find safe places. And they stay when they find them. They need the water. The water keeps them alive. But at the hint of danger, they run. If cornered, they attack. If hurt, they send out a cry that only other rats hear, warning of the danger. Thoughtful, shy, and how they love to play...

(VASQUES begins to run and leap in the sand. LUCIA enters and begins to run and jump behind VASQUES. Then ROCKET enters and watches them play.)

LUCIA: This fun, fun, Kee-kee. Kee-kee fun. Click. Click. Nice to play.

ROCKET: Very nice.
(VASQUES & LUCIA are startled by ROCKET. VASQUES picks up LUCIA and begins to run off with him.)
Hey, you don't gotta be afraid of me! Come on back. Shoot! Why are they always afraid?
(HE picks up one of the rats by the tail.)
You're not afraid of me, are you? We're old friends by now.

*(HE takes out his bottle of clear liquid and sprinkles some on
the rat and lets it go.)*
There you go. Tell your friends. There's more where
that came from. And the stories I could tell you...

(Lights cross to the salt mounds.)

SCENE 4

CUT-CUT
Christmas Eve. Night. The Salt Mounds.
*BELEN is rocking LUCIA on her lap and telling him a
story. They are both heavily made-up and dressed in once
fancy little girl dresses that have been altered to make them
more sexually revealing.*

LUCIA: Tell the pieces one, Belly. I love cut-cut
pieces.

BELEN: Okay, Lulu. But then you gotta go to sleep.

LUCIA: No sleep. Monsters come. Click, click, Belly.
Belly beautiful. Tell cut-cut please.

BELEN: Lulu beautiful too.
          *(SHE strokes his face and kisses
          him gently on the forehead.)*

Okay...There was a time when everyone's heart went blind and the sky turned black. It was the beginning of the judgement and every one who did not fear God was to be destroyed. A certain, evil woman with five children saved herself from the angel of destruction by offering pieces of her children to Heaven. She took an ear from one, an arm from another, and so on for every child she had. And so her children didn't look like other children. Oh, not at all.

LUCIA: Not at all.

BELEN: And she crossed the state line into Indiana, leaving them to find their own way in what was left of the world. These little ones looked different—their eyes never closed, and smelled different—like dried blood and dirt, and even sounded different—more like dogs than children. They howled and ran in packs, sniffing the ground underneath them, always searching for their missing parts—never able to stop and close their eyes until they found them. They looked under train tracks, and inside buses. They swam along the edge of every body of water, looking for themselves on the bottom. They dug caves in the sides of mountains. Their eyes were always searching. They even tried to make new parts from the loose pieces of wood and metal they found. But no luck. Nothing ever fit.

LUCIA: Nothing ever fits right.

BELEN: After years and years of searching, they grew so tired that they had to lie back on the ground and rest. That was the first time they looked up into the sky. And when they did, it opened up and snowflakes fell slowly down to them. They opened their mouths and captured them on the edge of their tongues. As they swallowed the snowflake, each one thought of the beauty of the snow. For the first time, they thought about something other than themselves. And smiled. And thought, "I am no greater than a snowflake, or a drop of rain,
or a grain of salt. Everything is a gift from God." With that, they each suddenly grew their missing part. The snowflakes were a reminder to never forget the power of Heaven.
(LUCIA closes his eyes.)
And the children finally closed their eyes and slept.
(Pause; then LUCIA suddenly opens his eyes.)

LUCIA: Did their mom cut them up?

BELEN: Yeah, I guess so.

LUCIA: With what?

BELEN: I don't know.

LUCIA: Why did she leave them behind?

BELEN: Because she could run faster without them.

LUCIA: Where is she now?

BELEN: Someplace dark. Someplace without children.
>   *(LUCIA closes his eyes*
>   *and finally begins to sleep.)*
That's right, Lulu-Lucia. Gotta take sleep when it comes. It's nice when it's only sleep that takes you.

(CUSTOMER ONE, whose face is masked in dark gauze, enters and beckons to BELEN. SHE gently places LUCIA's head on a mound of salt and walks to CUSTOMER ONE, slowly removing her blouse as SHE moves. CUSTOMER ONE fondles her breasts, and suckles them, reaching beneath her skirt.)

CUSTOMER ONE: *(Almost a whisper)*: Who taught you to move like that? You move from the inside out. You move like sweet air over wildflowers. I could come just feeling you move like that. Don't gotta get inside that. So small and delicate. I don't think I could get inside there. Can I get inside there?

(BELILAH enters.)

BELILAH: You ain't paid for that.

CUSTOMER ONE: You said I could be alone with her.

BELILAH: That was before you started talking about
entering. Entering costs.
>   (To BELEN)
Get your blouse back on.
>   (SHE quickly does so.)
Your time's up, pal. I'm saving her for something
special.

>   (BELEN moves to LUCIA and curls up beside him.)

CUSTOMER ONE: She's no innocent. No one moves
like that is innocent.

BELILAH: I trained her well. But she's still got the
membrane—last time I checked.

CUSTOMER ONE: I got a fifty.

BELILAH: Not enough. You could have one of the
boys for that.

CUSTOMER ONE: No. The last one shit all over me.
What do you feed them anyway?

BELILAH: I don't like cursewords in my house. Time for you—

> *(Taking out a knife)*

—to go.

CUSTOMER ONE: Don't expect me back here.

BELILAH: I have no expectations. That's why I'm happy. People think happiness is something you work for. Like a goal. Don't have any, so whatever I get is right. That's the only justice I know.

> *(CUSTOMER ONE exits.*
> *BELILAH sits across from LUCIA & BELEN.*
> *GRACE watches from the shadows.)*

Lucia don't sleep like that when you're not around. You got powers, and I'm gonna get them outta you, girl, and put 'em into me. Don't think I'm gonna let you keep them forever. And once I know there's no telling what might happen.

> *(SHE digs in the salt and pulls out a sleeping bag, shakes it*
> *out, and places it over LUCIA & BELEN.)*

Sleep tight. It's almost Christmas.

> *(BELILAH sings, GRACE disappears from view.)*

"It came upon a midnight clear,
that glorious song of old.
From angels bending near the earth to touch their harps of gold!
Peace on the earth, goodwill toward men, from Heaven's all gracious King!

The world in solemn stillness lay, to hear the
angels...sing."
You sure are two pretty children...
>   (Calling to VASQUES, who appears
>   from inside a salt mound.)
VASQUES! Keep an eye on them.

>   (HE nods. SHE exits.
>   Lights cross to GUADALUPE &
>   GRACE on the bridge.)

SCENE 5

BUTTER BUTT
Later that night. Christmas Eve, 11 p.m.
GUADALUPE & GRACE on the bridge trying to attract
customers. GRACE keeps trying to put her arm around
GUADALUPE.

GUADALUPE: Quit that!

GRACE: I'm just trying to keep warm.

>   (SHE tries again and HE pushes her to the ground.)

GUADALUPE: Next time I'll crack open that stupid monkey head of yours.

GRACE: *(Picking herself up)* You know you like me, Lupe (Loopy). I seen you look at me when I take a piss.

GUADALUPE: I look at you because you piss where you sleep. Even dumb animals know better than to do that. I just can't believe you do it. But everytime, you just start squirting, and then you sit right down on it.

GRACE: I like how it feels. It's all warm and from straight inside me. It's like a warm part of me has turned into this precious water and I wanna enjoy it as long as I can. Boys don't value their bodies like girls do. No, bob sir-ree, you sure don't. A girl's gottta care for her skin, and her nails, and her hair. Sitting in piss keeps my butt smooth as butter—
    (SHE flashes her butt at him.)
See? See any pimples? In-grown hairs? Cooties? You don't, do you?

    (HE pulls her skirt back down.)

GUADALUPE: Stop it.

GRACE: Doesn't my butt look good to you?

GUADALUPE: It's just a butt to me. Just any old butt. Here comes a car.

GRACE: Let them offer first—that's how you tell the cops from the customers.

GUADALUPE: You don't gotta tell me my business, Gracie. I know what I'm doing.

(A car's headlights approach slowly, come to a stop, we hear a Christmas carol blaring from the car radio, then a beer bottle comes flying out of the car at them. Then the car races off.
THEY avoid getting hit.)

GRACE: Shucks! They almost got me that time.

GUADALUPE: I wish they would have.

GRACE: You don't mean that.
        (SHE tries to kiss him, HE pushes her away.)
Who you saving yourself for?
        (No response)
There's nobody can understand you better. Nobody else knows how to hold you. It's like this—
        (SHE puts out her arms hugging the air.)
a full warm woman's hold. People without arms can't give you that.

GUADALUPE: Shut up!

GRACE: Anyways, you know it's a sin. If you love her, your babies'll come out retarded. They'll come out like they mother. Your sister's got Cancer. She's gonna—

GUADALUPE: I said shut up!
(HE slaps her. SHE starts to cry.)
Why can't you leave me alone?!

GRACE: I'm sorry. I just—love you.

GUADALUPE: You're bad for business, Gracie. You're gonna get us both in trouble. Why don't you just go away? Nobody wants to buy your lame equipment anyway.

GRACE: I'm the one who's watching your back. Without me you'd be scared stupid.
(Pause)
Maybe you just don't understand love. I always forget how young you are. You poor baby, you don't know you love me because you just haven't figured it out yet.

GUADALUPE: Yeah, that must be it. I get sick to my stomach when you come close enough to smell—so that must be love.

(Pause)

I'm sorry I hit you. But you made me.

GRACE: Why's your ear all funny like that?
        (SHE reaches out and touches it, HE jumps.)

GUADALUPE: Don't touch it!

GRACE: It hurts you, huh? Maybe I can speak to Belilah and she can find you a doctor. Would you like that?

GUADALUPE: No. And it don't hurt—not exactly.

GRACE: What's it do then?

GUADALUPE: Tingles, but bad. Like pins sticking in my head. It's like nothing I really feel, but something I remember feeling.

GRACE: Maybe your mama touched you there before she give you up. I wouldn't'ta given you up for nothing. No bob sir-ree. Your sister, maybe, but not you.

GUADALUPE: Here comes another one. Let me do this one alone. I don't need your tagalong butt bothering me.

GRACE: No, bob sireee. You know the rules.

LUPE: You—
       (GUADALUPE swings to hit GRACE
         but then changes his mind.)
—get on my last nerve, Gracie.

   (Headlights flash. GUADALUPE moves to the car to negotiate as GRACE circles the car to read the license plate.)

GRACE: JHX137. JHX137. JHX137. Repeat anything three times and you're bound to remember it.

   (Both LUPE & GRACE get in the car and disappear into darkness as BELILAH crosses onto the beach.)

SCENE 6

CLEANING RITUAL
Christmas Eve, late night.
BELILAH standing on the beach, looking into the water.
SHE takes off her shoes, polishing them one at a time. She dips the first shoe into the river and then wipes it with a rag.
As SHE does the first one, we see ROCKET in the bar,

alone, brushing his hat. A light captures each one of them in their cleaning ritual BELILAH is thinking about disappearing. ROCKET is thinking about how peaceful it would be to disappear.

BELILAH: It soothes my feet to wash my shoes. My steps are firmer in clean shoes. You have to have clean shoes on Christmas morning or the angels can't find you. I wonder where angels live in the winter?

ROCKET: Brushing my hat clears my mind. Gotta keep a clear head in a place like this.

BELILAH: I bet it's a place where disappearing is better than being.

ROCKET: Got to be ready.

(BELILAH catches the reflection of VASQUES in the water. Light on ROCKET fades as SHE speaks to VASQUES.)

BELILAH: I told you never to follow me. How come you don't listen, boy?!

VASQUES: I listen. But sometimes I hear things coming out of people's heads that makes me scared for them.

BELILAH: Did you hear this coming?

(*SHE bops him on the head as
the bells of a distant church toll.*)
Huh?! Hear the ringing in your head of my fist upon it?

VASQUES: Sounds like church bells.

BELILAH: Those <u>are</u> church bells, Vasques. When are you gonna get some sense?

VASQUES: When I need to.

(*BELILAH takes his hand as
they move toward the salt mounds.*)

BELILAH: You should be home watching the other kids. You know what you're supposed to do.

VASQUES: Gracie and Lupe found a date, and everybody else is asleep—but you.

BELILAH: And you. What you smiling about, boy?

VASQUES: Nothing.
(*HE swings their hands happily.*)
It's Christmas.
(*Lights cross to LUCIA in front of the field house.*)

SCENE 7

GIVE IT AWAY
Christmas day. Morning.
LUCIA sits in front of a field house collecting garbage to turn into jewelry. HE has plastic rings from bottle tops, bottle caps, socks, newspaper, aluminum gum wrappers, aluminum foil,
Styrofoam cups, etc. With a needle and thread, HE strings together a necklace. HE speaks to ANGIE, his doll made of garbage. Once HE begins speaking, we see GRACE sneak behind him. SHE speaks as if SHE were ANGIE, a softer, sweeter voice.

LUCIA: This one's for Belly, because she's my friend. Click, click. She's pretty and she talks soft and tells sweet stories. Not as sweet as your stories, Angie. Yours are the best. And you got nice hairs too, nice for braids and ponytails. Not like mines. Mines are "incorgable," that's what Belilah says.

ANGIE(GRACE): Don't listen to that mean old thing, baby. You got fine hairs. Real fine.

LUCIA: What's fine?

ANGIE: Soft and straight and sugar brown—like sweet grass blades in the winter—like the ones over by the train tracks.

LUCIA: Yeah? But they don't stay brown though.

ANGIE: Maybe your hair will begin to change color too. People got seasons, just like nature. Yuh, they sure do.

LUCIA: What season am I? Click, click.

ANGIE: You're in summer.

LUCIA: But it's Christmas. How—

ANGIE: Nature's in winter, but little boys are in summer.

LUCIA: I'm not a boy.

ANGIE: Oh? What are you then?

LUCIA: Click, I don'know, click. I used to be Lucian, but now I'm Lucia.

ANGIE: People got the right to be anything they want...You know what I heard yesterday?

LUCIA: What?

ANGIE: I heard that Belen say all kinds of crazy things about you.

LUCIA: She not do that, Angie. She love me.

ANGIE: She has a funny way of showing it. She told Belilah that you were talking to a customer without setting no price. You know how mad that makes her.

LUCIA: But I wasn't talking to nobody... Why'd she say that?

ANGIE: I don't know, baby. But she's reminding me of Arlene...you remember, Arlene?

LUCIA: She a bad—Click, click—a bad girl.

ANGIE: You should be careful of that Belen. She's got a witchy-poo way about her. Too many secrets. She ever tell you her secrets?

LUCIA: What's a secret?

ANGIE: Something somebody tells you and you ain't ever supposed to tell nobody else.

LUCIA: Like you talkin' to me. I know I can't tell nobodys. Because laugh at me, yes?

ANGIE: That's right. Can't have that. Did she?

LUCIA: I don' think so.

ANGIE: Don' think so, huh? If she tell you something like that, you tell me, okay? We gotta keep an eye on that girl.

LUCIA: Witchy-poo?

ANGIE: Yup. Did you bring me a present?

LUCIA (*HE takes out a necklace made of bubblegum wrappers and other metallic papers.*): I hopes you love it.

ANGIE: Oh, baby! I do. I do. It goes so well with my dress, don' cha think?

LUCIA: Oh, baby! Yeah! I do. I do.

ANGIE: You're such a good, sweet, talented boy. You make the most beautiful jewelry of anybody. Only a beautiful thing could make such beautiful things. You got a heart that sparkles. It's like a star.

LUCIA: LuLu Star?

ANGIE: LuLu's a twinkly goody cupcake. You're good on the inside—where nobody but me can see. I can see it because I know how you made me. I still feel your gentle fingers running over each stitch in my face. I can see because you gave me my eyes. Cut'em out of a magic picture book you found just over there.

LUCIA: You 'member that?

ANGIE: I can't ever forget it. I trust you with my life. We're family...And you know who you can always trust?

LUCIA: Angie. I trust Angie.

ANGIE: That's right, LuLu. I brought you something too. Look inside my head.

> (*LUCIA checks ANGIE's head and*
> *pulls out a long thin blade.*)

LUCIA: Wow...pretty. Prettier than the last one. You find?

ANGIE: Yes. I'm just like you. I find beauty because you taught me where to look. But be careful now. It's real sharp.

LUCIA: Lucia know. I cut make better jewelry now. Cut some cans and make some earrings, long and thin. Perfect earrings now. Now don'gotta use my teeth. They was beginning to hurt. Hard to cut with jus' your teeth.

ANGIE: Shouldn't use your teeth like that. You could pull 'em out or they might get rotten or something. Then where would you be?

LUCIA: Then where I'd be?

ANGIE: Up ugly creek with a mirror for a paddle.

LUCIA: Huh?

ANGIE: So you like it?

LUCIA: Oh, yes, sweetie pie Angie, my angel!

ANGIE: Good...it's my secret gift. Remember what a secret is?

LUCIA: Yeah...I can't tell nobodys.

ANGIE: That's right...Why do you always come here? I mean, and not go in? Just hang around the outside of this old nasty field house with all those nasty old kids inside. How come?

LUCIA: I don'know. Jus'ta watch, I guess. I see all
them kids with their Mas and Pas going in there to
play. And with nice clothes and nicer toys. Sometimes
they forget 'em and leave 'em and they become mines.
And I like lookin' in the windows and watching 'em
play. They got like fine things in there. Like almos'a
palace or a castle, like fairytale pretty stuff. And even
they garbage is good here. Shiny stuff. I don'know
how people can throw away such good stuff—like
sneakers! I found me one but I ain't never found the
other one. One day I'll find the other one. I made a
bracelet for Gracie, and this other necklace for Belly,
and a watch for Lupe from here.

ANGIE: A watch?? How'd you make a watch? Show
it to me.

LUCIA: No. Click, click. That's for him, Angie. He's
gotta be the one sees it first. How come you the only
one talks?

ANGIE: How come you always say click, click?

LUCIA: Sometimes my head goes off. On and then
off. I gotta turn back on, don't I? Let's sing, huh?

ANGIE: The one I taught you from last week?

LUCIA: Yeah! How's it again?

ANGIE: (Sings "Give It Away" by the ChiLites; GRACE does an elaborate dance behind LUCIA) "What's the sense in—

LUCIA & ANGIE: (Singing together)
—giving you loving when you're gonna give it away, give it away. What's the sense in giving you kisses when you're gonna give it away, give it away. Give it away! Give it away!. Oh, my baby, give it away! Oh, my honey, give it away! Oh, sweet darling, give it away!
                    (GRACE exits.)
I love you no matter what you do. Baby, Baby.
Baby, love was meant for two, I know, I know, I know I was meant for you.
What's the sense in giving you loving when you're gonna give it away, give it away."
Yeah! That's a sweetie cupcake song, huh?
                (No response from ANGIE)
Angie? Are you sleeping now? You sleep.
                (HE rocks his doll.)
Sleep, sleep. We'll be quiet for a little...then you'll talk again, won'ya? Yeah...sleep.
Only. Click, click. Gotta keep myself awake.
Somebody's always watching. Yeah...

(HE curls up on the ground protectively around ANGIE,
putting the blade back into her head.
Lights cross to the church.)

SCENE 8

TO BE REAL
December 25, Christmas afternoon.
ROCKET sweeps the church aisles.
HE sings to himself.

ROCKET: *(Singing Cheryl Lynn's "Got To Be Real.")*
"What you find got—
What you feel got—
What you know got—to be real!
What you find got—
What you feel got—
What you know got—to be real!
Oooh, your love's for real now!
You know that your love is my love—
my love is your love—
Our love is here to stay."

(FATHER CZEKAJ enters the church.)

CZEKAJ: Good song, Rocky.

ROCKET: Yeah. Sorry if I bugged you, Father. But I like keeping myself company. It's too quiet in here sometimes.

CZEKAJ: It doesn't bother me. I like company too.

ROCKET: Yeah. But you know what bugs _me_, Father? You calling me Rocky—my name's not Rocky. It's Rocket—like the real name of the squirrel on Bullwinkle. _His_ nickname was Rocky.

CZEKAJ: Is that how you got your name?

ROCKET: Yeah. I loved those cartoons—and I'm fast like that Rocket J. Squirrel. See? I almost got this whole church done in two hours. And churches breed a whole lot of dust. You got all kinds of wood and marble surfaces here. You got your pews, your railings, the altar. Even the crucifix gathers dust—and that green stuff too.

CZEKAJ: Mold?

ROCKET: Yeah. That.

CZEKAJ: It gets moist in here sometimes. Leaky roof. Poor insulation. It's hard to insulate stained glass.

ROCKET: Yep. And this is about the windiest place I ever been that's inside, so everything blows in eventually.

CZEKAJ: Yes. Everything.

ROCKET: Tell me something. What is it you do here all day?

CZEKAJ: Lately, I've been making a lot of phone calls.

ROCKET: There's a phone in here?

CZEKAJ: In my office.

ROCKET: Tell me something else. Did you ever drink holy water?

CZEKAJ: No. Did you?

ROCKET: Yeah. A couple of times. What do you guys put in it to make it smell like that?

CZEKAJ: I don't really know. I think it's just water that's been blessed. Why do you drink it?

ROCKET: I like it. I don't know. It tastes good to me. I get cravings for it sometimes.

CZEKAJ: I wondered where it was all going. I thought there was a leak.

ROCKET: I didn't take that much. And isn't it supposed to be took?

CZEKAJ: Most people just fill up a small bottle.

ROCKET: And it's safe, I mean, it doesn't have all that bad stuff in it. Does it?

CZEKAJ: It's safe. Yes. Is the water bad where you live?

ROCKET: Terrible. It tastes like dirty pool water—like after somebody peed or something—oh, excuse me, can I say peed in here?

CZEKAJ: I think it's okay. But maybe you could cut down on the drinking. I mean, whole gallons are disappearing. That's maybe too much to take. Okay?

ROCKET: Okay. You really never drank it?

CZEKAJ: Really. Never.

ROCKET: Hhm...that's interesting. I mean, it's such a temptation and everything. But I guess you guys keep a lot of things in check, huh?

CZEKAJ: I guess so. You clean a lot of churches?

ROCKET: No. Uhuhn. Just this one. It's my what you call charity work. Usually I clean parks. I mean, I work for the city doing that. And one time I came by here and saw how dirty it was and thought here's something I could do. Like cleaning my soul too or something. So then I started coming every week. It's been almost a year now I been doing it.

CZEKAJ: I know it's been almost a year. But I thought someone from the archdiocese sent you. I never thought to ask, because you never said anything about it. I mean, about getting paid.

ROCKET: Yeah, well, money's not the half of it, Father. You know what I mean?

CZEKAJ: Yes, I know. Thanks for doing it. Was it really that dirty? I was paying someone to come in once a month before you started showing up and I never noticed the dust.

ROCKET: I guess you wouldn't—being a priest and all. I mean, it's a worldly kind of thing, isn't it?

CZEKAJ: Or maybe if there's so much dust over everything you begin to get used to it.

ROCKET: Could be true for you, but for me, never. I'm a dust magnet. It comes to me and then I can't ignore it. I always listen to dust.

CZEKAJ: What does it tell you?

ROCKET: All kinds of things. It tells me about the people living around it. Hair, bits of cloth. Pieces of fingernails and dead skin. All get caught in the web of dust. I can tell how many come through, where they sat, if they kneeled. Sex—I mean, man or woman or child. I can tell how much or how little someone weighs from the dust that forms around the impression that their bodies left behind. I can tell a lot.

CZEKAJ: So you're like a detective of dust.

ROCKET: Exactly. Doctor Dust. Did you ever see the Bullwinkle cartoon where Bullwinkle is the heir to an English fortune?

CZEKAJ: I missed that one.

ROCKET: That's too bad. You could catch it on video though. You can catch anything on video.

CZEKAJ: I know. That's how I knew you were taking the holy water.

ROCKET: Oh...so you knew and was pretending not to.

CZEKAJ: I wanted you to tell me yourself. I knew you would if you had the chance.

ROCKET: Yeah, well I didn't think it was such a big deal. Anyway, in this episode, Rocket J. Squirrel has to help Bullwinkle remember who he really is and bring him back to Minnesota. Has to remind him of his humble roots—and I thought it was like a Jesus Christ kind of story—so I thought maybe you knew it.

CZEKAJ: Sounds like I should.

ROCKET: Should is a word only a mother uses.

CZEKAJ: Should maybe shows you care though—like a mother.

ROCKET: But it robs the "shouldee" of power. The power to choose and decide what's right for them. You gotta let people make their own mistakes. That's the only way to learn.

CZEKAJ: I like you, Rocket. I'd like to see you at mass sometime.

ROCKET: I make my own mass. When I'm here by myself cleaning.

CZEKAJ: I'll let you get back to it then. Nice talking to you.

ROCKET: Nice talking to you too. And listen, I'll try and cut back on the water.

CZEKAJ: Sounds good. And would you mind taking off your hat in here? I know it's old-fashioned, but—

ROCKET: *(Taking off the hat)* No problem.

CZEKAJ: *(As HE exits)* And Merry Christmas. Peace be with you, Rocket.

ROCKET: Same to you, father.

> *(CZEKAJ exits. ROCKET gets back to his sweeping and puts his hat back on.)*

ROCKET: I think God wears a hat. Some think it's because he's losing his hair—but I know better. He just has so much love, he has to keep it under wraps— or it would explode.
> *(Sings/hums "The Hustle"*
> *and dances as HE sweeps.)*
Pam-pah, pam-pah, pumparah, pum-pum.

Pam-pah, pam-pah, pumparah, pum-pum.
Pam-pah, pam-pah, pumparah, pum-pum.
Pam-pah, pam-pah, pumparah, pum-pum.
Pam-pah, pam-pah, pumparah, pum-pum.
Pam-pah, pam-pah, pumparah, pum-pum.
Pahh! Do the Hustle!

(HE repeats this as lights cross to the river.)

SCENE 9

BEAR DANCE & XMAS FISH
Christmas evening.
*BELEN & GUADALUPE walk to the river carrying
buckets, fill the buckets and GUADALUPE carries them to
the furnace area as BELEN follows him. They begin to wash
by the fire. GUADALUPE helps BELEN take off her
clothes and then disrobes himself. THEY wash each other
with pieces of their clothing. When THEY get to their
genitals, BELEN turns away and washes herself shyly, as
GUADALUPE watches her. Then HE turns his back to her
and washes himself. SHE begins to wash his back, and
smiles, then places her back against his and begins to rub his
butt playfully with hers.*

GUADALUPE: The bear dance!

BELEN: Yeah. We used to always do it when we were just little kids, huh? But it's still fun to do, ain't it?!

GUADALUPE: Yeah...it's still fun to do.
            (BELEN suddenly gets embarrased
            and puts her clothes back on.)
Hey! Those aren't even dry yet.

BELEN: I know. But they'll dry on just as fast. I'm getting cold.

(SHE sits down by the fire with her clothes on.
GUADALUPE picks up his clothes and sits next to her,
covering himself with them. THEY sit in silence for a
moment letting the fire warm them. Then BELEN gets up
and moves to a salt mound and lies back on top of it,
watching the sky. GUADALUPE moves slowly to join her.
THEY each speak their inner thoughts aloud.)

BELEN: I see the rest of my arm in the shape of the clouds at first light. At first light, I see the clouds and they call me, with my own real hand—not these dumb fingers I have on Earth.
In Heaven, I'm whole. We're all marked with something.

GUADALUPE: Same blood, minutes apart. Born same womb, a thin layer of skin separating us from entering each other, swallowing ourselves up to become one. In my sister's eyes, I see myself in their beauty. Her eyes are gentle firelight. I want to burn with her. Inside her.

BELEN: Lupe was kissed on his ear by an angel. He don't let no one but me touch him there. It don't hurt when I kiss it. When I kiss his ear, I can hear his thoughts. And they scare me because I know I feel that way too. When someone else touches me, I pretend it's him.

(THEY turn toward each other.)

GUADALUPE: What are you thinking?

BELEN: Something. That makes me smile from deep in my stomach. Does your stomach smile like that too?

GUADALUPE: Sometimes. Belen?

BELEN: Yeah?

GUADALUPE: You know what I wish?

BELEN: What?

GUADALUPE: That it was just you and me left. Just you and me and the whole world just ours. Then we could spend every minute—just alone together. You and me.

BELEN: What we would do? All alone like that? You think we'd fight?

GUADALUPE: No. Not us. We'd make peace. All the time. We'd get a little dog. And he'd watch us and bring us food.

BELEN: What kind? Pizza?

GUADALUPE: Yup. And Polishes. And Strawberry cheesecake. And reefer.

BELEN: You got any?

> (GUADALUPE takes out one and
> lights it and hands it to BELEN.)

GUADALUPE: Don't waste any. It's the last one I got.

> (THEY pass the joint back and forth between them in
> silence, trying to make each other laugh with the faces
> THEY make as THEY inhale.)

BELEN: How's a dog gonna do all that anyway? You think dogs know the difference between cheesecake and chocolate cake?

GUADALUPE: Oh, yeah. Definitely. They know everything. I heard about this dog that could tell the future.

BELEN: *(With a smile)* Yeah?

GUADALUPE: *(Aside)* To make her smile—that would be a selfish act of love. Her smile's just like mine.
(To BELEN)
Yup. You could ask him questions and he'd nod once for no and twice for yes.

BELEN: What if you asked a question that the answer was about when or why?

GUADALUPE: You have to be specific with a dog. No one really knows when or why anyways—not about things that count anyways.

BELEN: I know some when and whys.

GUADALUPE: You're not a dog.

BELEN: So this dog was like a ouija board?

GUADALUPE: Something like that. And he could also tell good people from bad—just from looking at a picture of them.

BELEN: I can do that too.

GUADALUPE: What do you see when you look at me?

BELEN: I see...
(Solemnly)
We're never getting out of here. What happens when they start coming to get the salt—when it snows or the roads get icy? What happens then? I don't wanna live under the bridge again. I still got the chills from last year. And my head hurts all the time now. I got the sound of cars buried in my brain. Running all over us. I wish we could get a house.

GUADALUPE: What kind of house?

BELEN: One with no rooms. Just big and open. Nothing dark anywhere. All light and filled up with yellow flowers.

GUADALUPE: I hate yellow. That's gotta be the ugliest color. Why do we need that color?

BELEN: What about the Sun?

GUADALUPE: The Sun's not yellow. It's orange. Orange is good. It's powerful. Yellow is weak. And ugly.

BELEN: Belilah wears yellow all the time.
                    (Pause)
You're right. It is ugly. Orange then. Orange peachy flowers. That smells better than cheesecake. Better than LuLu's skin.

GUADALUPE: LuLu's skin? What's good about that anyway?

BELEN: Didn't you ever smell him? He's still got baby smell on him.

GUADALUPE: I don't get that close.

BELEN: Why not? He loves us.

GUADALUPE: He's a freak.

BELEN: No, he's not. Why do you say that?

GUADALUPE: Anything don't got no sex is a freak. That's just a fact, Belen. You watch out for him. I think he's crazy. Talks by himself all the time. Dresses all crazy. He's spooky.

BELEN: Not to me.

GUADALUPE: Maybe you're spooky too.

BELEN: You know what I like to do? Pretend he's our baby. He'd make any girl proud to be his Ma. Don't you think it's fun to pretend he's our little poochie baby?

GUADALUPE: No.
    (Kisses BELEN on the neck)
I don't like to pretend.

BELEN: That tickles.

GUADALUPE: Yeah? How about this?
 (HE takes her deformed arm and kisses each finger.)

BELEN: Feels good. You're the only one touches that part of me. Everybody else is scared to.

GUADALUPE: I love every piece of you, Belen.

BELEN: You're supposed to. You're my brother.

GUADALUPE: Don't you love me too?

BELEN: When? Or why?

*(THEY kiss each other's hands sweetly. BELILAH &
VASQUES appear over the mound and watch as the lights
dim on GUADALUPE & BELEN and come up on THEM.)*

BELILAH: What did I tell you? Unnatural acts. This
is significant, Vasques. Keep an eye on them. It might
be time for some adult supervision.

VASQUES: Yes, Miss Belilah.

BELILAH: Might be time to show them something
they've never seen before. Just to remind them who
runs this place. Did you finish your rounds?

VASQUES: Yes, Miss Belilah.

BELILAH: They don't make 'em like you anymore.

VASQUES: No, Miss Belilah.
                    (Pause)
How long I been with you anyway?

BELILAH: How old are you?

VASQUES: Twenty, I think.

BELILAH: About that long.

VASQUES: About?

BELILAH: Exactly that long.

VASQUES: That's a long time...Was I a good baby? I mean, did I cry a lot?

BELILAH: You were an exceptionally quiet baby. In fact, I often thought you were dead. I had to throw cold water on you to get any reaction at all.

VASQUES: That's why probably I like to still wash in cold water. Other people complain in the cold, but I like it. I wouldn't want to live anywhere else.

BELILAH: We're gonna have to find some temporary lodging soon. Even salt doesn't last forever.

VASQUES: Depends on how much it snows, huh?

BELILAH: That and other things. That and a few other things, Vasques. We have to pick up a new one this week. To make up for last week's runaway. Arlene had such potential. Children don't understand how much they're worth. That's my job, I guess. To take the useless and make them useful again.

VASQUES: I don't know what I would have done without you.

BELILAH: I don't know either...the circus maybe. Or carnivals. Those arts are dying out though. It's not easy to get a job like that—especially if you look different. Oh, well, little man. Let's just thank the stars we found each other.
> *(SHE kisses him on top of his head.)*
You were a gift to me. On days like today, I cherish my gifts.

VASQUES: (Shyly handing her a package wrapped in newspaper) Merry Christmas, Miss Belilah.

BELILAH: Vasques! You didn't have to get me anything.

VASQUES: I hope you like it.

BELILAH: (Opening the package; pulls out a fish) Oh my Lord!

VASQUES: Do you like it?

BELILAH: It's a fish.

VASQUES: Yeah. I caught it myself. In the river.

BELILAH: In this river?

VASQUES: Yes.

BELILAH: Have you been eating things from this river again?!

VASQUES: No...

BELILAH: You're just like your father.

VASQUES: He's a hero. He died in the flames. In the flames of Heaven. You told me—

BELILAH: Your father was a drunken fool who fell into that furnace when he was supposed to be working. Working so I could have my baby in a nice clean hospital, like he promised me. He was gonna save me. And then he died. All I had to eat then was fish from this river. And then I had you.

(BELILAH throws the fish at him and exits.)

VASQUES: That's what I thought.

(Lights cross to the church.)

SCENE 10

<u>CONFESSION</u>
December 26, morning.
GUADALUPE in the church confessing. HE is in a
confessional booth with FATHER CZEKAJ seated in the
dark beside him.

GUADALUPE: I—I don't know how to do this.

CZEKAJ: That's alright, son. A lot of people don't know how.
                (Pause)
Are you Catholic?

GUADALUPE: I don'know. I think so.

CZEKAJ: Your parents don't go to church?

GUADALUPE: I don'know.

CZEKAJ: You don't have to be afraid. You can just start talking. What grade are you in?

GUADALUPE: I'm—I'm supposed to be in seventh, I think.

CZEKAJ: Hmmm...so you got left back?

GUADALUPE: Huh? No—I don'know.

CZEKAJ: Okay...Do you mind if I bless you?

GUADALUPE: No, I guess not. Is that what you do?

CZEKAJ: I try to. It's what you do in confession. I mean, that's how it starts. Okay?

GUADALUPE: Okay. Whatever. Bless me.

CZEKAJ: I bless you in the name of the father, the son, and the holy spirit. Amen. Say amen.

GUADALUPE: Amen. How come there's nobody else here?

CZEKAJ: I guess everybody was good this week.
                    (More seriously)
Not that many people come anymore. What did you want to tell me?

GUADALUPE: I don'know.

CZEKAJ: Did something happen? In school? Or with your Mom and Dad at home? I won't tell anybody. I'm not supposed to. This is between you and me and God. Okay?

GUADALUPE: Okay...

(Pause)

CZEKAJ: You still there?

GUADALUPE: Yeah. Can't you see me?

CZEKAJ: No. Can you see me?

GUADALUPE: No...but I thought maybe it was like a trick mirror or something.

CZEKAJ: No. No tricks. Old-fashioned confessional. I just see some light and a shadow of you.

GUADALUPE: That's good. I—What do I call you?

CZEKAJ: Father. Or Father Jan. My name is Janusz.

GUADALUPE: What kind of name is that?

CZEKAJ: Polish.

GUADALUPE: Okay. Whatever. Father Jan. Father Jan, I—I love her.

CZEKAJ: Love is good. But you know the Church asks that you wait till you're all grown up and married. That's when love is best.

GUADALUPE: I want to marry her. But Grace says it's a sin. So that's why I thought I should ask.

CZEKAJ: Marriage is a blessed sacrament. But you have a lot of years ahead of you. You're only what eleven or twelve?

GUADALUPE: Thirteen.

CZEKAJ: Thirteen. Still too young for such a big thing. If you and Grace wait—

GUADALUPE: I don'wanna marry Grace. She's a pain. It's Belen, I want.

CZEKAJ: Oh. Well, if you and Belen wait, you can have a wonderful wedding right here.

GUADALUPE: Yeah?

CZEKAJ: Yeah. But wait son. Don't be so impatient to grow up. There's plenty of time.

GUADALUPE: There is? But I don'know how to tell time anymore.

CZEKAJ: Believe me. There's time. Anything else on your mind?

GUADALUPE: No...I guess that's it. Is it over?

CZEKAJ: Unless you have something else to say.

GUADALUPE: Okay. Bye Father Jan.

CZEKAJ: Good-bye, son. But will you do me a favor?

GUADALUPE: Maybe.

CZEKAJ: Come to church sometime. Stop in and say a prayer. He listens.

GUADALUPE: Then He knows everything already?

CZEKAJ: Just about.

GUADALUPE: Good. I jus'wanned Him to know.

CZEKAJ: Say a prayer to yourself before you leave, okay? I bless you in the name of the Father, the Son, and the Holy Spirit. Go in peace.

GUADALUPE: 'Bye.

(GUADALUPE runs out of the church back to the Salt mounds. FATHER CZEKAJ steps out of the confessional and sees only his fleeing back.)

CZEKAJ: I wish they were all so easy...
> (*HE sits on a pew and speaks to the Cross.*)
Sweet Jesus, why am I always here alone?

(*Lights cross to the Calumet Park field house.*)

SCENE 11

LAVENDER GLASS
Later that morning.
LUCIA, dressed in a tattered blue dress, plays
with dolls HE has made from pieces of garbage.

LUCIA: Play, play. With sock man and the erasergirls
and my favoritest Angie. Click, click. I hear things
going off in my head. It's a hard click. It's not a gun,
but it's like a gun. My thoughts...Click.
> (*BELILAH enters pulling LUCIA roughly onto*
> *her lap and beginning to spank him viciously.*)
NOO! LuLu good. Click! Click!

BELILAH: Not LuLu! Not ever LuLu, sweet. I called
you, Lucia, because you're like the child who held the
four secrets of Fatima, secrets of the precious virgin
predicting all kinds of nasty things.
> (*Pinching the tattoo on his hand*)

I gave you that heart myself. I asked Vasques to mark you so everyone would know you were a child of Mary. But no more. No more. I heard you were giving it away. You know the rules. You know you can't get respect without paying a price.

(HE shrieks once more as SHE continues to beat him, but then stops and takes the rest of the beatings in silence. Feeling his butt.)

You'll always feel tight like a virgin from this end. From this end, you're a smooth piece of lavender glass. So beautiful it hurts to look. So beautiful it makes you want to break it in many pieces too small to find...but one day, a little piece shows up—under a fingernail, or deep inside the hard part of your right foot...My hands are covered with you, deep, bloodless wounds—that's what you've given me. That's all you've given me lately.

Do you think I like beating you? Well, yes, I do. But only because you deserve it. Yes, you do. You do, do, do. I told you not to go talking to people without my say so.

(SHE pushes him off her lap onto the floor.)

That's enough for now. Just remember who keeps you alive. I wouldn't do this if I didn't love you.

(SHE kisses him gently on the cheek and wipes his tears.)

Go wash your face. You got a date soon.

(HE exits holding on tightly to his dolls.)

LUCIA: *(To ANGIE, his doll.)* You was right, Angie. She been click-click telling on me. Telling lies. Click.
(Pause)
Click. Lies. Maybe Belen don't really love me no more...

(Lights cross to the salt mounds.)

SCENE 12

TONGUE ALPHABET
December 26, afternoon.
GUADALUPE, LUCIA, GRACE & BELEN are picking who is "it" for a game. GUADALUPE leads the choosing off. HE counts off using his balled up fists to count against the others balled-up fists.

GUADALUPE, LUCIA, GRACE & BELEN:
My mother is dead. Your father is red. My sister wants minks. My brother he stinks. One, two, three, four. You take the floor—you stupid whore!

*(GRACE is "it"—SHE almost always is.
The others run away from her.)*

GRACE: Hey, come on! I was "it" last—That's not right. You kids don't—You didn't count it right. Stupid counts as one—You can't go making it—

Shucks! You can't do that. C'mon now. Come back.
I'm not gonna play with you googles no more. Come
back!

> (BELEN returns and tries to take
> GRACE's hand in apology.)

BELEN: Don't be mad, Gracie.
We were just playing.

GRACE: Don't be all kiss-make-up with me, Belen.
You should—I know you know better. You're
supposed to be—shucks—all friends with me and
everything. Din't I 'bout teach you everything?! Din't
I?

BELEN: Yeah, I guess—

GRACE: You guess? You better guess some more. I
coulda let Belilah teach you. Then you wouldn't have
no guesses left. She woulda kicked them all outta you.

BELEN: Yeah, I guess—

GRACE: You guess again?? Who taught you how to
champ the bit?

BELEN: You did.

GRACE: And the speedy cream?
                    (BELEN *nods yes.*)
The tongue alphabet? The firemaker?
The Chocolate dip?

BELEN: Yeah, but I never wanted to know. I just had
to know.

GRACE: Under the salt's where you'd be now without
me.

BELEN: I wish I was. I always wished I was. I open
my eyes in the morning and I know I'm cursed cause I
still see out of them.

GRACE: There's people with more better reasons to
wish for that. Like me. I'm worse off than you about a
million times.
BELEN: How come you don't go away?

GRACE: I could go anytime I want.

BELEN: I would go if I could.

GRACE: So?

BELEN: There's just no other place I know. Lupe's
always looking at his maps, making a plan. He's got
them memorized so when the time comes we'll know

how to go somewhere. But we don't know where somewhere is. We got the names but which way are they? We don't know—yet. But when we got the east-west thing figured, we're gone.

GRACE: Good luck!

(GRACE exits and GUADALUPE enters with a map, LUCIA follows him.)

LUCIA: Hey! Look what I got! Hey!

GUADALUPE: Stop following me around, freak!

BELEN: Don't call him that.
            (Pullling LUCIA to her)
Show me what you got.

LUCIA: No. LuLu don'want no mores.

BELEN: Come on. Lupe wants to see—Don't you, Lupe? Please.
GUADALUPE: Okay. But then you gotta see this new map I found. It's almost perfect.

BELEN: Go ahead and show us, LuLu.

LUCIA: It's just jewels—I made them. For you.

(LUCIA hands them each their gift—
a necklace for BELEN, a watch for LUPE.)

GUADALUPE: What's this supposed to be?

LUCIA: A watch. For time.

GUADALUPE: A watch? It's just an old bottle cap with junk scratched into it tied to a string.

BELEN: It's beautiful. I knew it was a watch right away.

LUCIA: You did?

BELEN: Yup. Let's see...It's two o'clock. Isn't that what it says, Lupe?

GUADALUPE: It don'say nothing to me.

BELEN: Put it on.

GUADALUPE: You put it on!
(HE throws it at her and runs off.)

BELEN: Lupe! He's jus'a little kid. Don'be like that. Lupe? Oh, well. I think it's the watchiest watch I ever seen.
LUCIA: How come he don'like me? Click, Belly, click?

BELEN: He don'know what he likes. I love my necklace. It's got so much green in it. I always wanted eyes like that—that color exactly. Maybe when I wear this, I'll look like I have 'em. People with green eyes got secrets.

LUCIA: You got secrets, Belly? Don't say yes.

BELEN: Nah. I just wish I had 'em.

LUCIA: Oh...You wanna play with Angie?

BELEN: Not right now. I'm so tired. I wish I could sleep all the way through one night sometime.

LUCIA: Yeah. Night's hard to sleep, huh Belly?

BELEN: Sure is.

LUCIA: Story?

BELEN: Which one?

LUCIA: Cut-cut piece—

BELEN: No, baby. I'm tired of that one. How about Bears and Others?

LUCIA: No. Cut-cut.

BELEN: How about Locks and Bolts? You like that one.

LUCIA: No. I want pieces!

BELEN: I don't feel like that one, okay?

LUCIA: No okay. No okay.

BELEN: Let's go lie down.

(BELEN exits, LUCIA slowly follows.)

LUCIA: No okay. No okay. No okay. No okay...

(Lights cross to GUADALUPE on the bridge.)

SCENE 13

SHOW ME YOUR MAPS
December 26, later that afternoon.
GUADALUPE sits alone on the bridge
reading his maps. GRACE enters.

GRACE: What cha'doing?

GUADALUPE: What's it look like? Finding somebody.

GRACE: Who you looking for? Mr. Indiana or Mrs. Wisconsin?

GUADALUPE: What do you know about who I'm looking for?

GRACE: Nothing. That's why I asked.

GUADALUPE: Are there any cars out there you can run in front of?

GRACE: Notice anything different about me?

GUADALUPE: No.

GRACE: New lipstick. Belilah gave me one of hers. You should be nice to me. She'll do anything for me.

GUADALUPE: Stop smiling like that. You're giving me the creeps.

GRACE: You should smile more, Loopy. You got nice teeth.

GUADALUPE: Anybody got nice teeth compared to you. You got the smallest teeth I ever seen in a human head. You're prettier with your mouth closed.

GRACE: You think I'm pretty?

GUADALUPE: No. But with your teeth all showing, you're worse.

GRACE: Show me your maps.

GUADALUPE: You really wanna see?

GRACE: Yeah. I never really seen one before.

GUADALUPE: Okay.
          (GRACE moves to sit beside him.)
This is where we are. And this is where I wanna go.

GRACE: That's kinda far. You shouldn't go alone.

GUADALUPE: I won't. As soon as Belen gets better, we're on our way.

GRACE: You won't get very far with her. She's slow. I'm fast.

GUADALUPE: I know.

GRACE: That's not really where we are.

GUADALUPE: How do you know?

GRACE: I can read, Loopy.

GUADALUPE: You're lying.

GRACE: Why would I?

GUADALUPE: Because you—just because.

GRACE: Yes bob sirree. Me. Me is who you're looking for—so come find me.

(SHE exits smiling.)

GUADALUPE: Lying bag of piss...
(Pause)
Maybe she'll teach me to read. I'll make her teach me.
(HE carefully folds his map and hides it in the salt. LUPE exits. ROCKET enters, digs in the sand and pulls out the map. Lights slowly fade to black as HE opens it.)

END OF ACT ONE

ACT TWO
SCENE 1

MS. LOVE
December 27, morning.
BELILAH in the church,
talking to FATHER CZEKAJ.

BELILAH: I've done a lot of this kind of work before.

CZEKAJ: Have you? What ages?

BELILAH: Pre-school to Junior High age.

CZEKAJ: That's quite a range.

BELILAH: Yes, well. Kids are kids I always say.

CZEKAJ: So how many hours a week do you think you'd like to give us, Ms. Love?

BELILAH: Oh, I don't know, father. Maybe eight hours a week. I have another job, but this is such important work, don't you think? I mean, everybody should give a little back, especially for the kids. And please call me, Belilah. I hate formalities.

CZEKAJ: Belilah? What an unusual name.

BELILAH: Yes. It's biblical.

CZEKAJ: I know...Your parents must have been very brave.

BELILAH: Yes. They were. They thought children should have names that they had to overcome. Builds strength of character. My brother's name was Judas.

CZEKAJ: Was? I'm so sorry—

BELILAH: Oh, he's not dead or anything—at least, I don't think so. I just stopped speaking to him when he became a cop. I don't trust policemen. I don't think any man with a gun is a good idea.

CZEKAJ: But some of them do good work, protect and serve. They couldn't all be corrupt surely.

BELILAH: Surely. Maybe it's just my brother who I don't trust. Anyway, when do I begin?

CZEKAJ: Do you have any references I can call?

BELILAH: Of course. I just didn't bring my address book with me, so I'll call you with a couple, okay?

CZEKAJ: Okay. Our after-school program will start up again after the holidays. So I look forward to hearing from you soon. Now if you'll excuse me, you can let yourself out.

(HE exits.)

BELILAH: Let myself out? Who raised him? Bad manners. I don't know if I like this one. But it's been so long since I been inside a church, maybe I just forgot how priests act. It is nice in here. Quiet. Feels like the inside of a fur-lined coat. Cozy. Until those children come back...

(As BELILAH exits through the church door someone
appears holding it open for her.
It is ROCKET, the custodian.)

BELILAH: Thank you, sweetheart. It's so nice when people behave in a courteous way, don't you think? Don't you think courtesy is the main thing we all need to keep going in this life?

ROCKET: Absolutely. Where does the word civilization come from? From civilized. To be civil is to pay attention to your heart. To some it may seem like I'm just holding the door, but it's heavy for a lady. And ladies are important—too important to let hold their own doors.

BELILAH: You're just a saint to help this old lady.

ROCKET: Old? I'd say you were in your prime.
Thirty-five? Thirty-six? What's in a number?

BELILAH: You are a charmer, Mr...?

ROCKET: Rocket. My friends call me, Rocket.

BELILAH: I'd love to be your friend, Mr. Rocket.

ROCKET: I'd like that. Can never have too many
friends, right?

BELILAH: Can I buy you a drink, Mr. Rocket?

ROCKET: Not right now thanks. I gotta work a little.
Work is like the Sun. You love to have it come up, but
sometimes you pray for it to go away. Some things are
better in the dark.

BELILAH: What is it you do, Mr. Rocket?

ROCKET: A little sweeping. A little plumbing. A
little of everything that takes a certain mechanical skill.
Skills are like stars—you yearn for a sky full of them,
and yet the one that catches your eye is only the one
that burns the brightest.

BELILAH: Oh. I would have thought a sensitive gentleman like yourself would be an artist—a poet maybe. You speak so...poetically.

ROCKET: Maybe we can get together tomorrow night?

BELILAH: Maybe. What time?
ROCKET: Ten?

BELILAH: Alright. Wanna meet at the Slide Inn?

ROCKET: Sounds good.

BELILAH: Good-bye, Mr. Rocket.

ROCKET: So long. See you tomorrow.

(BELILAH kisses his cheek.)

BELILAH: You remind me of someone.

ROCKET: And who would that be?

BELILAH: I'll tell you tomorrow. And by the way, I love your hat.

(SHE hurries off.)

ROCKET: It's been a long time since I got one of those. A kiss on the cheek is like the wings of a glorious white dove brushing gently across your face.
(Pause)
I gotta start stealing from better poets. Time to sweep.

(Lights cross to CZEKAJ.)

CZEKAJ: *(Reading Genesis 19:26; ROCKET enters quietly behind him.)* "But his wife looked back from behind him, and she became a pillar of salt."
(Closes his bible; Pause)
I wonder how many people know her name.

ROCKET: It's Belilah, isn't it?

*(CZEKAJ looks at ROCKET
as the lights cross to the field house.)*

SCENE 2

THE BOYS
December 27, afternoon.
Outside the field house. LUCIA speaks to his doll, ANGIE.
GRACE enters quietly behind him.

LUCIA: *(Putting a new dress that HE's just finished making from cloth scraps on ANGIE.)*

There. You look like a goddess in this dress. Or a saint. It's almost all white like they like to wear. Click. Click. Yeah, they like white.

ANGIE (GRACE): *(GRACE speaks for ANGIE in her sweet, Angie voice.)* Yeah. I look like a living doll in this dress. You always know how to make me feel better...

LUCIA: You don't feel good? Why, Angie, why? It's such a beautiful day. Almost no wind today. Almost feels warm in the Sun.

ANGIE (GRACE): I don't know, Lulu. Just sad today. I get that way sometimes. I'm a moody morsel.

LUCIA: Me, too. I'm a moody morsel too. Click. Sometimes. Click.

ANGIE (GRACE): Tell me a story.

LUCIA: Belen's the one tells stories, Ange. Not Lulu.

ANGIE (GRACE): Ugh! How can you even say her wicked ugly stupid name to me?! I hate her stories. I wanna hear your story.

LUCIA: But I don't got no stories. Click. Click.

ANGIE (GRACE): Aw, sure you do. Like...I always wanted to know where your "boys" went.

LUCIA: Boys? Whatdya mean?

ANGIE (GRACE): You know—What used to be between your legs.
Who clipped your jewels, Lulu?
Or were you born like that? Without them?

LUCIA: *(Highly agitated)* CLICK! CLICK! NO, ANGIE! Why you wanna know that for?! Click. Click. WHY?

ANGIE (GRACE): We're friends, ain't we?

LUCIA: Yeah, but—

ANGIE (GRACE): Friends tell friends everything. Every little thing and every big thing. And it makes me sad that we have secrets between us. You share your secrets with your friends and then the friends don't tell nobody else or else they stop being friends.

LUCIA: I—click, click—don'wanna, Angie!

ANGIE (GRACE): Alrighty then. I'm gonna stop being your friend right this minute. Put me down and walk away, Lulu. Because I can't go around with you no more.

LUCIA: NO! Don't be like that. You know I love you.

ANGIE (GRACE): I don't know any such thing—if you won't tell me stuff. How would I know?
(Kind of sing-songy)
La-la-lah! I don't got no kind of friends. All alone waiting for what God sends. La-la-lah!
Used to have a friend named Lulu, but he's gone and left me, boo-hoo!

(Long pause)

LUCIA: Five years ago. Click. Click. Five years ago, I had a sister.

ANGIE (GRACE): So?

LUCIA: She...went away. To Heaven. Click click click click click click click click—

ANGIE (GRACE): Sssh! Calm down now. So she went to Heaven?! That happens sometimes, God bless her soul. That happens. What's that got to do with the "boys"?

LUCIA: It was my fault, Angie! Mine! I was supposed to be watching her—and I didn't. I was watching cartoons—and she got out of the house. Click. Click.

ANGIE (GRACE): Hmmm...But you was too young to be watching somebody else. That's not your business, to be watching somebody else. Nope. Poor Lulu. So, you got punished?

LUCIA: I punished myself. I wanned to turn into nothing, Angie. I just—
            (Crumpling up into a ball and
            hitting himself in the stomach)
Nothing. Nothing. Nothing.
            (HE continues to repeat "nothing"
            under his breath as ANGIE speaks.)

ANGIE (GRACE): Hey! Hey, that's enough! Stop saying that! You got too much work to do. Too much good work to go dying on me. Who would make me pretty dresses if you weren't here? Who woulda even made me without you? That's just selfish. Just stop.
            (LUCIA stops.)
Better. You're better off now anyways...So...was you trying to stab yourself? And then the knife slipped or something?

LUCIA: No. My mom and dad cried so much for her. Click. Click. Every day they cried for her. They said boys were stupid. Boys were good for nothing. For them I'd do anything...

ANGIE (GRACE): Jeez, I guess so. Are you a he or a she now? I think you're more he than she.
LUCIA: I'm just Lulu. Click. Click.

ANGIE (GRACE): And that's the way I like you, baby. Just Lulu is just fine by me.

LUCIA: We're friends click again click?

ANGIE (GRACE): Mmmm...let me think...Uh...yes. Again friends. Now don't you feel good telling me? I feel real good now. That was a very interesting story.

LUCIA: Angie better? Angie the best! I want you to always be best than me.

ANGIE (GRACE): Don't worry, honey. I always will be...Show me.

LUCIA: No. There's nothing to see.

ANGIE (GRACE): Please!

LUCIA: But it's real ugly down —

ANGIE (GRACE): I said, Please! Pretty please. Just a peek. I promise I won't scream or nothing.

LUCIA: *(Picking up the doll and putting her head down his pants)* Okay. If you want—whatever you want...

ANGIE (GRACE): *(Peeking down his pants from behind and covering her mouth when SHE speaks so it sounds like she's talking from inside there)* Oooh. It's not so bad. There's just some scars and stuff. I think it's beautiful.

> *(Pulling the doll out; GRACE uncovers*
> *her mouth and giggles to herself)*

LUCIA: You do?

ANGIE (GRACE): Sure. I don't got nothing down there either. That's what's nice about being a doll. You're a living doll too.

LUCIA: Thanks!
> *(HE kisses ANGIE sweetly.)*
I love you, Angie.
> *(GRACE exits.)*
Angie? You must be all tired. Click. Click. Me too.
> *(HE closes his eyes, holding ANGIE*
> *tightly to him and rocks.)*

LUCIA: *(With his eyes still tightly closed)* She was real pretty, Ange. You woulda loved her. Except she didn't have much hair. One time I painted her head with shoe polish so she'd be beautiful. My father locked me in the closet for it—but I know she liked it. We could speak without saying nothing. I could look into her eyes and I'd hear her words in my head. She liked being a helmet head—that's what the polish made her look like. She looked at me through the keyhole of the closet and told me that and told me not to cry. I mean, I could see her eyeball in the hole and it spoke to me. When I close my eyes now, I think I still can hear her. That's the way I stay alive. It's only with my eyes open that I begin to click off.

(Pause)

You're my best friend—after her. Her name was Angie too...

> *(ROCKET enters as LUCIA stoops to pick up some forgotten toys scattered around the field house.)*

LUCIA: Beauty. Beauty rope. Make a nice necklace for somebodys.

ROCKET: *(Holding up a sneaker)* Look what I found.

LUCIA: Wow! You lucky rascal! Mister's real lucky. LuLu needs 'nother one of those.

ROCKET: *(Handing him the sneaker)* Here. It's yours. I already have a pair. See?

           (HE points at his feet.)

You keep it.

LUCIA: Wow! No mister never give me anything, without—click, click—never...

ROCKET: Looks like you found some good stuff today.

LUCIA: Yep. A lot of dumb-butts leave all they good stuff behind. And then it's mine, right? All mine. You collect too?

ROCKET: Yep. But I throw away the stuff I collect— not like you. You make beautiful things.

LUCIA: How you—click, click—know that??

ROCKET: I seen you around.

LUCIA: Yep. I been around. You must find a lot of good stuff.

        (Pointing to the field house)

You got the keys to that place?

ROCKET: You don't need keys when you're a Rocket. Follow me.

LUCIA: What? You a bu'gler?

ROCKET: Nope. I just know how to get into things.

LUCIA: Like magical?

ROCKET: Yep. Kinda exactly like that.

LUCIA: You sure are a lucky rascadiddly, Mister.

ROCKET: Call me Rocket, okay?

LUCIA: Okay. Mister? Why you so nice? You take me inside?

ROCKET: Sure. Come on.

LUCIA: No! Click, click! I mean in—
            (HE points at ROCKET's heart.)
here. And—
            (HE touches ROCKET's arms.)
—hug with clothes.

ROCKET: Sure. Come on.
            (ROCKET sits on the ground and
            LUCIA sits on his lap and hugs him,

putting his cheek against ROCKET's.)

LUCIA: Yep...that's sweetie cupcake, mister. You got kids?

ROCKET: Not yet.

LUCIA: I could be...maybe.

ROCKET: Maybe.

LUCIA: You make fun of LuLu? Click, click.

ROCKET: No fun. Truth.

LUCIA: I got me 'nother sneaker, but it different color. But that's good. Lots of color is good.

ROCKET: You are a sweet young thing, LuLu.

LUCIA: Yep. Sweetie cupcake, LuLu.
Wanna play a game?

ROCKET: Sure.

LUCIA: *(Jumping up in excitement)* It's called "find twenty dollars" game. You reach in your pockets and you pull out what you got and you give me half. Okay? GO!

*(ROCKET reaches into his pocket
and pulls out some lint.)*

ROCKET: *(Holding up the lint)* That's all I got—but you can have half.

LUCIA: Thanks, mister. You work here?

ROCKET: Yeah. I like it too. What do you wanna be when you grow up?

LUCIA: I dunno. Not what you are anyways. I mean, I already pick-up garbage, so I want something real different. Jus'one thing, I think. I got too many conficts. That's what Miss—what some girl told me.

ROCKET: Do you believe her?

LUCIA: Yeah, maybe. I dunno. No.

ROCKET: You'll figure it out one day.

LUCIA: I squeeze my eyes and hope so. Click. Click.
     *(Taking one of ROCKET's hands
     and comparing it with one of his.)*
Wowwee! You got biggedy hands. You could probably kill an elephant or something.

ROCKET: Probably. But why would I?
          (*Holding LUCIA's hand*)
Hands are for holding.

          (*Lights cross to the bridge.*)

SCENE 3

Crispy Chicken, Chomp-Chomp, & The Fall
GRACE teaches GUADALUPE how to read.
THEY sit on the bridge railing as GRACE
traces the letters of the alphabet
into his hands with her saliva.

GRACE: (*Pointing at a letter of the alphabet SHE has drawn on his hands*) Repeat what I just said.

GUADALUPE: (*Kind of bored*) "The letter "R" is a round, rascally letter. It makes the sound "rruh" like in run or rabbit." When are we gonna get to the reading part?

GRACE: You got to know your letters before you can read, google. Everybody knows that.

GUADALUPE: I guess I'm not everybody. And stop calling me "google"! What the hell does that mean anyway?

GRACE: If you could read, you would know what I mean, goog—I mean, Loopy.

GUADALUPE: Okay. What's next?

GRACE: *(Drawing an "S" on his hands)* The letter "S" is a sassy, sunny letter. It makes the sound "esss" like snake or snuggle.
> *(SHE snuggles up to him.*
> *HE pushes her gently away.)*
Or snot.

GUADALUPE: C'mon. Quit it! Just teach me okay?

GRACE: I can teach you something you will never forget.
> *(SHE gets up and starts to shimmy all around him.)*
"S" like in—
> *(SHE kind of sings, thrusting her*
> *pelvis in his face on the word "pop".)*
"Shimmy, shimmy, cocoa pops.
Shimmy, shimmy, pop."

GUADALUPE: You're just plain annoying, Grace. That's the letter "P" for plain and "A" for annoying.

GRACE: That's amazing, Loopy! You're really getting it. I'm a better teacher than I thought.

GUADALUPE: You're not bad—as a teacher I guess.

GRACE: Is that a compliment? Or do I need to clean my ears?

GUADALUPE: You always need to clean your ears.

GRACE: I wouldn't be talking about ears if I was you, Mr. Raggedy Monster Ear. Forget it! I'm not gonna teach you nothing else.
>*(Turns to make a fake exit, turns back)*
Well, ain't you gonna stop me?

GUADALUPE: Whatever. Let's just get through this alphabet thing, okay?

GRACE: Kiss me first.

GUADALUPE: C'mon! Stop it!

GRACE: C'mon, Loopy...just one little wittle kiss. And then I'll teach you anything.
>*(SHE puckers her lips and closes her eyes.)*
I'm waiting...
>*(Pause)*
I'm still waiting.
>*(Pause)*
How long do you expect me to wait?

GUADALUPE: *(Grabs her hand and kisses it)* There. Finish, okay?

GRACE: That's a start. Maybe I'll finish—tomorrow.

(GRACE exits. GUADALUPE traces the letter "G" into his hand.)

GUADALUPE: "G" is for the google Grace. And the double google Guadalupe...
> *(Rubbing the spit off his hand roughly*
> *and following after GRACE)*

Gracie! Let's finish it now. I gotta figure this all out soon.

(Lights cross to the beach.)

SCENE 4

FUDDLE-FIDDLE
GRACE finds a dead fish on the beach.

GRACE: Ooowee! What a big ole fuddle-fiddle fish!
> *(Poking it with her foot)*

Just about dead too. But something's still moving around in there.
> *(SHE bends over it and begins to*

tear into the fish with her hands.)
What is all this commotion?! I guess I'll jus'hafta find
out.

    (As SHE tears into it, SHE pulls out a dead rat.)
Oohweewah! That's what killed you. Fish ain't
s'posed to eat rats. And what's this?

    (Continuing to pull the fish apart,
    SHE finds a belt with a star buckle.)
Oh, my goodness! And it looks like it would fit me
jus'perfectalicious.

    (Noticing something moving inside the fish)
Oohweewahwee! This is the spookiest thing I ever
seen. Baby fish coming out of a dead mother. You
ain't got no mama no more, you poor dumb
things...But I could be! Yeah! I'll tell you what I'll do
for you spookadelic fishies! I'm gonna take you to
Belilah's and put you in some water. I know you'd
like that 'cause you're the staring-est fish I ever seen
and there's a lot to see in her house—believe you me.

    (Running off trying to keep the baby fish in her hands and
    get them to BELILAH's before they die.)
Dang! You're the jumpiest bugaloos too!

    (GRACE exits humming as ROCKET enters humming.
HE notices her and watches her walk away. Then HE moves
over to the fish, pulling it off as lights cross to the Church.)

SCENE 5

THE WEATHER
Late afternoon.
In the church.
The ALDERMAN MOROSH sits
in a pew talking to FATHER CZEKAJ.

CZEKAJ: It's nice of you to come by. Is there an election coming up?

MOROSH: I understand that remark. People are so used to politicians being after something. But not me. I would love to help you re-build your church. A church is the spine of a community. None of us would stand without you—I mean for anything worthwhile.

CZEKAJ: I would appreciate any help you could give me. Even just an extra policeman outside during the Saturday night mass would help. People are scared to leave their homes now when it's dark. That's what's killing the church. People still believe but they just don't leave their homes any more, if they can help it. That's what you could do.

MOROSH: I'll do my best, father. When do you hear confession?

CZEKAJ: Every Saturday afternoon. I don't like to do it too much before Sunday. Things always happen on

Saturdays. Especially when people aren't working. Seems like it's getting easier to do harm—to yourself as quickly as to others.

MOROSH: Do you think—I was reading this book, Nostradamus and his predictions. And you know how the weather's been so crazy lately? Do you think...

CZEKAJ: ...it's the end of the world? No. But I'm not allowed to worry about that anyway. I mean, if it is I've got my soul in order so there's nothing to worry about. What about you?

MOROSH: Me? Worried? No. I mean, the weather is really bothering me. Summer is so hot now and winter, deadly cold. Just this week ten more homeless people froze to death in my ward. That kind of stuff bothers me. But I wouldn't say I was worried exactly.

CZEKAJ: If it is the end of the world, there's not a lot we can do about it. Except love each other. Trust in God. Stuff like that. I wouldn't let it bother me too much...

(With a smile)

So I'll see you in church this week?

MOROSH: *(With a nervous laugh)* You bet. I'll sure as—I'll be there. I'm serious about the building too. Just let me know.

(*MOROSH exits.*)

CZEKAJ: Sure thing.
     (*MOROSH is gone.*
   Turning to speak to the Jesus on the crucifix)
I bet I'll never see him again...Although, he did seem pretty scared about this weather thing.
     (*Lights cross to the beach.*)

SCENE 6

VAMPIRES

GUADALUPE standing on the beach, staring straight ahead as CUSTOMER THREE gives him a blowjob. All we see of CUSTOMER THREE is his back as HE kneels in front of GUADALUPE, and his arms and hands with long fingernails grasping GUADALUPE's torso.
GUADALUPE
submits to this act without expression.

CUSTOMER THREE: *(Finishing him off and reaching for his lips)* Aren't you going to say anything?

GUADALUPE: *(Pushing CUSTOMER THREE away with his foot)* Quit that!

(LUPE zips up and puts out his hand. CUSTOMER THREE puts some money in his hand as ROCKET appears behind him. CUSTOMER THREE sees ROCKET and walks off quickly.)

GUADALUPE: *(Defensively)* What are you looking at?

ROCKET: The water. What about you?

GUADALUPE: Nothing—most of the time.
                    (Meaning sex)
You looking for something?

ROCKET: Only when something's looking for me.
        (Taking out his vial of water and taking a swig)
Mmm. This is what keeps me going.
Wanna try?

GUADALUPE: You think I'm stupid or something?! I don't know what's in that stuff.
                    (Pause)
What is that—like acid?

ROCKET: Nope. Although on some, it could work like acid. That's what happens in vampire movies anyway.

GUADALUPE: Yeah? I never seen a vampire movie.

ROCKET: Didn't miss much.

GUADALUPE: I believe in them though.

ROCKET: Why's that?

GUADALUPE: I believe there's people who can only sleep in the daytime because they can't look at themselves in sunlight—and at night they go around sucking on other people. Yeah, there's a whole lot of people like that.

ROCKET: (Holding up the vial) Maybe you need to carry some of this.

GUADALUPE: No. Really. What's it do to you?

ROCKET: Whatever you need it to do.
GUADALUPE: Yeah?
                    (Pause)
Do you get a headache after?

ROCKET: No.

261

GUADALUPE: Feel like you're gonna throw up?

ROCKET: No.

GUADALUPE: Upset stomach?

ROCKET: Nope. None of that.
> *(Looking up at the sky)*
That's unusual. The moon is rising in the East—like the Sun.

GUADALUPE: The Sun rises in the East?!

ROCKET: Yep. Always has.

GUADALUPE: I'll try a bit of that stuff.
> *(ROCKET hands him the vial.*
> *LUPE takes a sip and hands it back.)*
Tastes like flowers. Does something happen right away or do you have to wait?

ROCKET: For me, it happens right away.

GUADALUPE: Oh...
> *(Closing his eyes)*
I feel something.

ROCKET: Yeah?

GUADALUPE: Yeah. I could just lie down right here and sleep. My body is rocking like a baby inside. Real slow. I gotta sit down.

(GUADALUPE slowly sits and pulls out a map. HE has it turned upside down. ROCKET looks at it from behind and turns it right side up, so it is in sync with the landscape.)

ROCKET: *(Pointing at the lake in front of them and then at the lake on the map)* East. The blue is the lake.

GUADALUPE: Oh...
(We see GUADALUPE figuring out the directions based on knowing which way is east.)
Wow! That stuff is powerful.

(GUADALUPE falls to the ground in a faint.)

ROCKET: *(Pouring water from the vial into GUADALUPE's deformed ear while reciting a modified version of the prayer to St. John.)*
I hope you understand the words I've poured into your ear.

(ROCKET exits as GUADALUPE continues to lay still for a moment. Then, GUADALUPE suddenly gets up.)

GUADALUPE: Belen! I got it now. Won't be much longer...

(Lights cross to BELILAH's apartment.)

SCENE 7

ANTICIPATION
In her apartment, BELILAH gets ready for her date. SHE speaks to the fish in the fish bowl.

BELILAH: Won't be much longer. He makes me feel like I'm on fire. That smile and those sashaying sidewise eyes—I'd follow him anywhere. He could be the one. What do you think? You seem to be thinking all kinds of things in that bowl of yours. The nasty way you watch me dress. And how you swim all happy when I sing. I shouldn't've let Gracie keep you here, but it being Christmastime and all—I just couldn't say no. I'm just too soft sometimes. That's my main problem.
(Pause)
You think he likes soft women? A gentleman like him usually does. I bet he likes a woman who laughs loud and sleeps soft. I'd make a pillow for him on every piece of me.
(Pause)

I wonder what he's thinking right this very minute.
This has got to be a special night.
                    (Pause)
I would pray now if I remembered how.
        (BELILAH closes her eyes for a brief moment
            then opens them, with tears in her eyes.)
But when I close my eyes all I feel are small fingernails
tearing at me, like rats scratching at my brain...He
could definitely be the one.

            (Lights cross to the Slide Inn.)

SCENE 8

THE DATE: PART ONE
Late evening.
At the Slide Inn, a local tavern, ROCKET sits drinking a
beer and waiting for BELILAH. ROCKET talks to the
bartender as HE waits.
The bartender, DOM, is CUSTOMER ONE
from the first scene.

DOM: Why can't Jesus eat M&Ms?

ROCKET: I dunno. Why?

DOM: Because they fall through the holes in his
hands.

ROCKET: Oh, man! That's really bad.

DOM: Why was Jesus crucified?

ROCKET: Why?

DOM: Because if he were stoned, instead of the sign of the cross, Catholics would have to go like this—
(*HE pounds on his own face and chest.*)

ROCKET: A visual. Very sophisticated, Dom. Got anymore?

DOM: Jesus was tired from wandering around the desert—decides to take a night off, pamper himself, check into an inn. Goes up to the innkeeper, puts three nails on the desk and says, Hey, Can you—

DOM & ROCKET: *(In unison)*
—put me up for the night?

ROCKET: Old. That's old. Way, way too unbelieveably old.

DOM: What can I say? I'm old. I know that's why you keep coming back. Telling tasteless jokes is an art—and I have finely mastered it.

ROCKET: There are some things in life, you just can't be proud of being good at.

DOM: Speak for yourself.

ROCKET: I always do.

DOM: Want a refill?

ROCKET: Sure. I think I'm being stood-up.

DOM: What time was she supposed to get here?

ROCKET: Ten.

DOM: *(Looking at his watch)* It's just ten now.

ROCKET: Women are supposed to be early. I hate waiting.

DOM: While you wait I got another one for you—

ROCKET: Oh, please, man. Enough. I gotta find a new bar. This place stinks like your jokes.

DOM: *(Walking away)* Suit yourself.

ROCKET: I always do.
      (BELILAH walks in wearing a red

jacket and a short red sequined dress.)
Wow! You look different.

BELILAH: It's not too much, is it?

ROCKET: Not for me.

BELILAH: You're who counts tonight.

ROCKET: What are you drinking?

BELILAH: I dunno. Something light. A Johnny
Walker red? Straight up, please. Ohhh..what the hey,
make it a double.

ROCKET: Hey, Dom. Bring the lady a double Johnny
Walker neat.

> *(DOM comes over and BELILAH*
> *and HE recognize each other.)*

DOM: Sure.
> *(HE quickly moves away to mix the drink.)*

BELILAH: Why Mr. Dom! It's so nice to see you
again.

ROCKET: You know this guy?

BELILAH: We met once or twice—at church, wasn't it?

ROCKET: *(To DOM)* You go to church??

DOM: Every now and then.
> *(Handing her the drink)*

It's on the house.

> *(DOM & BELILAH exchange a look.*
> *THEY'll keep each other's secret.*
> *An awkward silence.)*

ROCKET: *(Making a joke)* So...what's your sign?

BELILAH: *(Seriously)* I'm a Virgo—just like the Virgin Mary. We even have the same birthday, September 8th.

ROCKET: I was just kidding. I don't really believe in that stuff—although mine is really accurate. I'm a Capricorn.

BELILAH: I knew it! Vulnerable, sensitive, down-to-earth. We're have a lot in common—astrologically speaking. Earth and earth. We're both Earthy-types. Passionate, yet grounded.

ROCKET: Yeah, well...Like I said, I don't know anything about those kind of stars.

BELILAH: Why did you ask me out for a drink?

ROCKET: You asked me first.

BELILAH: Oh...maybe I did. Was I too forward, Mr. Rocket?

ROCKET: It's Rocket—just Rocket.

BELILAH: So...Rocket, what do you look for in a lady friend?

ROCKET: The same thing I look for in a man friend.

BELILAH: Silly! I mean a close lady friend, like one you fall in love with.

ROCKET: *(Quoting from the Bible, Proverbs 30:18-19)* There are four things that are too mysterious for me to understand: an eagle flying in the sky, a snake moving on a rock, a ship finding its way over the sea, and a man and a woman falling in love.

BELILAH: That's—that's—just beautiful. It could be from the Bible, it's so beautiful. Did you write that? I swear you're a talented man, Rocket.

ROCKET: Yes...but it's hard sometimes to have so many ideas and words in your head—there's just not enough time to get it all down—on paper. My main problem is time.

BELILAH: I know. And it all goes so fast. We always have to make time for what's important...like I left work early just to see you tonight.

ROCKET: That was very generous. What do you do?

BELILAH: I...run a little candy store—with my children. They're all good, helpful kids. Not like some these days.

ROCKET: How many kids do you have?

BELILAH: Just about enough let me tell you!

ROCKET: Yeah. They can be a handful. I don't have any—being a son is enough trouble.

BELILAH: Are your parents still with us?

ROCKET: Yes. But they kind of gave up on me. I was real young the last time I saw them.

BELILAH: That's a shame!

(From the jukebox we hear Thelma Houston's "Don't Leave Me This Way")

ROCKET & BELILAH: *(Simultaneously)* I love this song.

ROCKET: Can I have this dance?

BELILAH: I would be honored.

> *(THEY dance. A lot of attempted fancy*
> *disco moves, but they're a little off.*
> *HE tries to dip her at one point and SHE falls, but THEY*
> *both continue like it was meant to be.*
> *DOM watches and shouts encouragement.)*

DOM: *(Sarcastic)* Wooh! I haven't seen moves like that in a long time...

> *(Finally the song ends. ROCKET &*
> *BELILAH are both out of breath.)*

BELILAH: That was wonderful! I feel about sixteen again.
> *(SHE reaches into the ice bucket behind the bar*
> *and grabs some ice and rubs around her neck*
> *and then between her breasts.)*

That feels good.

ROCKET: Looks like it does.

BELILAH: (Pulling at the front of his shirt and placing ice on his chest) How's that?

ROCKET: *(Pushing her away)* Cold! Stop that!

BELILAH: You're the shy-type, huh? I wouldn'tve guessed that.

ROCKET: I'm nothing but surprises.

BELILAH: Buy me another drink?

ROCKET: Okay. But I can't stay too much longer. I gotta be at work at six.

BELILAH: Then we might as well stay up all night.

ROCKET: I don't think so.

BELILAH: It's unusual to meet somebody who likes the same music.

ROCKET: Yeah, I had a really hard time believing in the 80s.

BELILAH: So did I. An era to forget. Let's drink to that.

ROCKET: Just one more.

(Lights cross to the salt mounds.)

SCENE 9

POTATO-BABY
Late night.
BELEN & GUADALUPE plan their escape.
THEY are huddled together in a salt mound.

BELEN: When are we gonna get out of here, Lupe? You promised it would be soon.

GUADALUPE: It will be. Look at this.
        (HE takes out a metro-map of Chicago.)
We are right here.

BELEN: But where are we going?

GUADALUPE: That I don't know yet.

BELEN: Oh, Lupe!

GUADALUPE: But I'll know soon—prob'ly by tomorrow. I promise we won't be here come New Year's. It's gonna be a real new year for us.

BELEN: I hope so.

(THEY *hear a snoring sound from behind them.*)

GUADALUPE: Who's that?

BELEN: Vasques. He won't leave me alone. He keeps watching me. It's giving me the creeps.

GUADALUPE: Awh, he's okay.

BELEN: No, he's not. He's not right in the head. Belilah says it's from all the fish he eats from the river. That fish is not for people to eat. They come outta there all weird colors. I wouldn't eat that fish.

GUADALUPE: Yeah, me neither. It's nice to be all alone like this. Lucky to have both of them gone.

BELEN: You think they're together?

GUADALUPE: Who cares?! As long as they're not here. Where's the freak?

BELEN: I don't know. He's not talking to me so much any more.

GUADALUPE: Good. Then you can spend more time with me.

BELEN: I spend a lot of time with you. Anyway, we don't always have to be together. You're my brother and no matter where you are you know I love you.

GUADALUPE: I don't know that. Not always.

BELEN: *(Kissing his face many times)* How about now? And now? And this? And a big one right here!

GUADALUPE: Let me hold you.
BELEN: You don't gotta ask.

(THEY hold each other tightly for a moment.)

GUADALUPE: You're so beautiful, Belen. Your skin feels so nice—like toasted marshmallows.

BELEN: Toasted marshmallows?! That sounds burned and gooey.

GUADALUPE: Yeah. So? I like burned and gooey.

BELEN: Whatever...but it don't sound very beautiful. Anyway, you saying I'm beautiful, is like you saying you're beautiful. I mean, us being twins and all.

GUADALUPE: But we don't look that much alike. Maybe we're not even related. Maybe the people who said they was our parents, really bought us at a baby factory and we come from two completely different places. Like you—you're probably from Egypt. And me—I'm from Alaska. And they took us and put us together and pretended we was theirs. We musta not really been theirs or they wouldn't've given us to Belilah. I don't think real family would've sold us like that.

BELEN: I haven't thought about them in a long time...at least, a week.

GUADALUPE: Yeah...you start to get over things. When you grow up, I mean.

BELEN: (Teasing) So you're all growed up now, huh? When did that happen? You wasn't supposed to do that without me.

GUADALUPE: I'm not.
    (HE kisses her passionately, SHE doesn't resist.)
So? What do you think?

BELEN: Different.

GUADALUPE: Different?

BELEN: Yeah...from when men kiss me. I mean they do the same thing—but it didn't make me sick to my stomach like it does with them.

GUADALUPE: I didn't make you sick. That's good...I guess. But that was all?

BELEN: No. I felt scared too. Like a small little shaky thing in my whole body.

GUADALUPE: Maybe that's not scared. Maybe it's— I dunno, something else.

BELEN: What else?

GUADALUPE: In love—like to be in love—not just love somebody like a brother. Like maybe we should get married or something.

BELEN: You can't marry your own brother.

GUADALUPE: Yeah, you can. I already asked God and everything. He said it was okay.

BELEN: He did? When did you talk to him?

GUADALUPE: I dunno...a couple of days ago, I guess. He definitely said yes. I mean, as long as you want to. If you don't want to—

BELEN: I don't know what I want. I want to get outta here, that's all. Maybe I could think better somewhere else. Alls I do here is tell myself stories. To keep my mind to myself. Anybody can do anything to me as long I still keep that for myself.

GUADALUPE: Tell me one of your stories.

BELEN: For reals?

GUADALUPE: Yeah, it's better than wasting them on freaky-deeky.

BELEN: Don't keep being like that.
                    (Pause)
There's this new one that just come to me. It goes like this: There was once a house that everybody was scared of. Nobody would go there because they thought their souls was gonna get sucked out of their mouths.

GUADALUPE: I know some people like that.

BELEN: And in this house—

*(LUCIA enters and listens unseen by GUADALUPE &
BELEN. A few moments later, GRACE enters behind
LUCIA.)*

—lived a little boy and girl who grew a garden inside.
They was afraid to go out because all the people on the
outside thought they was witches, because they lived
in such a dirty old house with no windows. But inside
it was beautiful. It was like a jungle. And they made
animals for their jungle from the old furniture and
newspapers—

GUADALUPE: And maps?

BELEN: And maps they had left from when they had
parents who really loved them, but went out to the
store one day and never come back, because they was
hit by a school bus.

GUADALUPE: I knew school was dangerous.

BELEN: Yeah...those buses anyway. But when they
didn't come back, the boy and girl had to make a
family without them. And food too. So they growed
the food right in their living room. They had corn and
potatoes and lettuce and strawberries and cherries.
Right there—as much as they could eat. So they never
went hungry, but they missed seeing people, so they
had a baby.

GUADALUPE: How'd they do that?

BELEN: You know...They grew one.
GUADALUPE: Like the vegetables? Like a Mr. Potato-Head baby?! Musta been cute.

BELEN: It sure was. It was the cutest baby they ever seen. Of course they never seen no other babies to compare him with—but still even from what they remembered on t.v. there was never a cuter baby. And it loved them so much, that the first word it said was "love." Not "Mommy" or "daddy" like other lame babies do—but "love."

GUADALUPE: That was one weird baby.

BELEN: One special baby. And the baby grew up and learned to use the plants in the garden to heal anything. That boy could cure coughs and headaches, and stomachaches. And when his mother got Cancer, he cured that too. And one time his father fell down the stairs and broke his back, and that boy figured out how to straighten his spine and his legs and made him walk again. This was a very wonderful boy. The boy was so wonderful that he gave his ma and pa the courage to leave the house again. They weren't afraid no more of the bad neighbors, who cursed them out and threw rocks at them. They was proud now and nothing could keep them from showing it. But one day—

GUADALUPE: Uh, oh! I feel the bad part coming up.

BELEN: —one snowy and icy day, the ma and pa went out to the church to give thanks for their beautiful child, and the neighbors got into the house and grabbed the boy, put him on a pile of wood, and set him on fire—

GUADALUPE: I thought your stories had happy endings.

BELEN: —they set him on fire, but he didn't burn. He became a part of the flames and shot into the sky like a rocket, and became a star. Now when the ma and pa want to see their baby, alls they gotta do is look up and there he is, twinkling and smiling. And the neighbors felt so bad about burning up their son, that they helped them re-build their house—and now they have windows to open and put their heads out and they all face North where their boy lives with the other stars of cold winter nights.

GUADALUPE: Hmmm...that was like a Christmas story, huh?

BELEN: Yeah. Did you like it?

GUADALUPE: Yeah, whatever. Pretty much. Except for that part about growing the baby, I believed it all. I mean, it's like something that could happen.

BELEN: Yeah. It's exactly something that could happen...

(Lights cross to LUCIA & GRACE.)

GRACE: That was a piss-fart of a dumb-ass story.

LUCIA: I think it was pretty.

GRACE: What are you doing over here anyway? You know you have a date.

LUCIA: I thought maybe, click, click, maybe he wouldn't come.

GRACE: It's your regular guy. He always comes.

LUCIA: I guess.

GRACE: (Pushing him roughly) Do I have to carry you over there?

LUCIA: I'll go. But how come you act like that?

GRACE: Like what?

LUCIA: Like Belilah. You don't have to act like her.

GRACE: I am my own woman, Lula, and nobody, especially not a little chiclet like you, needs to tell me how to act. Get to work!

LUCIA: I guess 'cause she's your ma, you can't help it.
GRACE: Get going. And leave that doll here. No customers like seeing dolls.

LUCIA: Mine do. They all like Angie.

GRACE: Just do like I tell you!

(LUCIA places ANGIE carefully in a pile of salt.)

LUCIA: Don't be lonely now. I'll be right back.

(LUCIA exits. GRACE waits for him to get out of sight and then picks up ANGIE.)

GRACE: You are an ugly hunk of stupid junk, Miss Angie. But you are so useful.
(SHE takes the knife out of ANGIE's head, and looks at it as VASQUES appears behind her, watching and listening.)
What's this? Dried up blood. What's that boy been doing with you, precious? Using you for his own

284

slicing. Maybe the "boys" are growing back. That would be something.

(*Licks the knife and then wipes it clean on her dress*)
Shiny. I like you all shiny. The only blood I want on this knife is Belen's. Then I'm gonna never wash it. I'll just keep it forever. In a box tied with one of those dumbass ribbons she always wears. It'll be a little memory box. And I'll put you right by Arlene's knife, so you won't be alone. She's not gonna die—she'll just be part of a new family—like in that little story of hers. She'll just be another star...

(*VASQUES covers his mouth to keep from shouting out. This is first true evidence HE's gotten that GRACE is responsible for ARLENE's death. Lights fade on GRACE and come up more brightly on him.*)

VASQUES: No, Gracie! Why?! Why are you doing this? And I helped, didn't I?! It was me who delivered Arlene's body to the fire. I thought we were saving the other children from having to see—from getting afraid. That's what you said. And now Belen's in danger too.
(*Pause*)
I gotta stay awake. I gotta trust my brain more. Now everything you tell me is a lie.
(*Pause*)
We can't be family anymore.

(Pause)

I remember how I cried when I saw you coming out of Miss Belilah. It was a miracle, I thought. I counted all your fingers and your toes. Checked all your limbs. And I cried...'cause you were normal.

(Lights cross to the Slide Inn.)

SCENE 10

<u>THE DATE: PART TWO</u>
Back at the Slide Inn.
After midnight, December 28th.
BELILAH is still talking and ROCKET is falling
asleep at the bar. HE nods off every now and then
and then stretches his neck all around, pretending like
HE was just doing that in the first place.

BELILAH: So I named her Grace, because she was such a great gift. And she had the littlest shoulders I ever seen on a human baby. Now kittens and baby rats got smaller shoulders but not like my baby—
        (HE nods off and then catches himself.)
Am I boring you?

ROCKET: No. I'm just really tired. And I live kind of far from here. Can't we finish the story of your life another time? I really have to get up early—

BELILAH: Alright. I don't want to keep you, from your bed. But my apartment's right around the corner, if you don't feel like going all the way home.

ROCKET: Naw, I'll go home. But thanks.

BELILAH: It's no problem. I wouldn't mind at all.

ROCKET: Naw, gotta get my uniform for work and everything. It's not the right time.

BELILAH: When is?

ROCKET: I never sleep with a woman on the first date. Then there's no place to go.

BELILAH: I didn't ask you to sleep <u>with</u> me—just over—my house.

ROCKET: It wouldn't be a good idea tonight. I had a great time, Belilah. But I'm going home. I'll walk you to your door though. Are you ready?

BELILAH: Now I feel all embarrassed. I didn't mean anything like that. Anything nasty. I just want you to be safe. We both had a lot to drink.

(*SHE starts to feel him up.*)

C'mon, baby. I know you like me.

ROCKET: (*Pushing her arms to her side and off him*) That's enough, young lady. I'm walking you home.

BELILAH: Can I see you again? I'd really like that.

ROCKET: Maybe. You know where to find me.

BARTENDER/DOM: (*As THEY exit.*) What a nice couple...Maybe I can get some freebies out of this.

(*Lights cross to BELILAH's apartment.*)

End of Act Two

ACT THREE
SCENE 1

FAMILY ALBUM
December 28, early morning.
GRACE and VASQUES looking at a photo album in
BELILAH's apartment.

VASQUES: Is that really him?

GRACE: Yup. That's your dad. Looks just like you too.

VASQUES: No he doesn't. He's so...weird-looking. Look at his eyes. Are my eyes like that?

GRACE: Yup. Exactly. Gives me the creeps.
            (Pointing at another photo)
Now this handsome man over here is my dad.

VASQUES: Hmmm...you don't much look like him. Are you sure these are our fathers?

GRACE: Sure.
            (Bopping VASQUES on the head)
And I look a lot like him thank you very much.

VASQUES: It's lucky I have a hard head. With all the bops you give me.

GRACE: Just trying to knock some sensibilities into you.

(Pointing at another photo)

 Look at this one! Ain't I cute? A cute little baby girl.

VASQUES: Are there any of me? As a baby, I mean.

GRACE: Nope. Belilah didn't have no camera when you was born. Poor as anything. But she got rich when I come along.

VASQUES: She's rich?!

GRACE: Yup! But nobody but me is supposed to know. She shares everything with me.

VASQUES: She really loves you. You don't have to hurt anyone when you got that kind of love.

GRACE: Yup. You love me too, don't you?

VASQUES: I guess I do. You're my sister.

GRACE: Half-sister. But don't feel bad about that. It's a good half.

VASQUES: I didn't ever feel bad about that. I just wish—

GRACE: Wishes are for babies. People who don't know any better. You know better. Ooh! Look at this one. I got on such a cute dress. I wish I still had that dress. It looked good on me.

VASQUES: It is a pretty dress. But that still don't look like you.
(Getting up)
I better—

GRACE: I bring you here, to Belilah's house to show you beautiful things. Share some family history. And alls you do is doubt me. How do you think that makes me feel?

VASQUES: I should go back now. Miss Be—lilah will miss me soon.

GRACE: She might notice you're gone—but she ain't gonna "miss" you, Vasques.

VASQUES: That's what I meant.

GRACE: Don't look all sad about it. She's always gonna take care of you. Don't worry.

VASQUES: Thanks for showing me the pictures.

GRACE: You're very welcome. Maybe you can come by again.

VASQUES: Maybe.

GRACE: You don't have to rush off all crazy like that, Vasques.

VASQUES: Yes, I do.

(VASQUES exits quickly. GRACE pours herself a beer, and traces love hearts on the beer can, then begins to sing a song she wrote herself.)

GRACE: "I found my suitcase empty, loopy, 'cause you are not my beau.
You don't see how I love you, stoopy—you treat me like a 'ho'.
I write these words on a cold beer can—my fingers writing love songs to my man—
I'd do anything for your love. Toot, toot. Anything, for your love..."

(SHE takes a deep swig of beer. BELILAH enters half-way through GRACE's following speech which SHE says to her reflection in a mirror or window, like she's doing a commercial.)

GRACE: This is a very good drink. It's got vitamins and protein and everything you need to stay alive. And it helps you sleep too. Not like vodka or gin— they keep you up. Beer is the lullaby of beverages.

BELILAH: *(Crosses to GRACE and bops her on the head as GRACE takes a deep swallow.)*
That'll knock you out too, Miss Steal-My-Beer.
    (GRACE cries out in pain, spitting out the beer.)
Go sleep with your brother tonight. Thieving wench...

*(Lights cross to ROCKET
and BELEN on the bridge.)*

SCENE 2

EPIPHANY

ROCKET on the Toll Bridge on his way home from dropping off BELILAH. As HE crosses it, HE hears the sound of someone crying. It's BELEN, under the metal grating of the pedestrian walkway.

ROCKET: *(Singing the BeeGees "Staying Alive" and doing his best Travolta moves)* "Oh, You can tell by the way I move my walk, I'm a woman's man—no time to talk.
You need love and—"
    (Hearing BELEN's sobs under his feet.)

Damn! What—
(HE stoops down and tries to lift the grating.
It finally opens and HE reaches down
and pulls BELEN out.)
Come on outta there, my little queen. C'mon now. It's
all over. You're okay now.
(Holding her as her tears calm down)
Little queen? Little queen, it's okay. Did you fall in
there and think nobody was ever gonna find you?
Huh? Is that it? But that's not what happened.
Rocket was right there.

BELEN: I couldn't get out. My arms—I coulda died
down there, mister!

ROCKET: But you didn't.

BELEN: (trying to walk, but stumbling)
Ow! I can't feel my legs no more.

ROCKET: (Gently rubbing her calves)
Rest a minute before you try to walk.

BELEN: I gotta get back.

ROCKET: You've got blood on your face.
(HE takes out a white handkerchief and
wipes her face. SHE stares at him a

moment recognizing her own words.)

BELEN: Who are you supposed to be?

ROCKET: They call me Rocket 'cause I like to pass through quickly and stir up a lot of dust.

BELEN: Okay. You don't gotta tell me.

ROCKET: I am telling you.

BELEN: That might be your name—but that's not who you are.
> *(SHE gets on her knees in front
> of him and kisses his feet.)*
I've been waiting for you.

ROCKET: I heard your voice.

BELEN: Why now? I prayed before. I pray all the time.
> *(ROCKET is silent.)*
So are you the star from the north sky of winter?
> *(ROCKET is silent.)*
If you're real, you'll save my family too.

ROCKET: Anyone who believes can be saved.

BELEN: They'll believe. I'll make them. Even if you're just in my mind, I'll make them.

(*BELEN runs towards the salt as ROCKET watches her. As SHE moves out of sight, HE covers his ears with his hands and closes his eyes for a moment. Then he begins to sing again—loudly —as HE walks toward the water.*)

ROCKET: "Oh, You can tell by the way I move my walk, I'm a woman's man—no time to talk..."

(*Lights fade on ROCKET and cross to GRACE and LUPE in the salt mounds.*)

SCENE 3

CRISPY CHICKEN, CHOMP-CHOMP, & THE FALL
LUPE is trying to sleep and GRACE is trying to tell him a story.

GRACE: There was once a very bee-oohtiful girl named Grace. She had one bed sheet that she embroidered with candy corn and Chocolate kisses especially for Christmas. She liked the red and green aluminum paper, even though that nasty ole Lula kept trying to steal her papers to make some nasty junk. This was a sheet she could only share with a prince.

LUPE: Shut up! I'm trying to sleep over here.

GRACE: Duh! This is a bedtime story. Anyways, she knew a prince and his name was Loopy.

LUPE: Can't even get my name right, dumb pissbag.

GRACE: Loopy was a bee-oohtiful boy—except for his snaggly-assed ear that was purple and kinda half torn off. And people laughed at him because he was messed-up looking—'cept for Grace. She was kind and gentle and loved him no matter what he said to her. And finally he couldn't stand no more how much he loved her and he said, "I'll marry—

LUPE: You couldn't tell a good story to save your life, Gracie. Belen's the only one who—

GRACE: I can do things she can't even imagine doing. Listen:
(*Singing*)
"Every bit of Grace is what you need to love.
She's a bit of lace—an angel from above.
Gracie's so fine— she got a figure divine.
When you look at her—you wanna say—
please be mine.

Ooh, Gracie, the stars are in your smiling eyes—
Ooh, Gracie, don't disgrace me—hear my humble
cries!
Let me love you, let me take you into my strong arms!
Let me hold you, love unfolds you into my sweet
charms!
Ooh, Gracie, the stars are in your smiling eyes—
Ooh, Gracie, you gotta face me and my lovesick sighs.
Ooh, Gracie...Ooh, ooh, Gracie...Oohoohooh, Gracie..."
What d'ya think?

>   (*LUPE is snoring and sound asleep.*)

You and me are sealed like if we was fried together in
a hot oil batter. That's us. Two crispy pieces of
chicken—yummy and ripe and hard like diamonds. I
know you couldn't eat a chicken that hard—but you
know what I mean. It's a chomp, chomp chewy kind
of love that could break your heart.

> (*GRACE quietly lays beside him. LUPE turns to her and
> puts his arm around her. SHE starts to feel him up. HE
> starts to moan in his sleep.*)

GUADALUPE: Mmm...Belen.

> (*BELEN comes back and sees GRACE slowly make her way
> down LUPE's body with her mouth. BELEN covers her
> mouth and runs off.)*

Belen...

(Lights cross to LUCIA & CUSTOMER TWO.)

SCENE 4

HOLY INNOCENTS &
SWEARS MEAN NOTHING
At the salt mounds.
LUCIA is kneeling in front of CUSTOMER TWO, who
holds LUCIA's head as LUCIA goes down on a lit flashlight
which the CUSTOMER holds between his legs as if it were
his penis. LUCIA does his business as CUSTOMER
TWO/ALDERMAN MOROSH quotes from the "Lives Of
The Saints". HE comes at the end of the prayer.

CUSTOMER TWO: Today is the feast day of the Holy
Innocents! Oh...holy innocents, martyrs and patron
saints of choirboys! Innocent victims who gave
testimony to the Messiah and Redeemer, not by words
but by your blood. You triumphed over the world and
won your crown without having experienced the evils
of the world, the flesh, the devil. GOD! Today we
recall that the Innocent Martyrs bore witness not by
words but by their death. OHH, Man! GOD! Grant
that our way of life may give witness to our faith in
You which our lips profess. Amen.
(HE grabs LUCIA's face in his hands
and makes him look at him.)
Say you liked it!

LUCIA: Liked it.

CUSTOMER TWO: Say it again. Say "I liked it, father."

LUCIA: I liked it, father.

CUSTOMER TWO: Say, "do it to me again soon, papa."

LUCIA: Do it to me again, papa. But papa, say you love me first?

CUSTOMER TWO: You know I do.

LUCIA: But say it. Click, click. Please, say it.

CUSTOMER TWO: I love you, son.

(*LUCIA suddenly hugs CUSTOMER TWO around his legs.*)

LUCIA: I love you too.

CUSTOMER TWO: I brought you something nice.
		(*Hands him a box wrapped in children's Christmas paper*)
I know you'll like it.

LUCIA: *(Opening the box; it's a red and green Christmas dress)* Wow...It's too beautiful for me.

CUSTOMER TWO: No, it's not. It's just right for you. You're a lovely thing, Lulu.

LUCIA: I am?

CUSTOMER TWO: Very delicate thing. Your hair feels like an angel's breath on my thighs.

LUCIA: Can I put it on?

CUSTOMER TWO: Sure.
 *(Pointing the flashlight at LUCIA and watching him
    disrobe. His underclothes are torn and soiled)*
We should get you some new panties too. Would you like that?

LUCIA: Oh, yes.
 (Turning to him and modeling the dress)
How's it look? I never had anything so new before.

CUSTOMER TWO: It's almost new. I gave it to my daughter but she's too fat for it now. So it's yours.

LUCIA: Wow...I'm lucky she's so fat.

(HE spins around in the dress as CUSTOMER TWO playfully moves the light from the flashlight to coordinate with his moves.)
I'm lucky, lucky, lucky. That's why they called me, Lucia.

CUSTOMER TWO: Take it off now.

(Reluctantly, LUCIA takes off the dress as the lights cross to BELEN confronting VASQUES at the bridge.)

VASQUES: *(VASQUES enters running, out of breath)*
Oh, thank goodness! I thought something happened to you.

BELEN: Where is he?

VASQUES: Who?

BELEN: So I was dreaming. There's nothing to believe in anymore...
   (Pause; turning to VASQUES in anger)
And you! Did you know what was gonna happen, when you put me down in there to die? Still, you did it with gentle hands. I fought and bit you, and still, you didn't hit me or nothing. Just put me down in there. Told me you was gonna come back and let me out, but I didn't believe you. You knew I couldn't get outta there by myself. I didn't think you was ever

gonna come back and get me. I thought you were my friend!

VASQUES: I am your friend, Miss Belen. I did it because I had to leave for a little while and I didn't want nobody to—something coulda happened that I didn't want to happen. I wasn't trying to hurt you, miss. I swear!

BELEN: Your swears mean nothing to me, Vasques.

VASQUES: You don't understand the kind of danger that lives here. I've seen it. I've seen it rip little girls into so many pieces, that you can't put them back together because they don't even look like a person no more. There's things here you don't know—worse than you can know—worse than you ever need to know.
(BELEN turns her back on him.)
Don't be like that...Please.
(No response)
I'm gonna sit right here and protect you—all night. It's okay if you turn away from me—as long as I can see you...

BELEN: Belilah's right. Might as well die. Because there's nobody...

(Lights cross to the church.)

SCENE 5

CULEBRA

December 29, morning
At the Church. FATHER CZEKAJ speaks with BISHOP
HARRISON. All that is clearly seen of the BISHOP are his
thumbless, long fingernailed hands. The BISHOP also
wears a large gold ring on his right hand.

BISHOP: This parish is in an unusual place. My driver got lost several times. He's not good with maps.

CZEKAJ: Oh, I'm so sorry. If I had known, I would have sent more detailed directions.

BISHOP: It doesn't matter. I got here.

CZEKAJ: Yes. So you did.

BISHOP HARRISON: Let me get to the point. Do you have any chocolate?

CZEKAJ: No. I'm sorry. I don't.

BISHOP: Doesn't matter. Just a little yen. I've been traveling so much lately. Anyway, I have some unpleasantness to discuss with you. I hope you're prepared. You requested another year at this parish, which was granted—

CZEKAJ: Thank you, your holiness. I know our donations have been down lately—my parishioners are poor—but more have been coming every week. It's really exciting. I feel a renewing faith here. I—

BISHOP: That's wonderful news. And I'm sure you've been very inspirational to them. But the problem is that, uhm, it's been decided, that this parish must close.
(Long Pause)
Aren't you going to say anything?

CZEKAJ: I've been expecting this for some time. So I—what is there to say, your holiness? It's a pity. Parishes like mine—unusual parishes, as you called them—do important work for the church.

BISHOP: How many times have you been robbed?

CZEKAJ: I don't remember.

BISHOP: I can tell you exactly. Twenty times. In the last six months. That's almost every week, Janusz. The church can't afford those kind of losses. It costs too much to keep your doors open. The money is better spent in other parts of the city. It's been decided. And we fear for you working alone here.

CZEKAJ: Do you? When do I have to leave?

BISHOP: The New Year's Day mass will be your last one. And then you have two weeks to arrange your administrative papers.

CZEKAJ: Well...I appreciate your telling me in person.

BISHOP: It seemed important.

CZEKAJ: Yes. It seems—Do you have a new assignment for me?

BISHOP: Not yet. We're working on that. I'm sure we'll find something to suit you.

CZEKAJ: This suits me. I don't want to leave here.

BISHOP: Yes...but you will. And God's work will be served wherever you go. That's the thing to remember.

CZEKAJ: God's work...Yes, of course.

BISHOP: I have to be going. I think an ice storm is coming. I'd like to be in the air before then. That traffic from O'Hare is appalling.

CZEKAJ: Midway's a better choice from here.

BISHOP: Too disorganized. And dirty. I prefer O'Hare. I saw Scotty Pippen at the airport a few weeks ago. My one exciting event of the New Year, I'm sure.
(With a smile)
Of course, we are almost in Indiana.

CZEKAJ: Yes...it's long way from anything down here. Where are you going?

BISHOP: Just a little Caribbean vacation. To Culebra.
(BISHOP hisses playfully like a snake. CZEKAJ is not amused.)

CZEKAJ: That's supposed to be beautiful.

BISHOP: Yes. It always is. So you'll hear from my office shortly. Good Luck, father.

CZEKAJ: Thank you. Drive safely.

BISHOP: I will. Carlos is an excellent driver. He was once Cardinal O'Malley's driver.

CZEKAJ: Nice car...nice new car.

(BISHOP exits. CZEKAJ sits in the front pew
and puts his hands over his eyes,
as the lights cross to the salt mounds.)

SCENE 6

<u>*LOSE SOMETHING*</u>
Later that afternoon.
LUCIA returns to the salt mound where he rested ANGIE,
but can't find her.

LUCIA: (Searching) Angie? Angie, click, click, where are you? I know I left you right here.

(GRACE enters, pretend casual)

GRACE: What's the matter, Lula? Lose something?

LUCIA: Angie's gone. Somebody musta kidnapped her!

GRACE: I'll help you look.
　　　(GRACE goes off as LUCIA keeps searching.)

LUCIA: ANGIE! ANGIE!

(GRACE returns with the doll.)

GRACE: Lookey who I found! She must have been blown away by the wind. Poor dumb thing!

LUCIA: Thank God, click, click, Gracie! I'm so happy you found her. I was looking almost all night. Are you okay, Ange? You look okay...Thank you, Gracie.

GRACE: I'm just glad I found her in time. She was lying out there on the road where the salt trucks go. They coulda just hauled her off with them, or run her little ole head over.
That woulda been a shame!

LUCIA: Yeah...I'm so sorry I couldn't find you, Angie. I'm not ever gonna leave you again.

(LUCIA hugs ANGIE tightly to him
as GRACE watches and smiles.)

(Lights cross to BELILAH & MOROSH.)

SCENE 7

THE DEAL
December 30, afternoon.

BELILAH & CUSTOMER TWO/ALDERMAN
MOROSH discuss business on the Toll Bridge.

BELILAH: This is a lovely spot. Don't you think, alderman?

ALDERMAN/CUSTOMER TWO: I never noticed. Well?

BELILAH: These things are delicate, alderman. I need time to think.

ALDERMAN: How much time?

BELILAH: I'll tell you tomorrow. New Year's Eve is a good time for decisions. It's gonna be hard to give up all his other business. You know you have to make it worthwhile.

ALDERMAN: I just worry about him. With other men. Men can be savages.

BELILAH: Don't I know it, alderman.

ALDERMAN: I wish you wouldn't call me that. I thought we had an agreement.

BELILAH: We do. But no one else can hear us out here. You carry a lot of stress in your neck, don't you?

You should let me give you one of my special massages—cures anything in your bones that don't crawl.

ALDERMAN: Just give me an answer. That'll help.

BELILAH: Come by tomorrow—with cash.

ALDERMAN: Of course.

(ALDERMAN exits. BELILAH smiles happily.)

BELILAH: He might just pay me enough to get a real apartment, and beds for everybody. This is definitely gonna be a great year. You get a better kind of customer, when you got beds. And the kids wouldn't get sick so much. Kids always have the sniffles...Beds are definitely a good investment.
              (Pause)
Lucia would want what's best for all of us.
              (Pause)
I'll pick up a little gift or something for him. He'll be fine.

(Lights cross to the VASQUES.)

SCENE 8

THREE FEET

A light captures each family member in various parts of the stage. We see: LUCIA, hugging Angie tightly; GRACE, trying on her star belt; GUADALUPE, comparing his maps with the landscape around him trying to match them up; BELILAH, dancing to music in her head; BELEN, lying in the salt, rocking and staring; and VASQUES, tracing his foot onto a piece of wood. HE does this three times. After VASQUES begins his third tracing, ROCKET enters. When ROCKET enters, everyone but VASQUES exits. Then VASQUES speaks as HE performs a ritual by the furnace. ROCKET watches him.

VASQUES: *(As HE breaks the wood into five pieces and throws them into the flames)* I do this so that my steps can help the others: My little sister needs help getting stronger.
My little brother needs help remembering who he is. My other brother must release his anger and learn happiness again. My other sister must see her true self so she can stop hating. And for my mother, I hope for her to love herself—and for everyone else to get their wishes...
(Pause)
...and for their wishes to include me.
(A moment of silence.)

ROCKET: That's a wonderful prayer.

VASQUES: It's not a prayer.

ROCKET: What is it then?

VASQUES: A letter. To my father. He reads wood when it's burning. I smell him in the ashes.
(*Showing his burn marks*)
He stains me with his answers. I like to be marked by him.

ROCKET: My father marked me too.

VASQUES: Where?

ROCKET: Nowhere you can see. His marks are thick and dark. Inside me.

VASQUES: Sit over here. It's the warmest place.

(ROCKET sits beside VASQUES
and together they watch the flames.)

(Lights cross to BELEN & LUCIA in the salt mounds.)
SCENE 9

COMFORT: PARTY PROMISED
December 30, late afternoon.

BELEN sits alone crying. LUCIA discovers her.

LUCIA: *(Touching BELEN gently on the arm)* Hey, Belly. Whatsa matter? I never seen you with wet eyes before.

BELEN: Hey, Lulu. It's nothing. Where you been? I missed you.

LUCIA: I dunno. Is that why you're crying? You miss me?

BELEN: Maybe. Maybe that's why.

LUCIA: I had a date. Look what he give me.
       (HE models the dress for BELEN.)
It's a beauty, huh?

BELEN: Yeah...I'd like a dress like that.

LUCIA: Maybe I make one for you.

BELEN: That would be real nice, Lulu. Come here.
       (HE goes to her and SHE hugs him.)
I love hugging you.

LUCIA: I love you hugging me too.

    (BELILAH, GRACE, & VASQUES enter.)

314

BELILAH: I got a surprise for you kids! We're gonna have a party! There's a lot to celebrate.
I'm getting us a nice big apartment. Wouldn't you like that?

BELEN & LUCIA: Yeah.

GRACE: *(So only BELILAH can hear)* We don't need to take her with us, do we, Ma?

BELILAH: You shush! Of course she's coming. She's part of this family too. Brings in more money than you do, missy.

(GUADALUPE enters looking sick.)

GUADALUPE: What's happening?

LUCIA: A party! For our new 'partment.

GUADALUPE: I don't believe it. When?

BELILAH: Soon. It's gonna be the best New Year's Eve party I ever gave.

VASQUES: First one, too.

BELILAH: You shush! Everybody shush! I gotta go plan it. You know how many other people in this world are planning parties for tomorrow night? Like just about everybody, everywhere. We're gonna be fine, kids! We're gonna be just like everybody else...

(SHE exits. The OTHERs look at each other. Even a small promise of home is incredible to them.)

GRACE: Well, I guess we better start packing.

GUADALUPE: We don't got nothing to pack.

GRACE: Oh, that's right. I better go pack.

(GRACE exits. VASQUES follows her.)

GUADALUPE: *(Approaching BELEN)* You gotta let me explain.

BELEN: There's nothing to explain. I saw it all.

GUADALUPE: But I was thinking it was you the whole time. I thought it was you. That's gotta count for something.

BELEN: It doesn't.

LUCIA: What happened? Click, click.

GUADALUPE & BELEN: Nothing!

GUADALUPE: I can read the maps now, Belen.
We're getting out of here tonight.

BELEN: She taught you a lot—and so fast. Maybe you
should take her. I'm staying with Lulu.

> *(BELEN runs off with LUCIA*
> *following closely behind.)*

GUADALUPE: I dreamed while she was doing me. I
dreamed you and me got married, Belen. And we had
that potato-head baby. And everything was beautiful
like the stars in the sky.
> *(Pause)*
And then I opened my eyes and saw Piss-bag. It made
me sick. I threw up like ten times.
> *(HE takes out his maps and rips them to pieces.)*
Stupid maps! Belen...I used to make fun of her name,
because it's like a city and whatever. I thought that
was pretty dumb. But it's where Jesus was born—so
it's gotta mean something good. Not like me—My
name is the stupid one. Like I'm supposed to be a
virgin or something.
> *(Pause)*
Without Belen, there's no place to go.

(Lights cross to the Slide Inn.)

SCENE 10

HEAVEN KNOWS
DOM is fixing himself a drink as ROCKET tries not to listen. The jukebox plays Donna Summers' "Heaven Knows."

DOM: I'll prove it to you. What has L.A. got?
　　　(ROCKET shrugs his shoulders.)
The greater Los Angeles arena. And New York? The tri-station area. But Chicago—we got what nobody else has. Chicagoland. Get it? Chicago—Land. See what I mean?

ROCKET: Uh huh.

DOM: That's right. Here in the middle it's nothing but a playground. An amusement park. And my place sits right in the middle of the whole shebingle. I wouldn't wanna be anywhere else in the world.

ROCKET: Me neither.

(The jukebox begins to skip. DOM goes to try to fix it. HE's hitting it and shaking it, as GRACE enters the Slide Inn holding a small fish bowl with a small fish in it. SHE

has draped it with a scarf. SHE spots ROCKET and goes
right up to him.)

GRACE: Hey, mister? You wanna buy something special? I got something special.

DOM: Get the hell outta my establishment! No selling on the premises.
   (Pointing to the "No Soliciting" sign on the door)
Can't you read?

ROCKET: Leave the young lady alone, Dom. She's not hurting anybody.

GRACE: Yeah! I'm not hurting anybody. Maybe you wanna see what I got too.

DOM: I double-dip doubt it. Come on now. Get out. I can't have young girls like you in here. You'll get me closed down, kid.

> *(GRACE unveils the bowl.*
> *It holds a small clown fish.)*

GRACE: (To ROCKET) This is a partickler special fish. See? See how it seems to smile right at you—even though you ain't doing nothing funny. Yup! It's about the most creepadelic fish around. And it's yours—
   (turning to DOM)

or yours—for the right price.

ROCKET: Those are rare, aren't they?

GRACE: Yes-bob-siree. There ain't another one of these anywhere near here. You'd have to go to some Carry-bean island to fish up one of these fish.

DOM: Why's it looking at me like that? Get it outta here!

ROCKET: Don't those kind of fish need ocean water to live in?

GRACE: Just a dash of salt in plain old water is enough for this weencie-weenie fish.

ROCKET: Really? Sounds easy enough. Don't you need this fish in your bar, Dom? Might dress it up a little. People like looking at living things in places like this.

DOM: You think so?

ROCKET: Sure. It's a relaxation tool.

DOM: You think so? I got other ways to relax my tool thank you very much, pal.

GRACE: If you look at this fish for long enough, you fall asleep. I just did. Had to wake myself up to go sell the little darling. What d'ya say, mister?

DOM: How much?

GRACE: Twenty—and I throw in the tank.

DOM: I'll give you five.

GRACE: I'm afraid I couldn't let you have her for that much. She's a mighty powerful fish...Fifteen?

DOM: Okey-doke. Ten it is. But it better stay alive for a while. I hate when pets die. It's un-un-

ROCKET: -settling??

DOM: Yeah—something like that.

> (DOM hands GRACE the money
> as SHE hands him the fish.)

GRACE: You be good now, Clowny. I'd keep you if I could, but now that we're moving and all, and your brothers are dead...Anyways, I jus'wanned to make sure you had a good home. This nice man's your new papa.
> (Pause)

Well...if no one gentleman is buying me a drink, I guess I'll jus' mosey...
>*(Neither man moves to buy her a drink.)*

I like a nice cool beer in the evenings...Don'you like a beer this time of night?

ROCKET: I don't drink beer.

DOM: Move along, kid. And I don't wanna see your backside in here again. Understand?

GRACE: It's time to move on anyways.
>*(SHE moves to exit but turns back*
>*with a word of warning for DOM.)*

Oh...don't touch her. She gets kinda angry when you do. 'Bye.
>*(to ROCKET)*

And <u>you</u> I'll see again.

ROCKET: Why's that?

GRACE: I feel it. I see how you're looking at me—like you're in a dream. And you meeting a pretty little chickalini like me—must be almos'like a dream.

ROCKET: Almos'.
(GRACE smiles one last time and exits. ROCKET takes out
>*his vial of water and has a sip from it.)*

She come in here a lot?

DOM: *(too empathically)* I swear I never seen her before.

ROCKET: Hmmm...
                    (Petting the fish gently)
If you touch her gently, she won't get angry. You try.

                    (DOM reaches into the tank
                    and notices something different.)

DOM: Hey! There's two fish in here. I got a bargain!

ROCKET: No one likes a lonely fish.
                    (DOM continues to pet the fish
                    as ROCKET moves to the jukebox.)
Lonely fish got nobody to play with. That's what makes them angry.
                    (ROCKET plays with the back of the jukebox
                    and the song comes back on.)
There you go.

DOM: How'd you do that?

ROCKET: Just touched it right.

(DOM moves over to the jukebox to investigate as ROCKET takes a swig of water and crosses to the church. Lights cross to the church.)

SCENE 11

BAPTISM BY CIGARS
New Year's Eve. Morning.
ROCKET & FATHER CZEKAJ
sit outside the church smoking cigars.

ROCKET: Like it?

CZEKAJ: Yes. Haven't had one of these in a long time.

ROCKET: You gotta loosen up, father. Too many spiritual thoughts can make you a ghost. If you stop living then what good is a soul?

CZEKAJ: You may have a point there, Rocket.

ROCKET: Of course I do. Good cigars are like fine women. I guess, that's something else you...

CZEKAJ: I had a girlfriend once. In high school.

ROCKET: What was her name?

CZEKAJ: Wendy.

ROCKET: Wendy?! Like the restaurant? No offense—I mean, yeah, Wendy, huh?. Wendys are good. Do you miss her?

CZEKAJ: Not her. I miss having somebody. You know, to talk to. I mean, besides God, and the occasional parishioner who takes the time to stop and talk.

ROCKET: Things change too quickly not to make the time. I love to talk.

CZEKAJ: I've discovered that—I mean, the time part.

ROCKET: So they're kicking you out, huh?

CZEKAJ: Yes. They're kicking me out. That's just how it feels. Like I failed.

ROCKET
Nah...sounds like economics to me. That's what the church is about, I think. Not God you understand, but the Church. That's why I don't come to mass. Don't trust it. But I think if it works for you, go ahead.

CZEKAJ: I don't know anymore. I don't know what works for me. I love serving God, but it seems like something else is at work here—someone else.

ROCKET: It could be worse. You could be a cop.

CZEKAJ: I did consider that at one point.

ROCKET: No. That's not for you. You might have to kill people and everything. You're not the type.

CZEKAJ: I'm going to miss our talks.

ROCKET: Why's that? Nobody is dying here. You know where to find me.

CZEKAJ: So we could be like friends?

ROCKET: We are—like friends.
                (Handing CZEKAJ another
                 specially wrapped cigar)
Smoke this one tomorrow. It's a special one. Always like to start the new year with a good smoke.

CZEKAJ: Thanks.

        (THEY sit together in silence, smoking.)

ROCKET: What if I told you a secret?

CZEKAJ: Have you been stealing water again?

ROCKET: No...I mean, there's plenty left. Don't worry about that. Listen, what would you say if I told you I was the messiah?

CZEKAJ: I'd say you were nuts. Why do you think you're the messiah? Who would want to be the messiah anyway?! What a lousy job! Saving people who stopped believing in you.

ROCKET: You still believe.

CZEKAJ: I have to.

ROCKET: Why?

CZEKAJ: A calling. I heard a voice once. Never heard it again. But I followed that voice. And look where it got me...

ROCKET: Will you do me a favor?

CZEKAJ: Sure.

ROCKET: Will you baptize me?

CZEKAJ: You've never been?

ROCKET: No. Never. Never wanted to before.

CZEKAJ: Really? So I—You feel I—

ROCKET: You could do me. And I could do you. That's how it's done where I come from. Friend to friend. No words. Just water.

(HE takes out his vial of holy water and pours some into CZEKAJ's hand. CZEKAJ makes the sign of the cross on ROCKET's head. ROCKET dips into the water and does the same to CZEKAJ. They look at each other for a moment and start laughing.)

CZEKAJ: I can't believe I'm laughing.

ROCKET: It's good to laugh.
            (Pause)
Do you remember this one?
            *(HE begins to sing Gloria Gaynor's
            "I Will Survive.")*
"First I was afraid I was petrified, kept thinking I could never live without you by my side. But then I spent so many nights thinking how you did me wrong—

 ROCKET & CZEKAJ: *(In unison)*
—And I grew strong!

And I learned how to get along.
And so you're back from outer space.
I just walked in and found you here with that sad look
upon your face!

ROCKET: *(Still singing)* We will survive!"

CZEKAJ: *(Dropping out of the song)* Will we?

     (BELILAH enters, looking for ROCKET.)

BELILAH: I knew I'd find you here.

CZEKAJ: I live here.

BELILAH: I mean Mister Rocket. I wanted to ask you
something—in private.

CZEKAJ: I'll be in my office. Come find me, okay?
We've got to finish our duet.

ROCKET: You got it!
        (CZEKAJ exits.)
So? What did you want to ask me?

BELILAH: I'm giving a little soirée—to ring in the
New Year—and I just wanted to invite you. To meet
my kids. It's been a while since they've had a man in
their life.

ROCKET: And you think I'm the man?

BELILAH: Maybe. I don't know. You could be a good influence. I can feel it. Meeting you was like a gift to me.

ROCKET: Was it?

BELILAH: I bet you're good with kids.

ROCKET: Some kids...maybe. Yes...I can't resist your invitation. We'll both come.

BELILAH: We?

ROCKET: I don't go anywhere without the father. He's kinda depressed. This party might cheer him up.

BELILAH: No. Can't you come alone? I don't think we have enough food...

ROCKET: I'll bring some. It'll be fine. Priests don't eat much.

BELILAH: But you? I bet you have an appetite that won't quit. Isn't that so?

ROCKET: Yeah. I do get a hunger on me.

BELILAH: I knew it...well. okay then. Bring him too. I'm not ashamed of my kids.

ROCKET: Who said you were?

BELILAH: Nobody. Just saying. I'm not. Do you remember where I live?

ROCKET: Sure. You were the tipsy one, remember?

BELILAH: Yeah. But I wasn't drunk. Just— enthusiastic.

ROCKET: Right. What you said.

BELILAH: Come at 11:30. But let's meet at the salt mounds. It's a tradition in my family.

ROCKET: Alright. But isn't that late for kids?

BELILAH: Not mine. They like the night.

ROCKET: I know—I mean, from knowing you.

BELILAH: You're very insightful.

ROCKET: Sometimes. Sometimes, I don't see hardly at all.

BELILAH: See you soon. I gotta get everything ready.

ROCKET: See you...
> (BELILAH exits.)
After I die, I wanna come back as one of the Chi-Lites—or Gloria Gaynor. Now that would be a miracle...
> (Calling to CZEKAJ)
Hey, let's finish that song, my friend!

> (Lights cross to the salt mounds.)

SCENE 12

THE PARTY
New Year's Eve at the Salt Mounds.
VASQUES sets up a small cassette player and plays Disco music, something like Walter Murphy's "Fifth Of Beethoven." BELEN, LUCIA & GUADALUPE are in their normal clothes, but look cleaned up and combed. GRACE has on a new dress. VASQUES wears a bowtie. BELILAH enters in a new dress and carrying some buckets of chicken and pop. LUCIA is putting the finishing touches on a homemade disco ball.

BELILAH: I got the pop for free! How about that?!
People can be so kind sometimes...Oh! And you put
on my favorite tape! Thank you, Vasques!

VASQUES: You're welcome, Miss Belilah.

GRACE: Thanks for the dress, Ma.
                    (Looking at LUPE)
Doesn't it look just witchy good on me?

GUADALUPE: Almost human.

*(The Children stand around awkwardly. THEY don't know
how to dance. LUCIA spins his disco ball and flashes his
flashlight on it.
BELILAH applauds.)*

BELILAH: You're just the most talented child, Lucia!
Now come on and boogie with me!
                    *(BELILAH starts dancing wildly.
The OTHERS try to imitate her moves.)*
Yeah! That's it! What a wonderful family I have.

GRACE: Dance with me, Lupe.

GUADALUPE: Get away from me, you skank.

GRACE: You know you liked it. You know you like
me.

GUADALUPE: I still feel like throwing up when I think about it.

(HE moves to BELEN, who moves away from him.)
I said I was sorry like about a million times now.

GRACE: Get away from her, baby. She know you love me best, that's why she's all crazy like that. C'mon, baby. Dance with me.

(GUADALUPE pushes GRACE away and continues to talk to BELEN.
BELILAH is in her own dancing world. VASQUES watches.)

BELEN: Stop following me around.

GUADALUPE: Not till you stop and talk to me.

BELEN: Okay. Talk.
GUADALUPE: Forget you then! You're stupid if you don't know how much I—

BELEN: How much you what?

(LUPE grabs her and kisses her passionately on the lips.
BELEN slaps LUPE. LUPE shakes BELEN.)

GUADALUPE: Don't pretend like you feel different than me! I know how you smell me when I walk near you. I see your face. I feel your whole body turn to me. I think we even breathe the same, like when you run too much, and can't catch up with yourself. That's us, Belen. You and me. There's nobody else.

BELEN: I know.

(THEY kiss again. LUPE moves BELEN towards the salt. In silhouette, we see them making love as the party continues. GRACE watches them go off together. GRACE goes to LUCIA and speaks so no one else hears.)

GRACE: You know, Angie told me to tell you something—when I found her. I didn't want to tell you, because it was so bad—but now I gotta tell you. She wants you to take care of Belen tonight. She said Belen is a poison, that we gotta cut out. She's gonna leave here with Lupe and leave you all alone. And she's gonna take your dress and—it was she who put Angie by the trucks to die. She's bad. Bad, Lula. Real bad.

LUCIA: Noo! Click, Click! That's not true! You stop it, Gracie! Click! You bad! Click! Angie likes Belen now. She tole me so. She did. She did!

GRACE: She did not, you little liar!

(SHE pushes LUCIA to the ground. BELILAH finally notices all the commotion.)

BELILAH: Leave that boy alone, Gracie. It's a party!
(SHE starts dancing again.)
Where's Rocket? It's almost midnight. I hope he gets here in time...

(ROCKET and CZEKAJ enter. THEY carry toys for the kids and flowers for BELILAH.)

GRACE: *(Indicating the flowers)* Are those for me? I just love flowers, mister. Bouquets make the skin on my legs glow.
(SHE lifts up her dress, showing her legs.)
See??

(BELILAH bops GRACE on the head.)

BELILAH: *(To GRACE, trying to keep calm and happy)* Those are for me, baby girl! Go over there with the other kids.

GRACE: But I'm not like them. I'm your first-born girl.

BELILAH: Go!
>   *(To ROCKET & CZEKAJ)*
Sorry about that. She loves to embarrass her mother.
Teen-age girls are the most unruly beasts in the
Universe.

CZEKAJ: *(Slightly drunk)* You look beautiful, Mrs.,
uhm, what was it? Oooh, I remember now.
Something scary...Delilah?

BELILAH: B̲elilah.
>   *(To ROCKET)*
I see you gentlemen had some festivities of your own.

ROCKET: He drank some communion wine. I tried to
stop him.

BELILAH: Well, he can't do anything else, so he might
as well drink. Welcome to our—place.

CZEKAJ: You live here? Doesn't it hurt your...your...

ROCKET: Eyes?

CZEKAJ: Yes. That's it. Eyes. Doesn't it?

LUCIA: No. We don't put it in our eyes.

BELILAH: My kids are such darlings—they can get used to anything.

LUCIA: Take me with you when you leave, mister. I gotta get Angie somewhere safe.

BELILAH: You shush, boy! Mister Rocket does not need a little pest like you hanging on him.
(BELILAH pushes LUCIA away and takes ROCKET's arm as VASQUES puts on
Donna Summers' "Last Dance.")
Can you believe what just came on?! That Vasques is a mindreader.

ROCKET: I know.

BELILAH: Wanna dance?

CZEKAJ: *(Stumbling forward)*
Yeah! Sure, I'll dance.

(CZEKAJ takes BELILAH and
starts to dance with her.)

BELILAH: I hate drunks.

CZEKAJ: I'm not—hey, I never—listen...Can you show me that move?

*(BELILAH dances reluctantly with CZEKAJ as GRACE
sidles over to ROCKET.)*

GRACE: Remember me?

LUCIA: He's my friend, Gracie. You go find your
own.

GRACE: Nobody wants to be your friend, Lula.
                    (Pause)
How's my fish doing?

ROCKET: Pretty good last time I looked.

GRACE: I bet she looked back. My fish were all well-
trained.

ROCKET: So you like fish?

GRACE: Oh, yeah. I'd be a fisherman, if Belilah
would let me. I like the way fish feel—it's like
touching glass that don't cut you.

*(We see the silhouette of LUPE and BELEN's lovemaking
become more active.)*

BELILAH: What are those nasty kids doing? Vasques,
go get them out here.

*(As VASQUES begins to move in LUPE and BELEN's
direction, the ALDERMAN enters.
HE carries a bag with clothes for LUCIA.)*
Look what the cat dragged in...How nice of you to join
us, alderman! I thought you might change your mind.

CZEKAJ: Twice in one, uhm, one, what's it called?
Yeah, one week. That's more than I've seen him all
year.

ROCKET: I didn't know you had such influential
friends, Belilah.

BELILAH: He just came by to drop off a little gift for
the kids. Isn't that so, alderman? If you gentlemen
will excuse us...

*(BELILAH takes MOROSH off by
the arm to the bridge to talk in private.)*

CZEKAJ: That's...strange. He never—never seemed
that kind to me.

ROCKET: He has some kindness, I think. It's just the
kind you can't see so easy.

(Focus shifts back and forth between BELILAH &
MOROSH, ROCKET & CZEKAJ, and LUCIA & GRACE.
VASQUES watches it all.)

MOROSH: I got it. All of it.
       (Hands BELILAH a wad of cash)
He can come with me now. I'm going to take him out
of here. Someplace where he can be happy.

BELILAH: He's happy right here.

GRACE: *(To LUCIA)* You better listen to me. I know
what you did to Arlene.

LUCIA: Arlene?! But she—click, click! Angie tole me
she was gonna push Vasques in the fire.

BELILAH: He's not going anywhere—not tonight
anyway. Get out of here! You're spoiling my party.

CZEKAJ: Why do you—what are they doing here?

GRACE: That's just a dumb ole doll, Lula. You're the
one who did it! I saw you. I was trying to keep your
secret, but I can't no more.

LUCIA: NO! Click! Click! No! Leave me alone,
Gracie.

ROCKET: Living. Trying to live. Open up your eyes, my friend. This is your flock.

MOROSH: We made a deal. There's no going back on it.

BELILAH: I can call the papers and tell them all about you. You don't want that. And with all these witnesses. A priest even. Leave the money and go!

> (ALDERMAN turns as if to exit but sneaks back to watch.)

CZEKAJ: Why do you—why is it—do you always talk in riddles?

ROCKET: Why does the truth sound like riddles to you?

(The church bells begin to toll. It's midnight. GRACE moves to LUPE and BELEN and uncovers them. SHE pulls a sheet off them which is stained with BELEN's virgin blood.)

GRACE: Looky here! A New Year's surprise. A gift. You should be ashamed with a priest here and all. Come look at this, Lula. This the girl you love so much? Bring that Angie over here too.

CZEKAJ: What—what's happening? Are you kids—?

BELILAH: How could you let this happen, Vasques?!
(*Bopping him on the head*)
I told you what you had to do. I keep telling you, but nothing gets in that stupid fishhead of yours!

ROCKET: How did <u>you</u> let this happen, Belilah?

BELILAH: Don't judge me. You don't know nothing about me!

ROCKET: I know how much love you want to give.

GUADALUPE: You can marry us now, Father Jan.

BELEN: We know which way the sun comes up—it always comes over the water.

> (*GRACE runs to LUCIA and struggles
> with him to get ANGIE out of his arms.*)

GRACE: Give that to me!
(*GRACE gets the doll away from LUCIA and looks for the
knife, but it's no longer in ANGIE's head.*)
Where is it, you little freak?!

LUCIA: (*Taking the knife out from under his dress*) This what you're looking for, Gracie. Click. Click. Angie went bad. Angie didn't know no better. I has ta save her. She jus'don'know.

BELILAH: Put that down, honey.

CZEKAJ: Wow! That looks—hey, give me that.
    (*HE approaches LUCIA.*)
Come on now! You could get—that could hurt.

LUCIA: I know. Click! Click! I been knowing. It hurts me too much. It's too much, Angie. I can't let you hurt nobody else.
    (*LUCIA stabs himself and falls onto a a salt mound.*)
Send me all nice to heaven, Vasques. I know you sent, Arlene there...with fire.

(*Everyone is stunned into silence, except ROCKET. HE approaches LUCIA and holds him. As HE does so, the sky explodes with lightning.*)

ROCKET: I'll take you little one...One more miracle. That's all I have left. I thought I would use it on myself this time. But I'm not finding the way anymore. There's no maps to where we need to go. All the maps lead to this place, and all the prayers too.

(*CZEKAJ approaches ROCKET.*)

CZEKAJ: What are you doing?! We have to call an ambulance!

ROCKET: Not for this little one. I was sent for him.
            (ROCKET gently puts LUCIA down
                and stands to face CZEKAJ.)
I have a gift for you.
                (Places his hat on CZEKAJ's head;
                as HE does so CZEKAJ falls to his knees.)
And the gift is the word. You have it now. Now, do you remember my voice?
Don't despair. I'll be back.

(ROCKET picks up LUCIA's dead body, and begins to walk
    into the river. The other children slowly follow, first
    BELEN, then LUPE, then VASQUES. GRACE follows
                        last.)

GRACE: I wish I had a song for now. My songs are easy to remember.

(GRACE walks into the river as BELILAH remains at the
    water's edge, unable to move any further. CZEKAJ
watches, still on his knees in a state of rapture. When all the
    children are in the water, BELEN speaks.)

BELEN: And then all the children followed Him into the water and it didn't swallow them up. In the water,

they were purified and the dead rose and the blind saw and the wounded wore clothes made of salt—
> *(Taking LUPE's hand, who takes VASQUES' hand who takes GRACE's hand.)*

—because nothing would ever hurt them again.

ROCKET: That's how the story really ends.

> *(ROCKET and the CHILDREN all disappear into the water, as a storm surrounds them, BELILAH watches helplessly, the ALDERMAN runs off, and CZEKAJ rocks and prays.)*

BELILAH: You cannot take my children from me! This is their home.
> *(BELILAH turns back to look at the Salt Mounds and slowly makes her way back to them and sits.)*

Home.
> *(BELILAH grabs a handful of salt and pours it over her feet.)*

Home...

> *(Lights cross to the tavern.)*

EPILOGUE

At the Slide Inn.
DOM speaks to FATHER CZEKAJ.

DOM: *(Talking to CZEKAJ who is seated at the bar, wearing ROCKET's hat)* Yeah, there's been all kinds of massacres here...Just yesterday a guy drowned himself along with five kids just two blocks from here. They thought this guy was Jesus and they followed him into the water during a storm. Yeah...he was a regular customer too. And that girl—they were such nice-looking kids too.
(Pause)
I need to change my clientele...Nice hat...
(Pause)
I didn't think you guys were allowed in bars.
(With an awkward smile)
Especially dives like mine.
(Pause)
Sure you don't want nothing?
(Pause; CZEKAJ takes out a vial of water.)
So? Are you a dealer or what?
(with a laugh)
Just kidding, father.
(Pause; DOM puts ice into a glass
and sets it in front of CZEKAJ.)

Maybe windows—would help. I can never get enough air. It smells like salt now.

(Lights slowly fade to black as CZEKAJ gently strokes the fish in the fishbowl as DOM watches.)

END OF PLAY

EL GRITO DEL BRONX

El Grito del Bronx was commissioned by the New York Shakespeare Festival/Public Theater, Shelby Jiggetts, artistic associate. It was nurtured by the Sundance Writers' Retreat at Ucross, Robert Blacker, artistic director, Sharon Dynak, executive director.

First Workshop: INTAR, (NY), December 2003, directed by Michael John Garcés;
Second Workshop: Hispanic Playwrights' Project at South Coast Repertory, (CA), June 2004, Juliette Carrillo, project director, Michael John Garcés, director.
Third Workshop: Goodman's Festival Latino, (IL), August 2006, with Teatro Vista, Edwin Torres, artistic director, Lisa Portes, director.
Fourth Workshop: hotInk Festival at NYU, January 2007, Catherine Coray, artistic director, Lorca Peress, producer, Candido Tirado, director.
University Premiere: NYU, Tisch School of the Arts, March 2008, directed by Candido Tirado.
West Coast Premiere: Miracle Theater Group, Portland, OR, April 2009, directed by Antonio Sonera.
World Premiere: Goodman Theater, Chicago, IL, July 2009, in a co-production by Collaboraction & Teatro Vista, directed by Anthony Moseley.
Excerpts from Luis Lloréns Torres' **El Grito De Lares** included in the text.

For Adam, Annie, Craig, David, Kia & Robert because
you know why.

Cast Of Characters

1977:
JESÚS COLÓN—14, a boy nurtured by rage

MAGDALENA COLÓN—12, his sister, tense & nervous. She walks with a cast on her right leg.

MARIA COLÓN—40, their mother, very tired.

JOSÉ COLÓN—45, their father, very hungry.

Voice of a MALE TV NEWSCASTER
Voice of a FEMALE TV NEWSCASTER
Voice of a PUERTO RICAN MAN on TV

1991:
PAPO—28, an inmate on death row. He is gaunt and pale. The adult JESÚS.

LULU—26, a poet; the adult MAGDALENA. She has a slight limp when she walks.

GUY NEXT DOOR—PAPO's neighbor on death row; a shadowy figure. All we see of him is his hands which change from scene to scene, sometimes black sometimes white, sometimes old, etc.

MARIA— PAPO & LULU's MOTHER—54, in
mourning.

*FIRST GAS STATION ATTENDANT—a white man
in his 20s.
*LAST GAS STATION ATTENDANT—a white man in
his 20s.
*AND ALL OTHER GAS STATION ATTENDANTS—
white men in their 20s.
*All played by the same actor, his voice sometimes
amplified and altered.

ELIZABETH the LAST GAS STATION
ATTENDANT'S MOTHER—a white woman from
rural Kentucky, in her 40s in mourning.

ED—28, a journalist. Jewish-American. Lulu's
boyfriend.

SARAH, ELECTROCUTED BOY's MOTHER—a
woman in mourning, African-American, 30s.

TIME: On LULU's October wedding day in
           1991, with some moments from the past
           also revisited between the years 1977 &
           1991.

PLACE: The Bronx, New York—in a 1st floor apartment in a five-story walk-up, and in a rubble-filled alley behind the building; Death Row in an Ohio Federal Prison— PAPO's cell; Darien, CT—in ED & LULU's studio apartment, and a park; and Lorain, Ohio—in a SOHIO gas station store, and a hospital room.

On the set, PAPO's jail cell shares the stage with LULU's full-length dressing room mirror. All the scenes move within or around these set pieces. Behind them the background reflects a starless, night sky. By the end of the play, the night sky should be filled with stars.

ACT ONE/SCENE 1

A Saturday in October, 1991.
In a shared space, including PAPO's Cell
on death row and LULU's dressing room
moments before her wedding.
LULU stands in front of a full-length mirror, wearing a
wedding dress. SHE studies
her image with disbelief.
PAPO stands in the shadows of his
cell dressed in his prison garb.

LULU: White is a funny color. It's so light it can blind
the world to who you really are. Gets caught in your
eyes. Reflects an emptiness—some say it's a way to
begin again—a clean slate. I say, it erases what used to
be there. And that's your soul.
(Pause)
But maybe that's what it is to me only. For my
Brother, it could different.
For my Brother…I hope it is.
(Speaking to her brother, PAPO.)
I wish you could be here.
(Pause)
That's a fucking lie. I mean, it wouldn't be, if you were
somebody else. Like you used to be when we were
kids. Before…everything.

(Pause, as SHE lifts up her dress and examines her scarred right leg. It is the leg that was once in a cast. SHE traces the outline
of the scar with her fingers.)

A bride needs somebody to give her away. I remember the last time I held your hand—how the bones of your fingers were so sharp they felt like they would cut right through my skin. There's too much blood between us already, I thought—but I didn't pull my hand away. I held your fingers even tighter, hoping to see some of that color that locks us in. A transfusion of love. Didn't need a white dress then, did I?

(Pause)

PAPO: Tell me the story, Lulu.

LULU: I forget big chunks of it. Those must be the important parts. They're the ones that scare me.
(WE hear an oboe and a cello begin to play.)
Sounds like they're starting without me.

PAPO: Is that what you want?

LULU: Tell me again how you ain't me, Papo.

(PAPO comes forward out of the shadows and dances with
LULU. THEY both watch their reflection in the mirror as
the music plays.
Lights cross to the COLON living room, 1977.)

ACT ONE/SCENE 2

In the Colón apartment in the Bronx, 1977.
A dog is in the alley singing a la mexicana, which is a high-
pitched howling.
MARIA, with one black eye, is decorating all the bathroom
fixtures with adhesive paper dots—
orange and black for Halloween.
JOSÉ is playing the harmonica so the dog has musical
accompaniment. HE raises his hand and the dog howls at a
higher pitch.

JOSÉ: Canta, perra. Canta, Papito. Canta para los
ángeles.

MARIA: I love when Halloween comes, because then
they all come—Thanksgiving, Christmas, Trés Reyes—
one after another—like pum-pum-pum.

JOSÉ: What about Labor Day? Why can't it start
there? The pum-pum-pum? September gives you
even more time to celebrate.

MARIA: Don't make fun of me, José.

(Making a pattern on the wall with the colored dots)
Where's Jesús? I need him to bring me the ladder.

JOSÉ: He's acting out the war for independence with his sister.

MARIA : The what??

JOSÉ: El Grito De Lares. They've been talking about this being like that all over again. On the news. Because of those kids who took over the statue. Even the English stations.

MARIA: I haven't put the tv on yet. Doña Clara said I should try to watch only at night because it's better for my nerves. Things that aren't true make you calmer. You always gotta go to sleep with some lies you know are lies so you don't get nightmares.

JOSÉ: Have you seen my hammer?

MARIA: I threw it out.

JOSÉ: Again?! You know I'll just go buy a new one.

> *(JOSÉ walks out slamming the door,*
> *but then opens the door and throws*
> *a shoe at MARIA, exiting again.)*

MARIA: NIÑOS!!

>*(No response)*

Coño! I'm always alone.

*(In JESÚS's bedroom. JESÚS plays "Don Cheo" and MAGDALENA plays "Don Aurelio" in the play **El Grito De Lares** by Luis Lloréns Torres. THEY both wear their father's clothes as costumes. MAGDALENA hobbles around on her cast. JESÚS pulls her up onto the bed as they continue reading their play out loud from the same tattered book. JESÚS holds the book and shows a page to MAGDALENA when it's her turn to speak.)*

JESÚS as DON CHEO: So, once more.

MAGDALENA as DON AURELIO: Again. And what's new? How are things?

JESÚS as DON CHEO: Vegetating. We only vegetate. Before, at least, one conspired—today one emotion, tomorrow another. But now, the most unbearable monotony.

MAGDALENA as DON AURELIO: Are there no longer secret societies? Nothing is plotted?

JESÚS as DON CHEO: If there are, I'm not aware. I already know you never had full confidence in me. Who doesn't see that! Because of my relationship with Frasquito...

MAGDALENA: Who's Frasquito? I never heard that name before.

JESÚS: Just keep reading.

MAGDALENA: If I don't understand what I'm talking about how can I be a good actor?

JESÚS: You'll be a good actor because I'm a good actor. I raise you up. Stop worrying.

MAGDALENA: You're not so good neither. I'm tired of this game. My leg hurts.

(MAGDALENA goes to the TV and turns it on, sitting herself right in front of it)

JESÚS: Come on, Maggie. It's like dreaming awake.

MAGDALENA: I don't like to dream.

JESÚS: Why'd you jump out that window anyway?

MAGDALENA: I'm gonna get outta here. As soon as I can.

JESÚS: What d'you mean?

MAGDALENA: I mean I got to get outta this house.

JESÚS: Papi better—

MAGDALENA: You know what I dream about? That I wake up and he ain't here no more.
> *(Turning up the volume)*
Listen.

VOICE of female TV NEWSCASTER: We are now on hour four of the occupation by Puerto Rican Nationalists of the Statue of Liberty. They demand that the United States end Puerto Rico's commonwealth status and allow it to become independent. Bill Stover is live from Battery Park. Bill?

VOICE of male TV NEWSCASTER: Thank you, Jenny. I'm here across the river from one of the most controversial takeovers in the history of Lady Liberty. The Puerto Ricans are not the first to take over her coppery crown but they are the most vocal. In fact, you can hear the shouting from here. Let's see how

some Puerto Rican New Yorkers are reacting to this takeover:
Sir? Sir, how does this political action make you feel?

VOICE of PUERTO RICAN MAN on TV: Beautiful. I never seen the bandera like that—so high. With Miss Liberty and everything. I think it should stay like that. Beautiful. Then I'd have something to look at.

MAGDALENA: You see? You see how important it is to be free?

JESÚS: Yeah. Now I see.

(MAGDALENA & JESÚS look at each other. JESÚS
reaches out to touch her wounded leg
as the lights cross to PAPO's prison cell.)

ACT ONE/SCENE 3

In PAPO's cell on death row,
in an Ohio penitentiary 1991.
PAPO kneels by the toilet, like he's praying into it. HE
speaks to something in the toilet, as if he is speaking to
LULU.

PAPO: I saw God today. The left side of his face was dead—I mean, it din't move or nuffin. Hanging all

loose like that, He wasn't all stupid like I thought.
Like I thought He'd look at me too hard and point,
you know how people point when they don't respect
you—right in your face—and you just want to cut their
fucking fingers off and stick 'em up their ass? Not like
that. He din't use his fingers at all—he din't have
fingers. They were more like paws, like a dog or
somefin. And that was cool wif me. Dogs are better
than most people. They only eat when they're hungry.
They only bite to protect themselves. And they kiss
you just for being there. So I told him, "Hey, I'm like a
dog too. Especially my hands. Sometimes when I look
at my fingers I see the nails turn hard and brown.
They fold under themselves so I can walk on them."
And after I tole him that. Then I could. So I did. My
back arched up and all the hair on the back of my neck
stood up like I was real scared of somefin. But I'm
never scared.

(Pause, as HE looks at his hands. ELIZABETH, the LAST
GAS STATION ATTENDANT'S MOTHER enters and
stares at PAPO.)

I guess you know that.

(Lights up on the GUY NEXT DOOR.
All we can see of him are his hands
hanging loosely outside of the cell bars.
When GUY speaks, ELIZABETH exits.)

GUY NEXT DOOR: Mmhmm. Some things can't be secrets.

PAPO: How long you been there?

GUY NEXT DOOR: It ain't how long but how much longer—around here.

PAPO: How long you been fuckin' nosing me up, motherfucker? Fuckin' faggot motherfucker. You got nuffin fuckin' better to fuckin' do? Smell this.
    (HE pulls down his pants and
    presses his buttocks against the bars.)

GUY NEXT DOOR: Mmmm…something smells good over there. Can you pass me some?

PAPO: *(Pulling his pants back up)* Not today.

    *(Silence. PAPO hangs his hands loosely
    outside the bars of his cell like GUY's.)*

PAPO: Where you from?

GUY NEXT DOOR: The Bronx.

PAPO: And what about that…Me too. That's fucked up.

GUY NEXT DOOR: Yeah. That's like fate.

PAPO: Fuckin'fate. Naahh. What the fuck is that?

GUY NEXT DOOR: Open up your hands and look.
It's all right there.

> (THEY each open their hands and examine
> their own palms, as lights cross to
> ED & LULU in their apartment.)

ACT ONE/SCENE 4

> ED & LULU's apartment in Darien, CT, 1991.
> ED & LULU are seated at a folding table eating breakfast.
> LULU finishes reading to ED something she wrote for her
> mother.

LULU: *(Reading the last line of her poem)*
What color was that dream you made for me?
I wish I had saved it in the folds of my hands,
so I could feel you in the places I hold on to.

> (LULU stares at ED waiting for a reaction.
> Finally, he speaks.)

ED: Your mother would have loved that poem.

LULU: So you hate it?

ED: I didn't say that.

LULU: No. You just didn't say anything. Come on. What?

ED: Why do you ask for my opinion? We write different kinds of things.
(She stares at him still waiting for a real opinion.)
Alright. I thought it was a little sentimental.

LULU: That is the meanest thing you ever said to me.

ED: What? There's good sentimental and bad sentimental. I think it would be impossible to write about your mother who recently passed without being sentimental.

LULU: So I shouldn't write about her?

ED: No. But maybe you should wait a little. Until you have some objectivity.

LULU: Hmmm…what else could you say.

ED: What's that supposed to mean?

LULU: I mean you're just a wannabe science writer working as a planning and zoning reporter on a lousy suburban newspaper. Why would I ask you about poetry?

ED: I've written poetry.

LULU: Yeah.

ED: Yeah. Most of it to you.

LULU: Yeah.
            (Smiling despite herself)
So…you did write some good poems.
            (Pause)
Maybe I'm just not good enough to write about my mother. Or anybody.

ED: Stop that bullshit. Nobody ever thinks they're good enough. But that's what we all fight every day, because the world tells you the same thing–like me, I can't write what I want to write. Not till I prove myself writing stupid stories about rich developers who want to buy a little piece of land and build twenty really ugly and expensive houses on it.
Wow, I'm on the cutting edge, huh? Real important stuff.

LULU: How do you do it? I woulda killed somebody by now.

ED: It's not in my nature, I guess. I try to focus on the long-range plan, which doesn't include jail-time for killing a rich asshole or a self-important editor.

LULU: Right. The long-range plan. What if you don't got any of those?

ED: You find one. You make one. You pray for one.

(Pause)

LULU: I still can't believe Mami's gone.

*(ED nods. A pause, as THEY
both reflect on MARIA's passing.)*

ED: I thought a lot about her today. This woman I went to interview had a look in her eyes just like your Ma's. I had to go to her house because her son got electrocuted.

LULU: The one on the Metro-North tracks? I heard about it on the radio.

ED: Yeah. But it wasn't the tracks. It was the overhead wires. He was trying to climb one of the utility poles. Four of them tried it, but he was the one who got to the top.

LULU: And you went to that poor woman's house?! You people are ruthless.

ED: I brought her flowers.
LULU: That was thoughtful.

ED: I was the only reporter there with flowers, so she let me in. Still didn't get the interview.
She thanked me for the flowers. Said I was the only person who brought her any. She was going to put them in a vase and then she dropped to the floor—like someone had hit her on the back of the knees with a sledgehammer.

(Lights cross to the SARAH, the ELECTROCUTED
BOY'S MOTHER,
on her knees, holding a bouquet of flowers.)

SARAH: I remember the first time he woke up without crying. I heard him in his crib talking to this old bear I had bought him at the Salvation Army. It had only one eye because I couldn't find two the same to put on there and I thought a one-eyed bear would be interesting. I put it right in the middle of his forehead because did you ever see that movie "Jason and the Astronauts?" Where there was this giant with just one eye and it tried to eat everybody. I don't know…I felt sorry for that giant. It's kinda nice—I think—that you could have one of something. Because then it's that much more important. It's so important to see.

(Pause)

Teenagers don't think.

(Pause)

Why did they have to say that—in the papers? Over and over how I was out of work. He didn't die because we were poor, did he? He just didn't think.

(SARAH sings a song.)

"There was one little boy…little boy…who could see through the clouds.
There was one little boy who could see through the clouds.
And his tears…and my…and his tears…kissed the sores on my arms
And placed a prayer there:
Only wings…only wings can make a man because…his dreams must fly."

(Lights grow to include ED & LULU as SARAH opens her mouth in a silent scream.)

LULU: Did she faint?

ED: No. I went over to help her up. But when I pulled on her arm, she didn't budge. It was creepy.

Like she went into a trance—rocking with her mouth open. I wanted to get the hell outta there, but I couldn't leave her like that.
So I just waited.

(Pause)

Finally, she turned to me—

SARAH: *(To ED)* Can you get me a double with cheese no onions at Wendy's? I'll give you money. It's just across the street.

(Lights go down on SARAH.)

LULU: Bendito! She was probably weak from not eating. You didn't take her money, did you?

ED: Why do you always assume I'll do the wrong thing?? She lost her son for fuckssakes.
I'm not an asshole.

LULU: You went to look into this woman's face and ask her how it feels to have her son turned into a french fry so you could write a stupid fucking story about it and you're sensitive, right? Fuck you.

(LULU runs out of the house slamming the door behind her. ED pushes his food away and puts his head on the table.)

ED: And I was gonna ask her to marry me. What is my problem?

(Pause)

I'm just so tired.

(Lights cross to PAPO who is pacing in his cell.)

ACT ONE/SCENE 5

In PAPO's cell, 1991.

PAPO is walking in the shadows of the bars of his cell like HE is walking a series of balance beams.
HE does this in silence for a while, then we hear the GUY NEXT DOOR's footsteps which mirror PAPO's. PAPO doesn't notice at first, but then HE does. And HE stops. So does GUY NEXT DOOR. PAPO listens, then starts again. So does GUY NEXT DOOR. PAPO starts to hop from one beam of light to the next. So does GUY NEXT DOOR. Then PAPO begins to hum a slow Latin dance song and begins to slow dance. GUY NEXT DOOR begins to dance too as the lights come up on him dimly. WE can only see GUY's back and hands—never his face. It is as if they are dancing with each other—a tight romantic dance.

PAPO: *(Singing)* "No quiero vivir sin ti, sin tus labios tan preciosos, sin tus ojos tan brillosos.
No puedo vivir…no, no puedo vivir sin tu alma en mis brazos tan bella, tan gloriosa.

372

Quedas conmigo hasta la muerte...hasta la muerte
dulce, mi amor."

*(THEY finish their dance with PAPO humming his song.
Then PAPO moves to sit in his chair, as GUY NEXT
DOOR moves to his own.
THEY un-zipper their pants in unison.)*

PAPO: I follow the veins on my arm with my tongue.
A long slow wet kiss. Smelling my hot spit, letting it
melt into my blood. Feeling my dick fill up. My dick
gets so hard when I do that. With my tongue. That's
the only time. Like I'm getting inside myself and my
blood is my come. There's blood in my spit now. And
when I pee there's red. But that's my love showing.
Everything about me is red now.

*(PAPO places his tongue on his left wrist and begins to
slowly move up his arm while his other hand reaches into
his pants.
GUY NEXT DOOR moves to the wall separating their
cells and presses his body against it as if trying to melt
through it. The lights cross to the COLÓN apartment in
the Bronx.)*

ACT ONE/SCENE 6

In the Colón apartment, Evening, 1977.

MAGDALENA, walking with difficulty because of her wounded leg, is turning on all the lights in the apartment. SHE sings the same song PAPO was singing in the previous scene as SHE does this. JOSÉ bursts through the door, falling on the floor. MAGDALENA tries to run out of the room,
but turns back when she hears the sound of her father's voice.

JOSÉ: Help me, niña.

> *(MAGDALENA helps her father drag himself to the sofa and backs away quickly.)*

MAGDALENA: Ay, Dios mio, Papi! What happened?

> *(JOSÉ's feet are bleeding profusely. They are almost completely severed.)*

MAGDALENA: What happened to your feet??!
> *(Pause)*
Did somebody cut them up??!
> *(Pause)*
You're gonna bleed to death, Pa! We gotta call an ambulance.

JOSÉ: No.

MAGDALENA: But you—

JOSÉ: I SAID NO, MAGDALENA!

MAGDALENA: *(Moving away)* I'm going to tell Jesús!

JOSÉ: *(Grabbing MAGDALENA by the hair)* NO!!
*(HE suddenly lets go of MAGDALENA
and she falls to the floor.)*
I'm just gonna close my eyes and wait.

*(JOSÉ slumps forward in his chair. JESÚS enters, his
clothes stained with blood, holding a blood-soaked paper bag
and goes quietly over to JOSÉ. HE closely inspects JOSÉ's
feet and the blood-soaked carpet around him.)*

JESÚS: Damn, that's a lot of blood.
*(HE dips his finger into the blood
and puts it in his mouth.)*
Damn…that's sweet.

*(MAGDALENA stays down
on the floor crying softly.)*

MAGDALENA: Oh, shit! Is he dead?!

JESÚS: Maybe.

MAGDALENA: Shouldn't we get somebody?!

JESÚS: We should—get somebody.
> *(Pause; HE tosses the bag at JOSÉ.*
> *It contains a blood-soaked hammer.)*

Here's your hammer, Pop.
> *(Pause)*

He won't hurt you no more, Maggie.

MAGDALENA: Oh, my God, Jesús! I didn't mean—
Oh, my God!

*(JESÚS begins to move to MAGDALENA who pulls herself
quickly away from him. THEY both stop moving as the
lights cross to LULU & MARIA in the Visitors' Sign-In
room at the prison.)*

ACT ONE/SCENE 7

1987.
LULU & MARIA in the visitors'
sign-in room at the prison.
MARIA hums the song "There Was One Little Boy…"
sung earlier by SARAH, the ELECTROCUTED BOY'S
MOTHER.

LULU: I don't like you going in there alone, Ma.

MARIA: *(Touching her rosary beads which are strung around her neck.)* I'm not alone.

LULU: Right. They won't even let you wear those in there, Ma. Give them to me.

(MARIA hands her the rosary.)

MARIA: How come you don't go to church anymore, mi'ja?

LULU: Look around, Ma. You see God here?

MARIA: Sure.
(Pause)
The virgin appeared to me once.
In a flowerpot.

LULU: That's the plant I gave you. That's not real.

MARIA: No. I know. The outside was a statue of the Virgin, but the real Virgin's face came on top of the fake Virgin's face and tole me to take the dirt out of her belly and just have it like that in the house like a statue.

LULU: Is that all she said? Isn't she supposed to say important things?

MARIA: If your belly was filled with dirt, wouldn't you think it was a 'mergency?

LULU: They're calling you to go in.
                    (Kissing MARIA on the cheek)
Be careful.

MARIA: I'm not esscared of my own boy. He's your brother, Magdalena.

LULU: I know. And please call me Lulu. I hate that name. Nobody can ever spell it.

MARIA: God knows the name of the Magdalene. Why don't you say a prayer for your brother? I'll tell him you're doing that.

LULU: Don't lie to him, Ma. I'll be waiting right here.

MARIA: This could be your last chance to see him, Magdalena. You're gonna feel sorry, you ain't never seen him before—before you move back to New York.

LULU: No, Ma. I ain't feeling sorry about that.
*(MARIA throws her another kiss and joins the other women
lined up to enter
the main part of the prison.)*

LULU: *(To herself)* She thinks I remember how to pray.

(Lights cross to PAPO's cell.)

ACT ONE/SCENE 8

In PAPO's cell.
JOSÉ has a father/son talk with JESÚS.
JOSÉ wears red rubber boots and a fireman's hat. PAPO is
holding his hands over his ears
like he is trying to block out sound.
PAPO looks like he's been crying.

JOSÉ: You don'listen too good, m'ijo. I tole you not to cry in front of her. Women do not like a weak man. If you act like a ma-mau in front of your mother she will have no respect for you. And you don'got nothing else left. To get from her I mean. She tried to not respect me, but I showed her respect with the back of my hand and my clenched fists. All those new teeth she got look good on her, but she knows she wouldn't look that good, if I hadn't broken all her teeth. You know that, right? She knows it too.

PAPO: Get outta here. Mami's gonna be here soon.

JOSÉ: Maybe she ain't coming today…maybe she missed the bus. You gonna cry if she don't come.

Pobrecito. You wanna cry on Papi's shoulder? Come here.

PAPO: Leave me alone. When are you going to leave me alone?

JOSÉ: I ain't going nowhere. I'll be right here— waiting for you. You hear that blood racing to the back of your head, pounding it like a bitch in heat. That's me. That sound won't ever go away.

(JOSÉ laughs softly moves to the back of the cell, as PAPO begins to chant with his eyes closed.
JOSÉ will remain in the shadows of PAPO's cell until LULU's visit in ACT TWO.)

PAPO: I pray. I pray. I pray. I pray. I pray. I pray. I pray. I pray. I pray. I pray. I pray. I pray. I pray. I pray. I pray. I pray. I pray. I pray.
        (Pause; HE opens his eyes.)
One day, my eyes won't open. That will be a good day.

(Lights cross to ED & LULU in the park.)

ACT ONE/ SCENE 9

In a park. 1991.

ED has his head resting in LULU's lap.
THEY lounge on a red picnic blanket.

ED: A park is the one place where all children look happy. Even if they're terrified coming down a slide. Or you swing them too hard.
(pointing)
Look at that little girl.

LULU: Mmhmm. Look at her smile. She looks—
(Pause; with a sad smile)
My brother used to smile like that. He used to say that the shadows of the leaves on his face—made him feel like a tree. We'd go to the park all the time. Just to feel those shadows.

ED: Are you going to go see him?

LULU: What do you mean?

ED: I mean…are you going to go see him? He's— where? In Florida, or something?

LULU: Don't know. We lost touch.

ED: I could help you find him.

LULU: No. That's not—I really don't want that.

ED: You talk about him all the time.

LULU: I do? Maybe. I been thinking about the stories he used to make me tell him.
> *(We see PAPO caught in the dark*
> *shadows of the bars of his cell.)*

ED: Tell me a story.

(SHE rubs ED's head gently as SHE begins to tell ED a story. PAPO seems to be listening too, as if HE is recalling this story from the past.)

LULU: Once upon a time, a long, long, long time ago, there was a beautiful Princess named Antonia. Her father ruled the Earth and her mother ruled the Sky. This left the Princess to care for all the animals of the kingdom. She fed them sweet blossoms from an ancient tree called the Flamboyan that cried when his red blossoms fell from his branches. But the Flamboyan sighed with contentment when Princess Antonia touched his limbs, because her hands could heal him with their gentle power to make things grow more beautiful in an empty place.
> *(Pause)*

One day, an evil Chupacabra put a spell on her father, and he began to chop down all the trees in the kingdom. With an axe stained with his own blood, her father severed all the limbs of the Flamboyan, and with his spit he made a poison to kill the roots. Soon there were no trees alive in the Princess' garden. She could no longer feed the creatures that depended on the blossoms to stay alive. They knew no other food, so they grew weak.

(Pause)

Her mother tried to help by making the wind blow fiercely so that fruit from other kingdoms flew into the Princess' garden. Princess Antonia tried to feed them the fruit of ripe mangoes and papayas, but they would choke when they tried to swallow it because everything turned into a bitter paste in their throats and would make their tongues burn. Animals fell to the ground all around her, slowly melting into the soil and becoming a part of the Earth. She decided to try one last meal for her friends. Sobbing she cut into the soft flesh of the palms of her hands and let the blood drip into the mouth of the youngest one, the Coquí, a small frog whose song was like the cry of angels. Suddenly, the Coquí opened her eyes. So the Princess squeezed more blood from her torn flesh and fed it to the dying animal. Slowly, the frog began to sing. It was a song that reached into Heaven.

(Pause)

This song let her mother whisper of her own sadness to the clouds that soon broke open, raining the Earth with the mother's tears. The power of the mother's water and the daughter's blood seeped life back into the earth. And trees began to grow again.

The Flamboyan grew the fastest and his limbs lifted
the bewitched father into the sky, while his roots
buried the axe where no one would ever find it again.

ED: That's the freakiest story I've ever heard. But so
beautiful.   No wonder Jesús loved to hear them.
                    (Pause)
Wow...Hon'?

LULU: Yeah?

ED: Are you gonna tell our children stories like that?
LULU: Maybe.
                    (Pause)
Maybe I'll leave out the blood and flesh stuff though.

ED: Okay.
            (HE snuggles more deeply into her lap
                and settles in for a nap.)
The sound of your voice is like a pillow.

            (Lights cross to PAPO's cell.)

ACT ONE/SCENE 10

In PAPO's cell, 1991.

PAPO is pricking his fingers with the stone-sharpened end of a spoon. HE draws a map of Puerto Rico on the stone wall with his blood. Lights change to include GUY NEXT DOOR, who is leaning against the bars of his cell, listening to PAPO, but we can only see his shadow.

PAPO: *(As HE mentions the towns, HE draws a star on the map where they would be.)* I never been to P.R. but I know that my Ma was from Cabo Rojo, by the ocean, and Papi was from the mountains in San Sebastian. I never seen no mountains. But Ma would take us to Orchard Beach every Saturday in the summer. I miss how she smelled—with all that oil she put on—like burning salt—all crispy like that too.

GUY NEXT DOOR: Don't you miss the ocean?

PAPO: Nah...I just cover my ears and scream and when the sound comes back to me—that's like the ocean. But I don't do it for too long. I start to choke when I listen to that inside my head. Like I'm drowning.
      (Pause)
If you wanned them to, would they drown you here?

GUY NEXT DOOR: I don't think so. I don't think they'll let you choose anything where somebody has to hold you down or touch you to do it.

PAPO: But somebody has to put the needle in.

GUY NEXT DOOR: But that's a doctor. They're used to putting needles in. You don't need any strength to put in a needle. Not strength in your arms anyway.

PAPO: I used to have really strong arms.

GUY NEXT DOOR: You can still have them, Papo. In your head, you can lift almost anything.

PAPO: That's how I did it the first time. With my fists. My fist went right through that fucking hillibilly faggot trash. It felt so good. I couldn't stop. On and on, I tore into his face with my fingers. I almost took his face all the way off. He was bleeding from every hole. Then I looked down at my shoes and I thought: those niggers used to be white. But they looked sweet now—sorta like firemen's boots, but like the hats they wear, you know. On my feet I had protection. His blood made my feet fireproof.

(Pause; HE moves to the wall
separating him from GUY.)

I held him in my arms until he died. I wanned to be real close. To smell the death on him. I needed to smell that—right on my skin. So that even when his soul left him, it still had to pass through me. That's what I wanned. It was like a hot wire. His soul went through my mouth. And that was so sweet.

*(The FIRST GAS STATION ATTENDANT enters. His
clothes and face are bloodied.
PAPO kisses the FIRST GAS STATION ATTENDANT.)*

FIRST GAS STATION ATTENDANT:
(With a stutter) Took me bah-by sssurprise. The whole
thing. I hate ssselling things to those pah-people, bah-
but I try not to let them know it. It's their sssmell that
bothers me mah-most. Like bloody water, like when
you cccut open a piece of sssteak done rare—ssso wet
it can make you gag, but take that first taste and you
cannot not eat it. You and the animal become one.
And once it's inssside you, the taste ssstays in your
mah-mind like the first sssong you ever sang. Good or
bad, it's there forever. I wah-was his first. But he was
ssstill hungry. Even the sssteak has to eat sssometime.

*(MARIA, ELIZABETH & SARAH enter each carrying a
baby and humming the song that SARAH sang earlier as
THEY rock the baby in their arms asleep.)*

(The lights cross to ED & LULU.)

ACT ONE/SCENE 11

*In LULU & ED's apartment, 1991.
LULU is frantically going through her purse.*

387

ED watches her.

ED: You're sure they were in there?

LULU: Yes, Ed. I'm sure. I'm sure those mother-sucking sonsofbitches took them.

ED: We should call—

LULU: Who?? The fucking cops!

ED: The paper. I could have them write a story—

LULU: Just shut-up with your fucking stories. Journalism is part of the fucking problem. Newspapers are too scared to say the truth about anything. So stupid shit-face pigfucking cops get away with shit like this.

ED: Did you get his badge number?

LULU: No.

ED: Lulu…

LULU: I tried to. But you know how I get. I got all nervous. They were treating me like such a fucking spick. And I'm so fucking stupid. Why didn't I get his freaking badge number?! I don't think of shit like that.

I'm not like you. Always with the details. I just yelled at him and then he frisked me, went through my purse and said I had to get in his car. And then I couldn't see his fucking badge. And then—
(She starts to scream. ED holds her and SHE begins to calm down.)

ED: Okay. Start again. Close your eyes and think. Is that all they took?

LULU: Yeah. Fucking wannabe macho shithead dildos. They just wanted to humiliate me.

ED: And they picked you out as a suspect because you were walking? That makes no sense, honey.

LULU: Because I was walking and was the darkest person around. Obviously, I'm a shoplifter waiting to happen. Steal from that pink and green nightmare?! I wouldn't even set foot in that ugly-ass dress shop for rich-bitches who wear tennis skirts because they want people to smell their pussies through white, gauzy material because they're too fucking cultureless to have a taste and smell of their fucking own. I hate this fucking town.

ED: I going down to that station and file a complaint. You stay here in case we need to call a lawyer.

LULU: You're gonna get yourself hurt, sweetie. Didn't you ever see "Gentleman's Agreement?" They like your people almost as much as they like mine here.

ED: No one is going to hurt me, Lulu.

LULU: Please don't go. It's not even that important. I'm really over it now. I was just—

ED: We have to do something, Lulu.

LULU: They were just birth control pills. It's kinda funny really...when you think about it.

ED: Yeah...I'm real tickled.

LULU: Listen, these people don't care about us, Ed. This isn't our place.

ED: That's why we can't let them off the hook. You gotta make your own place. If you give it up to them, then nothing changes.

LULU: Some things don't change. Everybody's not my family. Everywhere isn't home.

(Lights cross to PAPO in his cell.)

ACT ONE/SCENE 12

In PAPO's cell, 1991.
PAPO is trying to melt a slice of cheese on a piece of bread
with a match. HE speaks to
GUY NEXT DOOR, who sits in his own cell
with his back to the bars.

PAPO: I love grilled cheese sandwiches. That's all I ever ate when I was home. I'd say "Ma, make me your speciality of the casa." And she would. My sister wrote me that I—that Mami's heart was always hurting with me locked up in here. Maybe that's why—can you die from that? A broken heart?
(PAPO remembers his mother, MARIA's last visit. HE moves into the memory as lights come up on his mother.)

MARIA: We never shoulda left the Bronx. But your father knew—

PAPO: My father is dead. Your husband is Papi's brother.

MARIA: Yeah, he's that too—but he loves you like a father.

PAPO: Ma, he loves you. He brought us out here and kicked me out as soon as he could. He didn't even let me come to the house and see you.

MARIA: I went to see you anyway. You always make things worse than they was.
You exhaderate too much, mi'jo.

PAPO: Exaggerate, Ma.

MARIA: Yeah. I been here 32 years and imaginate. I understand everything real good though…Anyway, Timo knew there was jobs out here. And as long as he had to work in a factory it might as well be a car factory because my husband, he likes cars.

PAPO: He still alive?

MARIA: Papo! You know he's the one brings me here to see you—

PAPO: You take the bus. You get here the same time each time with all the other bus ladies.

MARIA: Anyway, Timo said it would be nice—like moving to the country. And I came from the country. So I thought it would be good for you. You was getting into so many fights after your father—God rest his soul.

PAPO: Don't start, Ma.

MARIA: And then I found those needles…I got scared
you might not come home one day. So we moved to
Ohio. I thought we'd have a little house with a yard so
I could grow some tomatoes and some flowers—but it
wasn't no damn house. The projects were in shorter
buildings at least. At least I didn't have to climb too
many stairs when the elevator broke. But it smelled
the same. Why do people do pipí in the hallway
where they live? Even the concrete walls turn yellow
after all that pipí. And there was still roaches.
They were just a little bigger. And people said they
was waterbugs—that sounded so nice. Like they were
more like fish or something. But they sure looked just
like big ole roaches to me.
(Pause)
Why did you kill all those people, mi'jo? I know you
ain't no monster—like they saying.

PAPO: I don't know, Ma.

MARIA: (Taking his hands and kissing them)
Your hands still smell like they did when you was a
baby. That's gotta be the best smell there is. Like fresh
bread dipped in warm milk with sugar. You smelled
like sweet bread pudding to me, Papito.
(SHE smells his hands again.)

But they so skinny baby. Don't they give you nothing
to eat? Here.

> (*SHE reaches into her purse and
> pulls out a grilled cheese sandwich.*)

I made it before I came, so it's not so hot anymore like
it should be. But it's all I could think to bring you.
They don't let you bring a lot of stuff in here. They
don't let you do nothing like a mother needs to do for
her son.

> (*SHE takes his hands again and
> puts them on her chest.*)

You're always inside here, mi'jo. I want you to
remember that, okay? And don'believe nothing your
sister says. She's full of shit. She's walking better
now. They gave her some special shoes that make her
walk better. "It's like having new feet, Ma, " she said to
me. I think it must be so nice to have new feet when
you still got places to go.

> (*SHE smiles, lets go of his hands and exits.
> PAPO holds his cheese sandwich to his chest
> as lights cross to ED & LULU's apartment.*)

ACT ONE/SCENE 13

In ED & LULU's apartment, 1991.
LULU is packing a suitcase in a fury as ED watches. On
the radio, the song "Chupacabra Mix" by Megamix plays as

a commuter train rumbles by making everything in the apartment shake.

ED: That's the last train to the City. It's too late to go anywhere.
>*(HE tries to unpack her bag*
>*as SHE continues to put stuff in it.)*

Come on now. Stop it.

LULU: You've known me for two years now and you still don't know me. You know how sad that makes me. I only moved to this fucked-up place to be with you. I left school to be with you. You told me it would give us more time together and I never fucking see you. You're always working and I'm stuck in this Connecticut wasteland. People here think I'm somebody's maid. The other day some stupid woman saw me coming out of the coffee shop and asked me if I was a nanny, because she needed somebody special to watch her twins. And what do you do think that meant?!

ED: What do you want me to say?
>*(Turning off the radio)*

You wanna get married or something?

LULU: *(Imitating him)* "You wanna get married or something." That's real fucking romantic.

ED: You make me smile in my stomach, Lulu. Will you marry me?

LULU: Right. You ask me when I'm half out the door and I'm supposed to take it seriously. No, Ed. I won't marry you. You're just afraid of being alone. That's not love.
>   *(ED starts to cry quietly.)*
I don't believe you.

ED: Why not? What do I have to do? I come home sometimes and you're so angry and I don't know why. And you won't tell me. I gotta tiptoe around you. Like I did something wrong. This is supposed to be my house too, but you make me feel like I'm a bad guest who just won't leave.

LULU: I'm leaving. I'm the one who's leaving.

ED: *(Placing himself in front of the door)* You're gonna have to kill me to get through this door.

LULU: Let's not do this. I can't tell you what's wrong because I don't know. I just know it's wrong.

ED: So you don't trust me?

LULU: I don't even trust myself.

ED: Because I'm white.

LULU: You ain't white. White is a state of mind. Jews can't be white no matter how much they try. It's not in their blood. They care too much. They cry too easily. They have issues with their mothers.
ED: And what's a white state of mind?

LULU: It's when you don't care because you think you don't need to, because there's no one else in the world more important than you. That's white.

ED: I love you so much I can't breathe sometimes when you're in the same room with me and I can't touch you. Will you marry me?

LULU: *(With a reluctant smile)* Maybe.

ED: Maybe that's the last time I'll ask.

LULU: You don't let me leave. Nobody else ever did that.

ED: Maybe you never missed the train before.

LULU: Is that your theory?

ED: More of an hypothesis.

LULU: I love you because you sleep with a dictionary by the bed instead of porno.

ED: What do you think's inside the dictionary?

(Lights cross to PAPO's cell.)

ACT ONE/SCENE 14

In PAPO's cell, 1991.
PAPO speaks into the toilet.
GUY NEXT DOOR listens.

PAPO: Yeah! He wanned to marry me. You know like they have these weird ass things. Like with two men. But I couldn't hang with that. It didn't make no sense to me. So what, then I have to have a maid of honor or something? I didn't understand. You don't gotta marry people you fuck, especially if they're men. No. That don't make no kind of sense. And it was so faggoty. I mean you gotta fuck. But a wedding ring. Fuckin'weird.
(Pause)
Are you still in there?

GUY NEXT DOOR: I'm here.

PAPO: You stay quiet so much. Don't you like to talk?

GUY NEXT DOOR: I don't need to talk.

PAPO: What else is there to do in this fuckin' place? Talk and jerk off. I can't even do that anymore. But the good thing is that since I'm dying they're not gonna kill me. I'm helping them out.
          (Pause)
Are you White? Sometimes you sound White. Sometimes Black. You change a lot for somebody who don't talk.

GUY NEXT DOOR: Yeah? Maybe I'm both.
          (Pause)
Sounds like he loved you.

PAPO: I guess.
          (Pause)
He was both. Had real pretty green eyes. I'm a sucker for pretty eyes. He got his sister to bring him a ring to give me.
     (Pulls the ring out from under his bed sheet)
I play with it when I'm in bed at night. I put it on my finger and I think I could be married with like five kids. And they would all be beautiful and smile with their whole face. You know how kids can do that? Just become a whole fuckin' smile. It's too much, man, how they can do that. I wish I could remember doing

399

that. I wish I could go back in time. But time don't
work on me like that.

*(Lights cross to a store in a Sohio Gas Station. PAPO
moves into this memory as it unfolds. JOHN, the LAST
GAS STATION ATTENDANT is counting cash at closing
time. As HE counts, we see PAPO enter checking the scene
out.)*

LAST GAS STATION ATTENDANT:
We're closed.

PAPO: Cigarettes?

LAST GAS STATION ATTENDANT:
We're closed.
            *(Starts motioning with his
            hands like PAPO is deaf.)*
Closed, amigo.

PAPO: Amigo? Do I know you?
LAST GAS STATION ATTENDANT:
Get out of my fuckin'store.

PAPO: Newports. Two packs.

LAST GAS STATION ATTENDANT:
Come back tomorrow…amigo.

PAPO: No.

LAST GAS STATION ATTENDANT:
So what are we gonna do here?

PAPO: It's up to you.

LAST GAS STATION ATTENDANT:
(Pulling a rifle out from behind the counter.)
Get the fuck outta my store you fuckin'spick trash.

PAPO: You got bullets in that?

LAST GAS STATION ATTENDANT:
One way to find out.

*(PAPO slowly approaches the LAST GAS STATION
ATTENDANT.)*

PAPO: Go ahead. I been waiting for this. Go ahead.
It's time. What you waiting for?

LAST GAS STATION ATTENDANT:
You people are animals. Nobody would blame me. It
would be so easy.

*(PAPO faces down the barrel, takes the gun away from the
LAST GAS STATION ATTENDANT and sits on the
counter his back to the ATTENDANT.)*

PAPO: You're so afraid of me and you don't even know me. This is the part I like. Where I get to make you shit in your pants. People don't like to shit in front of other people.

But I don't mind it.

You know where shit comes from? From inside your head. If you kept all those things inside there your mouth would fill up and it would pour from you. And forget about kissing anybody. Shitting keeps you from being lonely. What's your name?

LAST GAS STATION ATTENDANT: John. We don't got any Newports.

PAPO: That's okay, John.

LAST GAS STATION ATTENDANT: You're him, ain't you?

PAPO: I waited my whole life to be a "him." You know any? I want to hear a song. In my head, I hear them all the time. Like I make a mass for myself except I'm on the cross too. I wish I could remember all the words to that Lamb of God song. You know that one?

JOSÉ & LAST GAS STATION ATTENDANT:
(*Singing*)

"Glory, glory, glory...Lord God almighty, Heaven and earth are filled with your sweet mercy."

PAPO: Lamb of God, who takes away the sins of the world, have mercy on us. That's about the prettiest thing anybody ever said. I never touched no lamb until we moved to Ohio. You can go right up to them and put your arms around'em and let your fingers get lost in all those warm curls.
>   *(Jumping off the counter and swinging*
>   *the gun in the ATTENDANT's face.)*
FUACATA!
>   *(PAPO kisses the ATTENDANT.)*

PAPO: *(Moving back to his cell)* That was the last one. They caught me because I started taking my time. I started to enjoy it too much–so God made sure I got caught.
>   *(Pause)*
I have sores on my dick now. That's where I was bit by God.

>   *(Lights grow to include MAGDALENA.*
>   *MARIA runs in screaming.)*

MARIA: Your father is covered with—

MAGDALENA/LULU & PAPO/JESÚS:

(In unison) We know.

MARIA: Jesús. I—I'm so sorry.

JESÚS/PAPO: Don't be sorry for him.

MARIA: I'm sorry for all of us.
 (MARIA begins to pray silently on her rosary as PAPO &
      LULU retreat to the shadows.)

(Blackout)
END OF ACT ONE

ACT TWO/SCENE 1

In the COLON Apartment, 1977.
MARIA sits on a chair trying to avoid putting her feet
down on the blood-stained rug.
SHE is eating from a take-out
dish of Chicken Delight.

MARIA: Niños? Don't you want any chicken?
  (No response from MAGDALENA & JESÚS)
Niños?
   (SHE tries to get up but can't.)
I had to go all the way to the Grand Concourse,
because the Delight over here closes early because they
was getting robbed all the time. That's a long walk.
The hardware store is closer than the Delight. That's
why I don't understand. Where all the blood came
from. Somebody musta busted his feet with that
hammer. They're gonna have to cut them off. They
was hanging off anyway.
    (Pause)
And you know, my husband never liked walking. I
don't know why he didn't take his car. He probably
stopped to play a number and…could be…somebody
followed him. They probably tried to rob him and he
wouldn't give them anything. He's stupid like that.
You don't argue with junkies. They'll just take an ice
pick and slice it through your head. Or a hammer.

(Pause)

That's what I tole the police.

(Pause)

Niños! Help me get off this chair!

(MARIA stands on the chair as the lights cross to JESÚS &
MAGDALENA watching the tv. We hear the theme song
to "Happy Days".
JESÚS turns off the tv.)

JESÚS: You know what? I'm always gonna be your
brother.

MAGDALENA: Even when you're dead?

JESÚS: What do you mean?

MAGDALENA: I mean when your soul goes to
wherever it goes to, do you think you'll remember
who you were? Or do you get to be somebody else?
Maybe you as my brother is just a body and your soul
belongs to God, so once you're gone I've got no right
to claim you.

JESÚS: Don't worry. Family's always got a claim.

MAGDALENA: That's what I thought.

(Lights cross to the jail cell.)

ACT TWO/SCENE 2

In 1991, PAPO's jail cell. A dream.
In the semi-darkness, we hear the whispered names of
PAPO's victims spoken by different women's voices, a
CHORUS of MOTHERS, WIVES, & DAUGHTERS

CHORUS OF MOTHERS, WIVES & DAUGHTERS:
(sometimes overlapping, sometimes in unison; once each
name has been said three times there is silence) David—
father; Alan—brother; Michael—son; Kevin—
son/father; Bob—brother/son; Roger—husband;
Lawrence—husband; Roy—father/ son; Craig—
husband/father; Joseph—brother/son; Len—son;
Peter—son; Owen—son; Kirk—son; Jake—son;
Ronnie—son;
Eli—son; John—son.

(Silence; as lights come up dimly on PAPO who is leaning
against the cell wall with his eyes closed as if HE is sleeping
in this position. ELIZABETH, the LAST GAS STATION
ATTENDANT'S MOTHER enters, carrying her murdered
son and places him in PAPO's bed. The bed gets soaked in
the corpse's blood. Blood even flows from underneath the
bed. After a long silence, ELIZABETH begins to speak to
her dead son as if he is lying before her in a coffin.
PAPO's eyes slowly open.)

ELIZABETH: What do you think of that wood?
> *(No response)*

I thought it was pretty. Matched your hair sort of.
Cherrywood. Smells like cherries too.
> *(SHE sniffs at the edge of PAPO's*
> *bed like it is her son's coffin.)*

Sold your truck to buy it. Couldn't bury you in the
truck. Though you mighta liked that. You used to
drive it all the way down to Kentucky to see me. I'll
miss that truck.
> *(Pause)*

I'll miss you driving that truck too.
> (Pause)

You wasn't a very good driver though…always
running into things on the road. I wondered why you
never could avoid any of those poor little souls.
Wheels always covered with bits of flesh and feathers
or fur. Sticky thing—a dead animal. A dead animal's
smell can stay on the chrome of your car forever—
metal grinds it in. I tried cleaning out them wheels
with tomato juice once but I guess that only takes out
skunk smell on a living thing. Didn't do nothing for
the car.
> *(Pause)*

I loved how you kept the tails of the pretty ones you
hit. That was something. Flew them from your CB
antenna like a flag. Prettier than the flag though.
Softer. Had a sense of style. I always admired that

about you. My son, John, knew how to do things right. First one in our town with a CB and an eight-track tape player. Even bought me a Perry Como tape to listen to when I was in your car. You worked so hard to make things nice for me.

(Pause)

Went North to make a good living with the car factories there and all. But couldn't get no job. Some stupid immigrant or maybe a nigger got it first. That's what you told me anyway. "Them people are like fire ants," you told me. "They come to your picnic and burn the skin off your knees." I try not to think badly of other people but Christ is gonna have to help me out of this one. Why did you send him to my son's gas station, Lord? That's what I want to know.

(Turning to look directly at PAPO and addressing him directly; HE shrinks to a squatting position as SHE speaks to him.)

I pray for your death. Every day. When I wake up. Every night. When I go to bed. "Hurry up and kill him, Jesus." I say to myself. "Kill him like he killed my boy." And I get the same answer back. "Save your own soul with forgiveness, Elizabeth. Your boy's not ever coming back." Not really a satisfactory answer from above. But that doesn't keep me from believing—even though he don't bring me any Perry Como tapes—God is all I have left. And you know there's some people He don't talk to at all so I appreciate the attention.

(Takes out a comb and begins to comb her son's hair which is matted thick with blood.)
They did okay with the make-up, but the hair is bad. You never used gel in your hair. I tried to put some Dippity-Doo on you once to get the cowlicks down, but you said other kids would make fun of you if you smelled like a girl. There's nothing worse for a young man, I suppose than smelling like he cares too much about his daily grooming.
(Pause)
Almost nothing worse anyway.
(Pause)
That's better. And a cowlick. Your hair never could be tamed. Need to go as you really were, so God knows what he's in for when you walk into those gates. Oh—and I brought you this.
(Places a note in the corpse's breast pocket)
Just in case. It's your fourth grade report card. It has Miss Clark's comments about you having such potential. She was the only one who got that right. Your other teachers were morons. God will want to see that card.
(Softly sings the same song as SARAH, the MOTHER of the ELECTROCUTED BOY did in ACT ONE as the lights begin to crossfade.)
"There was one little boy, little boy…who could see through the clouds…"

(The lights cross to LULU in her apartment.)

ACT TWO/SCENE 3

In ED & LULU's apartment. 1991.
LULU is cutting articles out of the newspaper.
ED enters quietly with a bouquet of flowers.
HE tiptoes behind her and places the flowers in front of her
making her jump.

ED: Surprise!

LULU: Shit! You almost gave me a heart attack.

ED: You left the door unlocked.

LULU: I did? I never do that.

ED: I know. You think a raccoon is going to get in here with you.

LULU: Hey, it could definitely happen. You know I saw that big fat one on the back steps last week going through our garbage.

ED: We got better cans now. The kind that lock. It should be okay.

LULU: (*Putting the flowers in a vase*) What's the occasion?

ED: You needed some flowers.

LULU: Needed?

ED: I wanted to give you some flowers.

LULU: Oh. Okay. Whatever.

ED: (*Referring to the article she was cutting out of the paper*) What's that?

LULU: Research. A couple of articles I want to keep.

ED: I did some research myself today. We can rent a hall at my alma mater for only $300 for 8 hours. For the reception. The wedding? Remember? Why are you looking at me like that?

LULU: City Hall. What do we need a party for?

ED: So we can invite family.

LULU: I don't have any family.

ED: What about that uncle who gave you money for college?

LULU: He's dead.

ED: When?

LULU: Recently.

ED: Why didn't you tell me?

LULU: Well, he was <u>my</u> uncle.

ED: I'd tell you if my uncle died.

LULU: Yeah. But you like your uncle.

ED: Why do you need that article?

LULU: You ask a lot of questions.

ED: I'm a reporter.

LULU: City Hall.

ED: Don't you think we deserve a celebration?

LULU: Whatever.

ED: Don't whatever me.

LULU: I'm a whatever type. If you don't like whatever, why do you want to marry me? I can just be your Catholic 'ho and you can marry a nice Jewish girl.

ED: Did my grandmother call today?

LULU: She calls every Sunday, Ed. She thinks I'm a lowlife, doesn't she?

ED: She's just old.

LULU: I didn't say yes. You can't rent a hall until I say yes.

ED: Whatever. What are you going to do with those articles?

LULU: I don't know. I just wanted to keep them. To re-read them. Understand them. I think they're about love.

(Pause)

One was about the Chupacabra in Mexico, on vacation with the coquí. "Monster leaves its Puerto Rican Paradise to Cruise the Gulf of Mexico with its little frog friend, the Coquí." Latino Urban myths, they call it. I believe in the Chupacabra though. How else can you explain all those cows and goats drained dry of their blood? And some people too. There's gotta be

something out there doing that. Like Dracula or
something, but more selective. Only happens when
you don't pay attention to it. Act like it can't touch
you and it touches you—big time.
Sucks you right down its throat.
                    (Pause)
I started writing again today.

ED: That's great.

LULU: Is it? I don't know anymore. Did you know I
was never who I wanted to be? Did you know I
wanted to be President?

ED: Did you know I wanted to be the first president
who was also an astronaut?

LULU: Did you know I wanted to be President so I
could help my brother?
                    (Picking up the paper again)
There was something else in the paper. About that
Latin King who was supposedly ordering murders
from his prison cell. They gave him the most severe
Life Imprisonment sentence ever. He can't see his
sister and mother again for forty-five years.

ED: Yeah. I heard about it. He'll be in isolation for all
that time. Wasn't he a murderer before he went to
prison? So you feel sorry for him?

LULU: I feel sorry for his sister and his mother.
(Pause)
I can't. Not yet.

ED: You're right. You do have to say yes first.

*(The lights cross to MARIA sitting
in a spotlight talking to a judge.)*

ACT TWO/SCENE 4

*In a judge's chamber in Ohio, 1987.
MARIA, in a tight spotlight,
is questioned about her son.*

MARIA: No, sir. I never tole him that. He learned it
by himself.
(Pause)
I don't know if it's true. I only believe my son is a
good man in his heart.
(Pause)
He didn't think they were. I don't know why.
(Pause)
Yes, Judge. I know what human means. He does too.
But he didn't see it in them, I guess. He's a sensitive
boy that way.
(Pause)

I'm not saying that he was right. I'm saying he thinks
he was right. He's not thinking clear.
His father died when he was young and you know a
boy needs his father or there's no one for the man he'll
become to be like. No footprints to follow.

(Pause)

I know that. But for him it's true. He don't know who
he is. He's never known.

(Pause)

I was born in Puerto Rico. He was born here. In the
Bronx, I mean.

(Pause)

I don't know. If we still lived in Puerto Rico, he
wouldn't have found as many people not to like, I
think. But who knows? Maybe he woulda found
more. Everywhere is changing.
It used to be so safe there and now everybody got their
gates and security guards.
Everywhere there's things to be scared of.

(Pause)

I know there's people scared of my son, but not me. If
you could let him live—

(Pause)

No, he din't. No mercy. Mercy is changing too. His
dying won't change anything, Judge.

(Pause)

Then I hope this makes them very happy. Let them
watch his soul get set free. And I'll be right there next
to them. I'm sure they'll like seeing me there too.

(SHE is fighting back tears.)
I'll be singing. He liked my singing. Whenever my
baby boy would cry, I could rub the space between his
forehead, just over his eyes and sing to him real close
so he could feel my breath on him. And he'd get so
quiet—just lookin'at me, his eyes wide and soft on me.
That boy could kiss wif his eyes, wif the look he give
you.

*(Lights grow to include PAPO in his cell listening to his
mother sing. The other Mothers
[SARAH and ELIZABETH]
appear and sing with MARIA.)*

THE MOTHERS: Why can't a boy's warm breath be
the air— Be the wind—
So his tears turn to rain?
Why can't a mother's love be the ocean—
Be the sea—That his sadness fills again and again.
Un niño que vuela remojado en lagrimas, puede llenar
el mar.
A boy who flies with tears can fill, can fill the deepest
sea.

*(Each MOTHER is captured in a spotlight.
THEY begin to speak.)*

SARAH : There was this playground I used to take him to. It had a globe of the world, that kids could sit on and spin.

ELIZABETH : He would sit on that world and spin and it was a movie or something. A little boy on top of the world—turning it at his own pace, making it move with the power of his laughter.

MARIA: He would go so fast sometimes, I got scared for him—that he was gonna fall. One time he did. Right on his face.

SARAH: But he just got right back up on it. A big smile on his face.

ELIZABETH: "I wanna go faster this time, Momma," he said to me his face full of mud and his hair covered in leaves.

ALL THREE MOTHERS: But that smile.

MARIA: I would help him get back on. And the spinning would start again.

SARAH: I thought all boys must want to go too fast like that.

ELIZABETH: I thought there was no better place on earth to be. His hair would stick straight up like a bolt of lightning from all that spinning.

MARIA: His face would get all red like he was on fire. I would tell him it was enough. I was essared with all that red on his face, that he would ehplode or someting.

ELIZABETH: Shoot! I'd help him spin faster. If that's what he wanted then I said do it. Spin till you fall, boy, if that's what you want.

ALL THREE MOTHERS: Never seen him that happy again.

(ELIZABETH & SARAH help MARIA out of her dress, underneath SHE wears a hospital gown. MARIA stares at her hands
as the lights cross to PAPO's cell.)

ACT TWO/ SCENE 5

In PAPO's cell, 1991.
PAPO examines his hands in the
florescent light of his cell.

PAPO: They got bad soap in this place. My hands are never real clean. You know the skin around my nails looks so dark—like it belongs to somebody else—somebody who bleeds from there. I used to help my Ma cut up vegetables sometimes. She hated cutting vegetables. She said she din't like their smell on her. That the smell of peppers would get into her blood and then when she peed or shit you could smell it—the peppers. But I thought, damn that sounds better than shit-smelling shit—You know what I mean? So me I loved to cut up those things. But it din't work on me like that. I guess you know that.

(PAPO moves his hands into the shadows outside his cell. GUY NEXT DOOR takes his hand and begins to file PAPO's nails with an emery board.)

PAPO: I thought they wouldn't let you have a nail file in a prison.

GUY: A file, no. But an emery board won't get you through any doors—even though it is an essential tool. Never underestimate the power of good grooming.
(As HE continues to file PAPO's nails, GUY begins to sing, "The Bare Necessities" from Disney's "The Jungle Book" a la Louis Armstrong.)

"Look for the bare necessities,
the simple, bare necessities.

Forget about your worries and your strife.
I mean, the bare necessities, mother nature's recipes,
grin and bare necessities of life."

PAPO: That was a good movie.

GUY: Yeah. But I liked "Cinderella" better. More
magic. There.
>   (HE tries to give PAPO his hand back,
>   but PAPO doesn't let go.)
All done.

PAPO: The only thing better than having your nails
filed is having your hair washed. My sister used to
wash mines. Maggie had great hands. The kind that
feel every knot and unknot it. Like yours.
>   (PAPO holds GUY's hand in a tight handshake.)
Thanks, man.

GUY: Sure. Anytime. The sound of the nail file filing
away always mellows me out.

PAPO: I like that sound because it cuts the silence.
And you know something real is happening.
Something you can touch.
>   (HE gives GUY's hand one
>   last squeeze and pulls away.)
When's your date?

GUY: In the Spring.

PAPO: You got some time then. I was set for this
month, but it got delayed because I got sick. So it'll
probably be November or December now. My lawyer
gave me the date, but I keep forgetting it.

GUY: Some things are better that way.

PAPO: Nah. Always better to remember…
*(Pause; HE lets his hand wander down to his crotch and
holds it there between his legs.)*
And you know what? Especially in the case of pussy,
because women remember so much more about dick
than we do about pussy that if you don't remember
any little detail, like—it was yay deep, or yay wet, or
she came yay many times. And yo, she likes the
horizontal flick not the vertical thrust. And yay, and
yo, on and on like that.
Don't you think?

GUY: Women are complicated that way. They have
expectations.

PAPO: Yeah. Guys don't have that. Expectations.
(Pause)
I thought they would let me have some books at least.
(Pause)

Maggie used to tell me stories. Right from her head.
Always cooled me out.

GUY: *(As HE tells his story the sound of a solo alto sax
plays in the background.)* Once upon a time, a long time
ago, there was a dinosaur named Jo-Jo, who played the
alto sax in an all dinosaur band. He was a hip cat
Bronto-dino who only hung with other leaf-eaters until
he fell for Gladys and her liquid chocolate eyes. Like
all of the other T-Rexes, she had real bad eyesight and
only ate meat. They made an instant electric
connection when their frames touched. He wore
shades because he played jazz and the ladies coming
to his club expected him to wear the night on his eyes.
Gladys wore light blue horn-rimmed glasses with little
sparkly jewels at the tips that made her eyes shimmer
and shake like morning sunbeams.
*(As GUY continues to tell his story,
PAPO curls up on his bed and listens.)*
He would never kill anything that was alive and
Gladys thought everything alive was hers to eat. Until
she met Jo-Jo and it was love at first note. When she
heard the sound of his saxophone, it made her forget
all about meat. But in the beginning, Jo-Jo wasn't too
sure about Gladys. He thought she might have eaten
some of his relatives, but still there was something
special about this girl. Oh, yeah!

(LULU enters wearing the horn-rimmed glasses and sits at the edge of PAPO's bed. SHE gently rubs his head like she is washing his hair.)

He couldn't get Gladys out of his mind so he decided to drop his juice on her egg sac. And Gladys, being a Latin dinosaur, got pregnant the first time they made sweet delicious prehistoric jam. A family! It was something Jo-Jo dreamed about, but it gave Gladys nightmares. What if she couldn't control herself and ate the baby she and Jo-Jo conjured from their magic love?? Every night Gladys lay awake staring at the egg about to hatch and thought about not eating it. Was it possible? Could she change the way of her tribe? The fate of her happiness lay in the life of one little dino-babe. And what if her baby was more like her than him and ate her father? Those questions would soon be answered for the ripe egg began to quake and slowly crack...

(PAPO sighs deeply and continues to sleep.
LULU exits.)

I wish I could fall asleep like that. But I'm the type that needs to stay up and watch the egg.

(Lights cross to ED & LULU's apartment.)

ACT TWO/SCENE 6

In ED & LULU's apartment in Darien, CT, 1991.
THEY are watching TV and eating popcorn.
On the TV is the sound of a music video, "Let's Talk About
Sex" by Salt N Pepa. THEY watch in silence for a moment,
exchanging amused glances.

LULU: *(Moving to sit closer to ED)* I like this song.

ED: Uh, huh.
                    (Pause)
Isn't Star Trek on now?

LULU: Dance with me.

ED: Uhnuhn.
             (SHE pulls him up off the couch.)
Man!
             (ED starts to do his one dance step,
                a modified twist.)

LULU: You are the only person I know who actually
still does the twist.

ED: If you want me to dance with you then you better
be nice.

LULU: I think it's adorable.

ED: *(Pulling her to the couch onto his lap)* That's enough.

LULU: When I was a little girl, I had this recurring dream that I was a featured dancer on Soul Train. I'd be dancing down the line and do some amazing moves that defied gravity and then some handsome boy would start dancing with me and we would be in perfect sync. Like we were twins or something, and then he would go to kiss me and then I would see my brother's face.

ED: Kind of a spell breaker, huh?

LULU: My brother always knew where I was. It sounds weird now. But it never felt weird then. Like we shared the same mental space. If I wanted to see the sunset over in Crotona Park, he would meet me there, and we never said anything about going. I would be in the library and he would be hanging out with his boys down the street and suddenly we'd both find ourselves in the park, watching the sun disappear. Don't you think that's weird?

ED: Define weird. Eerie? Strange? Otherworldly?

LULU: It is really hard living with a human thesaurus.

ED: I'm serious. How do you define it? How did it make you feel when he showed up in the park?

LULU: Safe.

ED: Sounds like he loved you. He probably still does. There's nothing weird about love.

LULU: You never met my brother.
> *(Lights cross to PAPO's cell.)*

ACT TWO/SCENE 7

In PAPO's cell.
PAPO is trying to teach the GAS STATION
ATTENDANTS how to shoot a gun.
The actor, who plays all the GAS STATION
ATTENDANTS, sits behind him. When PAPO changes
which ATTENDANT HE is speaking to HE shifts position.
The ATTENDANT stays in one place, but his voice changes
each time he speaks. Perhaps it is amplified or distorted each
time with a microphone. In PAPO's head all the GAS
STATION ATTENDANTS are in the room with him. HE
cannot distinguish one from the other except by voice.
PAPO never makes eye contact.

PAPO: With shotguns, it's important to hold it close to your body so that it don't jump when you pull the trigger. This keeps it more balanced and easier to hold for longer periods of time. If you wanna be ready

to shoot, you have to keep it locked into your body—
like another arm. And then you don't get no surprises.

FIRST GAS STATION ATTENDANT:*(With a stutter)* I
preferred handguns. Ssshotguns are so ha-hard to load
and not as accurate a ssshoot.

PAPO: But the good thing about shotguns is that you
will hit the target—maybe not exactly where you
planned to, but you will hit it.

(*JOSÉ enters from the shadows to stand beside the GAS
STATION ATTENDANT.*)

JOHN, LAST GAS STATION ATTENDANT: Yeah.
You hit it alright. But the smell stays on your hands-—
of the gunpowder.

JOSÉ: I like clean hands.

JOHN, LAST GAS STATION ATTENDANT: That's
why I never liked working in a gas station. Always
had the smell of work on me.
Hands that smell like gasoline give people headaches.
The ladies don't like it at all, amigo.

PAPO: It's like a high for me. That smell takes me
places. Places I could only go in my dreams. There
was no place I could really go.

JOSÉ: But that's what I gave you.

PAPO: A chance to go on a trip to my own island. This island was surrounded by gasoline and I could light a match and make it all burn—anytime…anytime I wanted.

JOSÉ: I had the match.

PAPO: I controlled the flame.

SECOND GAS STATION ATTENDANT: But you can't really have power over fire, Mister.

JOSÉ: That's where you were wrong.

ALL the GAS STATION ATTENDANTS & JOSÉ: Fire is stronger than everything.

PAPO: I tried—I was trying—

THIRD GAS STATION ATTENDANT: Yeah. You tried, pal. But you couldn't get close to the fire.

JOSÉ: You were already burning up.

PAPO: All I saw was white.

FOURTH GAS STATION ATTENDANT:
But fire doesn't have any color.

JOSÉ: It just burns.

PAPO: That's how I saw you all.

FIFTH GAS STATION ATTENDANT:
They talk about red-hot and white-hot, but most fire is
kinda blue.

JOSÉ: And it's still real hot.

PAPO: I tried to erase you.

JOSÉ: You can't make all that color go away.

SIXTH GAS STATION ATTENDANT:
There's too much history behind it.
Too much already burned.

PAPO: You're not real.

JOSÉ: I can only speak for myself.

SEVENTH GAS STATION ATTENDANT:
I sure the fuck was real. I had tickets to see AC/DC in
concert that Friday at the Agora in Cleveland. I was

gonna take my girlfriend, Tina. She likes that stuff more than I do. I think she was planning to break up with me—until I got those tickets.

PAPO: You have to do things for women.

JOSÉ: That's the truth.

EIGHTH GAS STATION ATTENDANT:
I gave Melody so much free gas until she married me.

PAPO: I don't need to know that.

NINTH GAS STATION ATTENDANT:
I was real too. And I had a kid. My baby boy had the biggest smile on his face all the time. I thought he was retarded the way he smiled so much. But the doctor said he was just happy.

PAPO: It's hard to believe that kids can be that happy.

TENTH GAS STATION ATTENDANT:
My kid is a terror—

JOSÉ: —just like his Pa.

TENTH GAS STATION ATTENDANT:
He's only four but he has about five girlfriends already. Women fall for those bad boys.

PAPO: Some bad boys. I was never that lucky.

ELEVENTH GAS STATION ATTENDANT:
You probably scared them away with all that
darkness.

PAPO: What do you mean?

TWELFTH GAS STATION ATTENDANT:
He means you look like one scary mother-fucker.

PAPO: I like that look.

THIRTEENTH GAS STATION ATTENDANT:
Yup. I shoulda seen you coming.

PAPO: But you didn't.

JOSÉ: Uhnuhn. Me neither.

FOURTEENTH GAS STATION ATTENDANT:
And I was so hungry. You got me right at closing
time. So I was getting ready to go have me some big-
ass dinner. My mother is a great cook. She makes this
chicken thing, that is out of this world.

PAPO: If I had let you eat something —

FIFTHTEENTH GAS STATION ATTENDANT:
Better to go hungry. Then there's still a hope for
something.

PAPO: What kind of something?

SIXTEENTH GAS STATION ATTENDANT
What he means is that it hurts less when you still think
you got plans.

PAPO: Like if—

SEVENTEENTH GAS STATION ATTENDANT: What
he means is that you weren't the last thing on his
mind.

PAPO: So then—

LAST GAS STATION ATTENDANT:
What he means is that you couldn't take that last
memory away, amigo. And that's like hope.

PAPO: I'm not sorry.

ALL THE GAS STATION ATTENDANTS & JOSÉ: We
know.

(JOSÉ lies down in front of PAPO.)

PAPO: My father—

(A light comes up on JOSÉ lying in a pool of blood.)

ALL THE GAS STATION ATTENDANTS:
We know.
(The light slowly fades on JOSÉ.)
History.

(Lights cross to LULU & ED in bed.)

ACT TWO/SCENE 8

LULU & ED in bed.
ED sleeps, LULU stares at the ceiling.
SHE is silent for a time and then SHE speaks.

LULU: What does it mean when they say that the
Universe is expanding?

ED: All the matter of the Universe was one and then it
became unstable sending all of its pieces out.

LULU: The big bang.

ED: Since then all these pieces have been pointing
away from this explosion—expanding outward.
Eventually it will come together again, imploding the
Universe. Then, maybe, the process will begin again.

(Pause)

LULU: Can you hear music in Space?

ED: Probably not. I mean, you might hear a natural music—like air rushing through your ears—

LULU: Like listening to a seashell. But people cut themselves on seashells.
(Pause)
Can there be a rip in the Universe?

ED: Yeah. They're called black holes.

LULU: How do they work?

ED: They pull the stars around them into their magnetic field and then suck them in.

LULU: They eat stars? That's like eating light. They sound like serial killers—walking around preying on the innocent, sucking them into their darkness—are black holes really black?

ED: Yeah. Because they're so dense that no light escapes them.

LULU: Yeah. It's exactly like that.

ED: What?

LULU: My brother. And me.
                    (Pause)
If I stay with you, I'm gonna pull you in too.

ED: I don't go anywhere I don't want to go.
          (Taking her hand and pulling her to him)

LULU: People have magnetic fields too.
                    (Pause)
When things on Earth die, I wonder what happens to
the Universe. Like does the order of things change
and so the balance gets messed up, bringing us closer
to the time when things reverse? We could explode
like tomorrow. Maybe that's what they mean by light
year, because as we get lighter we get closer to
exploding.

ED: Light means fast. I was taught that it was like
going around the equator seven times in a second.
That's a light year.

LULU: That's fast.
                    (Pause)
How do we know that we're not on the end of that last
rotation? This could be it. So long, pal.
          (SHE puts out her hand and

HE takes it and shakes it.)

ED: *(HE takes her hand and tucks it under his cheek and closes his eyes.)* We better get married soon. Before the explosion.

LULU: I'm going away for a few days.

ED: When?

LULU: Saturday.

ED: Today's Thursday.

LULU: I know. I just decided.

ED: Are you going to tell me where?

LULU: To see my brother.

ED: Oh. Good.
                    (Pause)
Shouldn't I come—

LULU: No. I gotta do this alone.

ED: Okay. For how long?

(Silence)

LULU: I'm hoping for a light year.

ED: That's one hundred and eighty-six thousand miles per second times the number of seconds in a year—just in case you were gonna ask.

LULU: *(Pause as SHE looks out the window)*
I like how we can sit in our bed and see stars.

ED: *(Taking her hand and pulling her to him)* Yes.

LULU: Wait.

*(LULU lights a candle and turns off the lights as THEY
hold each other and
stare out the window at the stars.)*

*(Lights cross dimly to PAPO's cell. JOSÉ still lies in the
pool of blood. PAPO sees MARIA who kicks and rolls JOSÉ
out of the cell and begins to wash her feet in the pool of
JOSÉ's blood. ELIZABETH enters and stares at them for a
moment. Then ELIZABETH dips her feet in it too.
PAPO watches the MOTHERS.)*

ELIZABETH: Mmmhmm. There's nothing like a good foot soak. I always say. Trying to raise a family and keep 'em in a straight line—that's the hardest work.

But I'm rewarded sometimes at night. With some water. When my boy was little he used to rub my feet after and then I'd toss the water over the top of him. "There you go, John the Baptist," I'd tell him. And he'd scream and run—he hated taking a bath. But I always got him with my foot water. Thinking back on it, it don't sound too sanitary but, well, we used everything we had for everything we could. That's how it is. I didn't blame nobody. Not even his son-of-a-bitch mother deflowering father. No. That's not me. Not who I used to be anyway. No one to pull me and my boy outta any hole if we fall in.

(SARAH enters. SHE has the one-eyed teddy bear tucked into her shirt as if SHE's breastfeeding it. SHE sees MARIA and ELIZABETH and moves to sit with her feet in the blood also.)

SARAH: I don't mind warm water—like this. Some people only want fresh, but I like it to stand around for a while. Getting all thick with the air. Some people don't like thick, but for me it's good. I used to fill the tub before I went out to get our check and Isaac used to mind it for me. I could always count on my Isaac to keep things right in the house.
(Pause)
But he spent too much time alone in there. He never played except by himself.
(Pause)

He loved trains. We lived right next to one, so he pretended that the train was his train and he was guiding all these rich people to their jobs. "Without me, they'd never get there," he tole me. I had to smile about that. If the rich people knew some little black boy was guiding them, they'd probably start commuting by boat. Better left a secret, between me and my boy.

MARIA: Families gotta keep some things secret.

ELIZABETH: This is like one of them crazy spas or something. The three of us here.

SARAH: There's a lot of us. We just can't see them. We don't look.

ELIZABETH: I don't wanna see 'em all.

MARIA: I pray for them sometimes. I pray for all of us.

(The MOTHERS all pray silently in their own way, as PAPO begins to pray too by dipping his finger in his father's blood and adding faces to his map of Puerto Rico, many faces. As the lights go from candlelight to florescent, the MOTHERS exit taking JOSÉ with them never to return.
PAPO moves slowly to his bed and lies down.)

Lights cross to the apartment in Darien.)

ACT TWO/SCENE 9

In the apartment in Darien, CT.
Late night.
ED is practicing opening and closing a small velvet jewelry
box which contains an engagement ring. Finally, LULU
steps out of the bathroom dressed for her trip to Ohio, a
packed suitcase in her hands.

LULU: You still up?

ED: Yeah.

LULU: How come?

ED: Waiting for you.

LULU: How come?

ED: They say three's the charm.
   (HE whips out the jewelry box and accidentally tosses the
                ring out the window.
        THEY both run to the window and look out.)
Oh, shit!
            (THEY pull back from the window.)
I think that raccoon got it.

LULU: Yes.

ED: Do you mean it?

LULU: Yes, except…

ED: What?

LULU: My brother murdered eighteen people and is dying of AIDS on Death Row. Maybe it was twenty people. I'm not sure. I'm not sure I'm not my brother.

ED: In Florida?

LULU: Ohio.

ED: Why didn't you tell me before?

LULU: I thought you'd run screaming out the door.

ED: I'm not in love with your brother.

LULU: You don't know who you're in love with! I've been lying to you, Ed. Don't you get it?!

ED: Don't you?! You're not him. And I'm not my grandmother. Sure there's pieces of them inside us, but then there's this new piece, this piece we made together out of all that stuff.

LULU: You don't care?

ED: Of course I care. I care about you. Why don't you care about you too? That's the part that breaks my heart. You always gotta make it so hard to love you.

LULU: It is hard.

ED: Not for me. Not ever.

(Lights come up on PAPO's cell.)

ACT TWO/SCENE 10

In PAPO's cell, 1991.
LULU visits PAPO.
It is her first and last visit.
PAPO is on his bed looking very sick.
LULU is dressed in upscale chic.
SHE examines all of PAPO's drawings, a Puerto Rican flag
with a Rheingold beer can in the star, and the large picture
window where PAPO has drawn palm trees and beaches
and sleek convertibles and many faces.

LULU: I like your paintings, Jesús.

PAPO: Yeah. I go by Papo now.

LULU: That was Papi's dog's name—the one he always made sing to us. The one you hated.

PAPO: I didn't hate that dog. I was the one who fed it.

LULU: Okay. Whatever. Are they going to starve you to death? You look like a stick.

PAPO: They give me food—I just can't eat it.
  (HE *fingers the material of her suit.*)
Nice. You look so different now. Like a woman. Like you work in a bank or something.

LULU: I do work in a bank. I'm saving up to go back to school.

PAPO: What for?

LULU: To learn about poetry. I always wanted to and now I can.

PAPO: Wow…That's crazy.

LULU: Poetry is crazy? I guess you would know.

PAPO: I mean crazy good.

LULU: Oh.

(PAPO has a coughing fit. LULU wipes the blood HE coughed up off his lips and chin.)

PAPO: Some people are scared to touch me. Especially if there's blood.

LULU: Whatever. Don't worry about it, Je(sus)— Papo. Papo. What an ugly name. People call me Lulu now.

PAPO: Yeah? That's an ugly name too. Thank you for coming out.

LULU: Whatever. You know I've been meaning to. And they won't let you have more than one visitor a month and Ma always wanted to come…Anyway…Now I can see you.

PAPO: You almost missed out.
                     (Pause)
How was the funeral? I begged them to let me go.

LULU: It was beautiful. And really sad.
                     (Pause)

I gotta ask you something. Did you—

PAPO: You don't want to know that.

LULU: I was there. That first time. When you first got the idea. I helped, didn't I?

PAPO: No. It's all mine.
                    (Pause)
Do you remember how one Halloween Papi painted a jack o'lantern face on that big lamp in the living room?

LULU: Man, that was so embarrassing. And then the ink didn't come off and we had it staring at us through Thanksgiving, Christmas. All the way until Easter, when I managed to break it.

PAPO: I thought I broke it.

LULU: Yeah? Maybe. Maybe we did it together.

PAPO: Like we did most things.

LULU
We wanted to be the Prince and Princess of Puerto Rico. Taino warriors back from the ashes.

PAPO: Stupid. We were such stupid kids.

LULU: I don't believe you did all that.

PAPO: I do. When they stop my heart, I'll believe it even more.
(*Pause*)
What was Mami wearing?

LULU: I put her in that low-cut green silk dress. The one she bought and Papi never let her wear.

PAPO: She liked that I bet.

LULU: Can I—can I bring you something from home?

PAPO: From home? Where's that? No. Nothing. They won't let you put anything nice on me anyway.

LULU: Right.

PAPO: You can go if you want to.

LULU: I don't want to go.

PAPO: Yeah, you do. You started looking at your watch.

LULU: Since you left home, I always look at my watch.

PAPO: Oh.

(*Pause*)

Are you married now? Mami said you was gonna—

LULU: No.

PAPO: Don't you love him?
LULU: Yeah. Maybe. I don't wanna talk about it.

PAPO: We gotta talk about something. Why'd you come? After all these years, you ain't come. What you need? To tell me you hate me. I know that already.

LULU: I don't hate you, Papo.

PAPO: Why'd you come? Did Mami make you promise or something?

LULU: I came because my brother was a sweet, gentle boy. And I wanted to find out what happened to him.

PAPO: Can't change the facts, Maggie.

LULU: You scared of dying?

PAPO: No. I'm scared of not dying. I need the rest.

LULU: You always was hard to keep up with.

PAPO: Yeah. But you managed. You could always slow me down with your words. You put them together so pretty. Making pictures with them. Like your tongue was a paintbrush and your spit the paint.

LULU: That mess sounds nasty.

PAPO: Not to me.

LULU: Were you sick before—

PAPO: I don't know. But they tested me in here. That's when I found out.   It din't make no difference really…since I was already gonna die. Except I miss tasting things. I lost that first. I don'understand it but it goes like that sometimes. Weird, the things you lose, huh?

LULU: Real weird.

> *(LULU takes PAPO's hand, noticing the torn flesh around his fingers.)*

PAPO: I tear at my fingernails until I bleed so I can draw on the walls. Sometimes I draw you.
The other day, I put you right there, standing under those trees looking at the moon.

LULU: You did?

(PAPO nods and THEY continue
to hold hands in silence.)
I'm sorry. That I never came before.

PAPO: Yeah…But I knew you was gonna come.

LULU: How did you know?

(PAPO takes four envelopes from under his bed, and spreads
them on the floor in front of LULU.)

PAPO: *(Referring to each letter by year and reading what*
he wrote on each envelope.
They are quotes from LULU's letters.)
Nineteen eighty-seven: "You're not my brother
anymore."
Nineteen eighty-eight: "I missed these subways. They
smell like lechon."
Nineteen eighty-nine: "I just met a guy who loves me
for me. Must be retarded."
Nineteen ninety: "You're breaking Mami's heart."

LULU: You saved those?

PAPO: Been waiting for nineteen ninety-one. I ask the
guard everyday.

LULU: I'm sorry—

PAPO: No. Don't be. It's good to wait for something. Keeps you…going. You was always like that for me.
(Taking LULU's hands.)
You were always my hope. Like you were gonna be somebody and I was gonna get to say, "Yup that's my sister." Everything good that I coulda been, you are. You had to come. So I could see something good that was a part of me. That's the only way to find peace.

LULU: I can't do nothing for you.

PAPO: Sure you can. Letting me look at you. Feeling your voice on my skin, instead of just inside my head. Just keep talking. That's all I want.

(PAPO closes his eyes.)
LULU: There's gonna be a full moon tonight.

PAPO: That's just what I wanted. Tell me a story about the moon.

LULU: I can't.

PAPO: You used to be able to tell a story about anything.

LULU: Moon stories always have monsters in them.

PAPO: So?

LULU: I don't want to tell those stories anymore.

PAPO: Maybe the monster can die in this one.

LULU: But they come back. They always come back.

PAPO: Not if you let them do what they want to do. I think Monsters like to lay under a tree and taste Summer rain pouring through those sweet leaves. Takes their minds off the hunger.

LULU: You tell one.

PAPO: I only know one story…
It was a fucked up time, when everything was dark and shitty. When a man couldn't prove he was alive without spilling blood. And three little boys saw this and kept seein' it, and seein' it, and they tried to close their eyes—but when they did—their fear filled up their throats so they couldn't breathe. They each waited for the sleep that never came.
What did come was the day they each had to walk the burning path.
The first one chose not to move—to stay a young boy forever. He turned to ashes and fed the fire. The second one chose to walk over the hot lava—he walked above the ground with his special feet meant not to take any heat.

And the third chose to travel below those hot rocks making the road buckle and cave—until he felt those footsteps above him—crushing him—so he reached through the earth and pulled the second one down to his level.

Then none of them was breathing anymore. Finally, all were back to where they came from.

And what about that?!…The miracle was that it was the same place.

And they all cried for freedom.

LULU: I want you back the way you used to be.

(LULU begins to cry.)

PAPO: For me, there ain't no goin'back. But you…you have time.

GUY: *(From the shadows of his cell, overlapping with PAPO's last line)* It's time.

(PAPO pulls LULU's wedding dress from under his bed. PAPO helps LULU dress in the wedding gown. Finally, HE pulls the veil out and helps LULU put it on. PAPO kisses her.
Then HE pulls the veil over her face. The lights come up on LULU's mirror as PAPO takes LULU's arm and walks her back to her mirror as if he's walking her down the aisle.

PAPO turns away from her and LULU watches him move away. GUY enters, dressed in a sky blue guayabuera shirt with clouds painted on it and dark glasses—like a hip human version of a Magritte painting. GUY meets PAPO as PAPO begins to collapse, catches him, and carries him off into the darkness.)

LULU: *(SHE lifts her veil, then SHE speaks.)*
Once upon a time, my brother, who could never reach the moon, turned into a Chupacabra, filling himself up with the liquid rage—that he knew before he could even speak. Its burning red edges finally burst from his fingertips turning him into flames. He burned souls into the night, hoping it would make him one with the moon. He shines now in all that light.

(Silence. LULU studies her image in the mirror. SHE adjusts her veil and her dress. SHE traces the scar on her leg with her fingertips. We hear an oboe and a cello play the music from SARAH's "Little Boy Clouds" song.)

LULU: It's about time.

(LULU checks her own breath against the glass of the mirror, as the night sky in the background fills with something like the Northern Lights. LULU turns to watch

the light show of stars and then turns to look at the door out of her dressing room.)

(Lights fade to black.)

THE END

FROM THE COUNTRY TO THE COUNTRY OF THE BRONX:

Da bronx rocks: A SONG

This piece was commissioned by Mabou Mines as part of an event entitled, *Song For New York: What Women Do While Men Sit Knitting*.
Music by Lisa Gutkin.
Performed by Elisa Bocanegra
With LaTanya Hall, Simotra Houston, Susan McKeown & Sophia Holman.

Developed with the help of a Rockefeller MAP grant and with workshops through New York Theater Workshop at Vassar College (6/05), Voice and Vision at Bard College (7/05),
Sundance@White Oak, (FL), 1/07, directed by Ruth Maleczech.

First Production: Mabou Mines, (NY), July 2007, at Gantry State Park in the East River, directed by Ruth Maleczech.

Excerpt from Talmud: Ta'anith, 2:1.

Thanks to Dana Mock-Muñoz de la Luna.

Intro:
(Note: Words in [brackets] are translations.)
SINGER or CHORUS: (Spoken in a whisper, muttered under music)
Metamorphosed deep-oceanic shale,
Metamorphosed Proterozoic to Lower Paleozoic rock,
"biotite-plagioclase-quartz-muscovite-kyanite-sillimanite-garnet" schist.

SINGER: *(Sung)*
The day I drowned
My eyes felt like this,
Wind-whipped river kicking up tears—
A wet air, face-drenched mist.
I'm in mourning
For my sister's soul.
My mourning's a place
beneath my feet.
El luto es una piedra
[Mourning is a stone}
Dentro de mi corazón.
{Inside my heart.]
Piedras perdidas en la memoria.
[Stones lost in memory.]
Piedras perdidas, en el río.
[Stones lost in the river.]
No la llores más, mi madre,
[Don't cry for her anymore, my mother.]
No la llores más.

[Don't cry for her anymore.]
Sitting on a hill of Inwood Marble—
green satin—
across from that child Manhattan.
Manhattan—so full of schist.
And now footsteps land on my chest.
Where do the scars of history rest?
Cutting class to spy the view:
Wondering how many feet polished
This old rock like new—
Kicking stones into this Harlem riverbed—
Defying white man's history of "don't you tread."
A stone pretends to be an arrow,
In my sadness-moistened hands.
Will my people leave treasures
buried in this new land?
Sung Refrain:
¿Patria, dónde estas?
[Country, where are you?]
¿Es esto lo que nos enseña la historia?
[Is this what history teaches us?]
No la llores más, mi madre,
[Don't cry for her anymore, my mother.]
No la llores más.
[Don't cry anymore.]

Verse One: *(V. 1,2 & 6 could have same melodies inspired by Lebanese, Cante Jondo, Albanian, Native American, Puerto Rican aguinaldo/ wailing/mourning songs)*

Sung:

At P.S. 58, I was told:

The Siwanoy Indians left us no word for this place.

In 1639, here comes the White race.

There are names though

That I've heard:

Mother Rock cries

Keskeskeck.

My mother cries too,

But only when she thinks we can't hear her.

Jonas Bronck, a Swede,

though some say a Dane.

A sea captain from the west,

carved into the Deep South

of your stone breast,

Near this "River of high bluffs" —

beside our Aquahung.

They gave your river his name.

when Jonas died dreaming—

dreaming of pale-skinned Galician women—

like the mother of my mother's bisabuela

    [great-grandmother]

I'm told. No one writes it down.

She died imagining love. He died imagining her.

I imagine her too, my skin stained with her vision of

the Sun.

Sung Refrain:

No lo llores más, mi Cielo.

[Don't cry for him {the Sun} anymore, my sky.]

No lo llores más.

[Don't cry anymore for him.]

Verse Two:
Sung:
Daughters' shoes are filled

With tears for their mothers—

Walking in her sorrow,

Pressing despair into others.

It's 1643,

and already nothing is free.

Anne Hutchinson,

why'd they name a parkway after you?

Did you stand here,

holding your child's hand,

exiled by Pilgrims—

dreaming of religious freedom?

Came —no fear.

God on your side.

Your God on your side.

Came without asking

the chief who mourned—

a wife whose scalp

was torn from her skull—

by a White man.

Chief Wampage buried a hatchet in your head—

taking your name when you were dead.

He also took your child, Susannah.

Annhook needed a new wife.

Spoken:

Reigning over "Lapechwahacking"—his tribe's blood

seeping into stone—

Annhook signs away his heart—parts with Susannah

and his half-breed son.

Little William—as his white family named him—

looked just like his father.

Little William—dreamed of an island filled with others

like him.

Sung: (A musical change)

I dream of an island like that—

An island where my father slept in a burlap bag once

filled with grain—

The island he left to find his wife and live without

pain.

Carrying photographs to remind him

of people whose names were already forgotten.

Faces with all races traced onto their dusty lines.

¿Patria dónde estás?

[Country, where are you?]

Does anyone find home again?

Sung Refrain:
Piedras perdidas en la memoria.

[Stones lost in memory.]

Piedras perdidas en el río.

[Stones lost in the river.]

Piedras que se quedan atrás con el *coquí.

[Stones that stayed behind with the coquí.

(*treefrog only in P.R.)]

Verse Three:

Spoken:

Imagining the prayers of the lost,

Stolen from their homes in 1760.

Chanting rhythmically over music inspired by Afro-Cuban,

Yoruban, Santeria, call & response:

Biko, omba dua.. Eleggua.

[*translation: *Please, pray. Eleggua: the orisha of the*

crossroads, honored at the beginning and end of all

ceremonies, He makes communication possible between the human and spirit world.]

Jindé. Eleggua.

[*Arise. Drum/Dance/the rhythm of life]

Tí jindé. Eleggua..

[*Arose. Drum/Dance/the rhythm of life.]

Lewis Morris. Jindé lá. [*Arisen.]

Sovereign rights. Kandé lá. [*Awoken.]

Declaration of Independence—Eleggua.

They fight for freedom—

Mó má—That I understand. [*I know.]

Too many slaves.

That I understand.

English and French take.

That I understand.

Louis invites George over the river.

Tory captives to deliver.

Naval strategy to plan—

That I understand.

A musical change:

Washington protects Manhattan from the English fleet,

walking the Morrisania streets—

into gun-fire, without blinking.

Securing the Bronx and its waters,

the first bullet-facing gangsta'

kept his head in a slaughter—

even the Indians were impressed.

Spoken:

That I understand.

By the time the British landed at Pell's Point,

once known as Lapechwahacking,

the Algonquin nation was gone.

I don't understand.

Can hope be born from disappearing?

A man's suicide upon the temple fence,

Turns a synagogue into a Pentacostal church.

Sung Refrain:
Piedras perdidas en la memoria.

[Stones lost in memory.]

Piedras perdidas en el río.

[Stones lost in the river.]

Piedras que se quedan atrás con el coquí. [Stones that stayed behind with the coquí.]

Verse Four:

Spoken over rhythms from an instrument such as the pandaretta or congas. Perhaps inspired by Bomba:
This is what I was taught about these once cobbled

stone—

streets where fortunes were sought and sown.

The Nineteenth Century embraces industry ending the

country life.

Edgar Allen Poe watches Virginia die of T.B.—his

cousin-wife.

The Civil War orders the new Irish men to kill or be

sent home again.

The new coal burning elevated train

sprinkles Third Avenue with coal-dust rain.

Bet on a horse at the "Grand Concourse"—

the widest paved street in the New World's complete.

The Borough of "The Bronx" is finally created,

When the 23rd and 24th Wards are mated.

Yiddish lives in the newspapers the intellectuals of

Kelly Street write.

Jews escape the pogroms of Eastern Europe to

continue their freedom fight.

100,000 people attend Sholem Aleichem's wake at his

Kelly Street home—

The man known as the Jewish Mark Twain says a final

Aleichem Sholem.

Trotsky was here.

Arthur Flegenheimer, becomes the Baron of Beer—

as Dutch Schultz—a name to fear.

"The House That Ruth Built" welcomes fans.

Babe Ruth's 60th home run is ran.

Musically begin a move to Mountain Jewish and finally to

Aguinaldo:

The Bronx Public School system does what's right—

hires Sarah L. Delany, the first Black woman to teach

in a school that's white.

Lee Harvey Oswald turns ten, but no one sees his hate.
Colin Powell comes from Trinidad to become Secretary

of State.

The Cross Bronx Expressway blasts through its heart,

neighborhoods destroyed, communities ripped apart.

Urban renewal takes its toll.

Sung Refrain:
Piedras perdidas en la memoria.
[Stones lost in memory.]
Piedras perdidas, en el río.
[Stones lost in the river.]
Piedras que se quedan atrás con el coquí. [Stones that
stayed behind with the coquí.]

Verse Five:

Sung as an Aguinaldo:

One eighteen-year old girl from the coquí's land,

Works in a dress factory and dreams of sand.

Spoken over music:

She meets a slender man who plays the guitar,

He writes her a song and their history is born.

They marry and teach three little girls to sing—

Ten, two and one—a family's begun.

She sews red trim onto curtains already hung.

In an apartment covered in crumbling paint,

He tells them stories of *chupacabras and saints.

[*goat-suckers:mythological beasts that drain

 animals—and tourists of their blood.]

They wanted to spin straw into gold,

Another American dream marked sold.

Scraping paint from the walls—

Covering beige with sky blue—

he works till his two-year old falls.

She and I had eaten flakes of lead.

She ate more—I was lucky, they said.

Sung/Cried/Gritos/Cante Jondo/High elongated ripple-effect

wailing:

Él lloró.   [He cried.]

Ella rezó.   [She prayed.]

Spoken no music:

Pain etched the lining of her skin.

She prayed. She asked for a miracle.

Spoken over music:

Three girls once well—now one must remain

in a Pell's Point—no, Pelham Bay—hospital wing.

There's a view of the bus stop through her

windowpane.

She'll see us if she could only remember to look.

After months had past,

Sung:

the second child came home,

spending hours—and now years—rocking.

The father worked nights.

The mother worked days.

The mother and father missed each other

In this house laced with sadness.

No way to stitch this fortune back together.

Spoken over music:

The father remembers how the wife used to smile.

The mother remembers how the daughter loved
dresses.

The daughter enjoys flipping through the pages of
books

feeling something she only remembers in her

fingertips.

Books with cloth pages are the best.

In 1965, a fourth child is born.

With her comes some kind of hope and a sort of
freedom.

Sung in a round, acapella, inspired by
madrigals/medieval motets & canciones:

No la llores, Mama. No la llores más.   [Don't cry for
her anymore, Mama.

Mira que tu hija a la gloria va.

Don't cry anymore.

Watch your daughter going to Heaven.]

Spoken:

On our flag it says:

**"FROM THE COUNTRY TO THE COUNTRY OF
THE BRONX"**

Where are we now?

Latitude: forty point eight five north.

Longitude: minus seventy-three point eight six six
west

Verse Six:

Sung with melody similar to V.1 & 2:

The 2000 census claims

4000 farmers from upstate

moved down to the Bronx—

but no one's heard from them of late.

Disappearing into the City's

Only mainland borough,

What could be their fate?

Perhaps they've gone fishing with sticks

harvested from along el río by hand—

The Bronx River is stocked with trout.

You could live off Keskeskeck's land again.

Bathe in Aquahung's waters.

Play the numbers now and then.

Eat jerk chicken and walk through the Zoo.

Smell the roses when the Gardens bloom—

and catch a ball game too.

Sleep on an Orchard Beach dune.

almost no gang activity there—they say.

Visit the only New England fishing village

outside of New England on City Island on the way.

But don't forget to visit some loved ones at Rikers,

okay?

Sung Refrain: {repeat music of earlier refrains}
No lo llores más, mi Cielo.

[Don't cry for him {the Sun} anymore, my sky.]

No lo llores más. [Don't cry anymore for him.]

Spoken over musical change to European inspired music:

In Seville, a gypsy housing project is known as "El Bronx."

In Milan, a tract of empty lots is called "Il Bronx."

A chain of hip-hop clothing stores in Europe is called "The South Bronx."

Here, we're The Bronx. Da Brahhnx.

Up to the Bronx—

The Bronx rocks!

Sung over European/Romanian Gypsy music:

In a Bosnian refugee camp, a brown man runs up to me—:

"You gypsy? You come to gypsy side and I make you tea."

"No, Sir. I'm Puerto Rican from the Bronx."

"No. You gypsy. Bronx come with me."

We had our tea.

You see? Throw one stone into the water and it all
rocks.

Lost Stones,

[Piedras perdidas,]

Stones lost in memory—

no more.

[Piedras perdidas en la memoria, no más.]

Music Out.

Whispered, but not too quietly and with overlapping, spoken

by the CHORUS as in the beginning of the INTRO:

You see? Throw one stone and the water sings—

one child feeling history on her fingertips.

Etched on this rock beneath my feet,

lives ending and lives beginning again.

The Bronx is home.

End for now…

AFTERWORD

My World Made Real

I wanna be a singer. I listen to the radio
all the time and I tell people's fortunes. I
mean, I sing wif the radio and it's like
telling a fortune `cause I can look into
somebody's face and know exactly what
song to sing at them and like it helps
them…I can do that for you, too. Gimme
your hand.

~Miriam in *Miriam's Flowers*, Cruz,
Shattering the Myth, p. 58

At the age of nine, I was certain that I was going to be
a rich and famous actress. I was also certain that I
would move to New York City to live a very
glamorous life and that I would take my mother with
me. I would share my big dreams with her and we
would plan our adventure. I took all of this very
seriously as I wanted nothing more than to see her
happy.

Twenty years later, I am home for the holidays and she
breaks down in tears, telling my brother and me that
she is lonely and unhappy. She can't stand the confines

of her home anymore. I instantly offer to move her in to my small apartment in Amherst, Massachusetts.

> "I am close to New York," I say.
> She shakes her head, "No."

She also refuses my brother's offer to move in with him. He lives nearby and has an extra room. We are both still trying to save her and we are all just as helpless as ever.

I understood from an early age that my mother felt trapped. I am sure that many things about our life made her happy. My father provided a sense of stability and a consistency that I don't imagine she ever knew before. She was one of nine siblings raised single-handedly by her mother in East Oakland. They moved a lot, dodging evictions notices, truant officers, and welfare workers at every turn. She was a young and strikingly attractive woman when she met and quickly married my father. Two years later, I was born and two years after that I had a little brother. My mother's life had changed dramatically in her early 20's and her feelings of isolation and disappointment sank into depression over the next ten years. A darkness settled in around her as did her increasing dependence on alcohol.

In 1995 I was taking a contemporary theater course. My professor had assigned *Shattering the Myth: Plays by Hispanic Women,* edited by Denise Chavez and Linda Feyder (Arte Publico Press, University of Houston, 1992). Miriam of Cruz' *Miriam's Flowers* was a young woman who grew up too fast. To mourn the death of her brother, she carves flowers into her arms and prays to her saints for suffering. She tries be a good daughter and to take care of her alcoholic mother through to the play's tragic end. In the final moments, we see the daughter cradling her deceased mother. Miriam carves roses into her dead mother's body so that she will be recognized as a saint when she gets into heaven.

With *Miriam's Flowers* in front of me, the world as I knew it had new meaning. My world was worthy of writing about and reading about. My world could be reproduced on the stage. The people, the places, the music, the things spoken and those things left unsaid. All of these things were written in a book and I held that book in my hands. The mothers who abandon their daughters, the daughters who love them unconditionally. The fathers present and absent. The children trying so hard to make sense of the world around them. The alcohol, the abuse, the dysfunction, and the hope for something different. The compassion and the humanity that we have for one another even in dire conditions. The hope. My world was made real by her plays. I saw myself and my world reflected back to me with new meaning. I was not alone anymore. If she could write these plays, then I knew that I could do anything.

At that time, I could not have felt more out of place. I had just returned to college as a single mom. I was living on my own and raising my then three-year old daughter. I was in the process of separating from a violent and abusive partner and two years before this I had dropped out of school. Needless to say, I was not a typical college student.

I had little in common with my peers even before I became a mother at age twenty. I was smart and had always done well in school but my life took an unexpected turn when I entered into my first intimate relationship at age 16. For four painful years I was terrorized by a young man that I thought I loved. Growing up, I was the quiet nerdy girl who wanted to fit in…I tried too hard. Throughout grade school, I befriended my teachers in my constant search for approval or any sort of attention from adults and authority figures. As the chasm between my mother and I grew deeper, I began to run toward anyone and anything that would dull the pain of rejection. I learned later that my maternal grandfather was an abusive man and an alcoholic. Even though my grandfather passed away before I was born, his legacy of abuse lingered in my family.

In graduate school, I encountered another Cruz play: *The Have-Little*, published in *Contemporary Plays by Women of Color*, edited by Kathy Perkins and Roberta Uno (Routledge, 1996). Michi and Lillian are two "girl-women" growing up in the mid 1970's in the Bronx. Theirs is a friendship forged out of tenderness and cruelty. Their paths diverge as Lillian's world closes in around her and Michi makes plans to leave for college. Despite all of her hardships, Lillian believes in God and the goodness of mankind. By the end of the play, Michi has said her final goodbye and we are left with Lillian, a young single mom who lovingly assures her bundled-up baby: "We got so much together, Joey…" As they sit in front of the open oven in their small apartment with all of the burners turned up on the stovetop, she hums "Baby mine" as the lights fade. At the University of Massachusetts Amherst, 3000 miles away from everyone and everything I knew and loved, I felt the same sensations all over again. Through Cruz' characters, I felt as if I had been written into existence.

During this time, I read everything I could get my hands on related to Latina/o theater. The dawn of the 21st century ushered in a boom of scholarship and the publication of anthologies of plays by Latina/o writers. This included *Out of the Fringe*, edited by Maria Teresa Marrero and Caridad Svich (Theater Communications Group, 2000), *Latina Performance: Traversing the Stage* by Alicia Arrizón (Indiana University Press, 1999), *Latinas on Stage* by Arrizón and Lillian Manzor (Third Woman Press, Berkeley, 2000) and during Alberto Sandoval-Sánchez and Nancy Saporta Sternbach's *Puro Teatro: A Latina Anthology* (University of Arrizona Press, 2000) and *Stages of Life: Transcultural Performance and Identity in U.S. Latina Theater* (University of Arrizona Press, 2001) These books built on the foundational scholarship and contributions to the field of Latino Theater set down by Jorge Huerta and Alberto Sandoval- Sánchez. As I moved through my studies, I began to shape this material into a course I now teach on the Latina voice in contemporary theater.

With a new job at the University of Massachusetts Amherst and the discovery that she and I had a mutual friend, I found my first opportunity to meet her. I had just been hired in a new dual-hire position as the program curator at New WORLD Theater (NWT) and a member of the dramaturgy faculty in the Department of Theater. NWT was a professional non-profit theater in residence at UMass dedicated to producing and presenting theater by artists of color. In

2005, I invited her to western Massachusetts to interact with young playwrights and respond to their work.

As her self-appointed host for that two-day visit, I learned a great deal and gained a dear friend. I was teaching a course on Latino Theater and asked her to speak to the students as we were reading her play *Fur* in the class. That day she read "Sand" to us. It is the first monologue in her collection of monologues titled *Telling Tales* (Eric Lane, editor, Penguin Books, 1993). Hearing the words aloud, I understood their power in a profound way. Watching her as tears streamed down her face, I had concrete evidence about the healing power of creativity. That day, I learned that it was okay to cry. I learned that it was ok to point out the ways the world had let us down. I also learned that I could continue to love and care for the people who may not have always understood or cared for me in the ways that I needed them to and I learned that I was not alone in this experience.

Telling Tales takes us in and around the neighborhoods of the Bronx with eleven potent monologues. Some of these serve as blueprints for her later work. The closing line from "Sand" makes its way into the opening scene of *The Have-Little* as does the admonishment, "She wasn't supposed to go on the roof." We meet Don José Maria Sotillo, her great-grandfather, and Sharon, her best friend, in the monologues "Yellow Eyes" and "Parchesi." These characters return in the full-length play *Yellow Eyes*, published for the first time in this anthology. With "Fire" and "Rats" we understand clearly the time and the location of this writing. It is the late 60's and early 70's, the Bronx of Cruz' childhood and she is writing about the devastation she sees all around her. Jeff Chang details this history as he chronicles the birth of hip hop in his book *Can't Stop Won't Stop: A History of the Hip Hop Generation* (St. Martin's Press, 2005). Suffice it to say that of the many factors at play, urban renewal policies and the tactics of benign neglect along with a devastating economic downturn meant white flight out of the Bronx and a dive into poverty for those who remained.

By the mid 1970's the South Bronx had lost 600,000 jobs and unemployment among young people had risen to 60 percent (Chang, 13). At this time, ownership of apartment buildings began moving into the hands of slumlords who quickly figured out that they could make more money by burning down buildings than by collecting rent. And the practices of "benign neglect" included letting the Bronx burn, cutting social services, education, health services, the fire department, the police force (Chang, pp 13-16). All of this came to a head in 1977 during a blackout that sent most of New City into darkness for 36 hours. The national attention the Bronx garnered after the looting and the riots of this blackout brought President Carter and Mother

Theresa to the Bronx. Chang writes that while standing amidst the devastation, Carter turned to Patricia Harris, the Secretary of Housing and Urban Development and said "softly, 'See what areas can still be salvaged.'" (p. 17)

Migdalia Cruz understood another kind of salvation and began writing about it with Maria Irene Fornes at INTAR, which she attended from 1984 to 1988 and again in 1990. For Cruz, encouraged by Fornes' charge to "write what you know best," the things to be salvaged were the people and the stories. In an interview for the essay "Violent Inscriptions: Writing the Body and Making Community in Four Plays by Migdalia Cruz," (*Theatre Journal*, The Johns Hopkins University Press, 2000. 51–66) Tiffany Ana Lopez shares an excerpt of an interview with Cruz that addresses criticism she has received from within the Puerto Rican community. Some are not comfortable with her depictions of Puerto Ricans dealing with poverty, homelessness, drug addiction and violence. Cruz' response to this perspective is clear and simple: "These are the people I find interesting and poetic and these are the people I love."

So, Cruz's plays are about pain, suffering, economic injustice, and her central characters are often negotiating highly dysfunctional family lives. The plays collected here and published for the first time are deeply personal and highly poetic, historical in content, and critical of the persistence and prevalence of institutional racism and classism in the United States. But her plays are also about much more and more importantly, she humanizes the intense social and political issues that concern her.

She depicts dreamlike worlds and the emotional connections between her characters drive the action. Each world that she creates for these characters to inhabit demands a fluid and malleable stage space. The mirror where Lulu dresses for her wedding and Papo's prison cell co-exist seamlessly for Cruz in *El Grito del Bronx*. *Salt* takes place "sometime in the near future" and the scenes move quickly and easily to and from "a church, a tavern, a field house, a shabby apartment and a beach" (Cruz, *Salt*, p. 3) and the salt mounds outside of South Chicago. Belilah Love and the children of this play have carved their living spaces in and around the mountain of salt. Past and present occupy the same stage space through the use of memory in *Yellow Eyes* and the play spans just over a century as José Maria recalls his life as a slave in Puerto Rico. The fluidity of *From the Country to the Country of the Bronx: Da Bronx Rocks: A Song* is evident in its title and the movement comes from her powerful blending of her family's personal story with nearly 400 years of Bronx history.

Migdalia Cruz writes about "those things" that one should not talk about, much less put on the stage. Her writing often challenges the reader with its strong images and harsh take on reality. The blood and the guts, her characters' vulnerability, and her courage to explore and expose this vulnerability is difficult to take at times. I walked away from *Salt* the first time I tried to read it. It took me three years to finally sit down and read it in its entirety. The content, however, is tempered by her ability to demonstrate an incredible sense of compassion for her characters in some of the ugliest moments of their lives. The potency of her words and the possibility of connection through such honest ugliness is a worthy reward. She tells the truth and exposes the human condition in its rawest forms and then forces theater practitioners to figure out how to put these stories on the stage. By doing this, she pushes the aesthetics of the American stage and our craft to new horizons. We must rise to her standards and produce these plays. It seems like a daunting task and the number of creative risk takers in our field seems to be shrinking every day. I remain ever hopeful to see more of her work on our stages and I am incredibly thankful for her voice. It helped me find mine.

I started to write stuff down, hoping—if not to
make sense of it, then to at least pay respect to
the memory of it, of us, of a small time in
history when all of us grew up too soon.
~Cruz, artist statement for
The Have-Little, in *Contemporary*
Plays by Women of Color, 106–7.

Priscilla Page

University of Massachusetts-Amherst

Notes on Contributors

MIGDALIA CRUZ has written more than 40 plays and musicals including *Fur, Miriam's Flowers, Another Part Of The House, The Have-Little, Lucy Loves Me, Dreams of Home, Telling Tales, ¡CHE-CHE-CHE!, Latins In La-La Land, Cigarettes and Moby-Dick, Lolita de Lares, Frida: The Story of Frida Kahlo* (libretto) and *Running For Blood: No. 3* (a radio play), that have been produced across the U.S. and in Mexico, Puerto Rico, the U.K., Greece, Canada, Egypt, and Turkey. Maria Irene Fornes' Playwrights' Laboratory at INTAR nurtured her.

New Dramatists sustained her. Latino Chicago Theater Company gave her a safe place to raise her voice. Awards, such as the NEA Fellowship, TCG/Pew Residency, the Sackler Fellowship, the McKnight Fellowship, Massachusetts Cultural Council, Connecticut Arts Commission, Kennedy Center's New Play and twice runner-up for the Susan Smith Blackburn Prize, made her feel appreciated. Support from Sundance, MidWest PlayLabs, Mabou Mines, Mark Taper Forum, Teatro Vista, Monarch Theater, Steppenwolf, and the Lark kept her plays growing. Migdalia holds an MFA degree from Columbia University and a BFA degree from Lake Erie College. She was born and raised in the Bronx. She is currently developing *Two Roberts: A Pirate-Blues Project* at the Lark (NY), and is adapting Petronius' Anti-Nero *Satryricon* to 21ˢᵗ C. America.

PRISCILLA PAGE is a dramaturg and writer whose main interests are new play development and translation. She is currently a member of the dramaturgy faculty in the Department of Theater at the University of Massachusetts Amherst where she is leading the efforts to institute the Multicultural Theater Certificate for undergraduate students. She worked as the program curator at New WORLD Theater, a professional, non-profit multicultural theater in residence at UMass Amherst, for five years. Her duties included serving as the resident dramaturg, overseeing all archival and documentation efforts, managing the Asian American Women Playwrights Archive, and supervising an on-going team of dramaturgy student interns. Her producing/dramaturgy credits include sash & trim written
and performed by Djola Branner and directed by Laurie Carlos, Crossing the Waters, Changing the Air written and directed by Ingrid Askew, and Lydia on the Top Floor written and performed by Terry Jenoure, directed by Linda McInerny. She serves on the national awards committee for the Association of Theater inHigher Education (ATHE) and co-

coordinates the Jane Chambers Playwriting Award through the Women and Theater Program at ATHE.

ALBERTO SANDOVAL-SÁNCHEZ is Professor of Spanish and U.S. Latina/o literature at Mount Holyoke College since 1983. He received his Ph.D. in 1983 at the University of Minnesota. He is both a cultural critic and a creative writer. His bilingual book of poetry New York Backstage/Nueva York Tras Bastidores (Cuarto Propio, 1993) was published in Chile. In 1993 Mount Holyoke College produced his theatrical piece Side Effects, based on his own personal experiences with AIDS. In 1994 he edited a special issue of Ollantay Theater Magazine on U.S. Latina/o theatre and AIDS. He has published numerous articles in books and journals on U.S. Latina/o theatre, Latin American colonial theatre and colonial identity formation, Spanish baroque theatre, Puerto Rican migration, images of Latinas/os in film and on Broadway, Latina/o theatre on AIDS, and Latina theatre and performance. He is the author of José Can You See?: Latinos On and Off Broadway (The University of Wisconsin Press, 1999) and co-editor of Puro Teatro: A Latina Anthology (The University of Arizona Press, 2000, in collaboration with Nancy S. Sternbach from Smith College); followed by a critical study, Stages of Life: Transcultural Performance and Identity in Latina Theatre also in collaboration with Sternbach (Arizona, 2001). He co-edited with Frances

R. Aparicio (University of Illinois, Chicago) a special issue on U.S. Latina/o literature and Culture, Hibridismos Culturales, in 2005 for Revista Iberoamericana, and he also co-edited (Jotopías/Patopías) with Ramón Rivera-Servera (Northwestern University) a special issue on U.S. Latina/o queer theater and performance for Ollantay Theater Magazine (2008). His present research and scholarship center on the staging of monstrosity, enfreakment, queerness, and abjection on Broadway and minority theatre. He is also working on trauma, memory, death, and mourning in Puerto Rican and U.S. Latina/o theatre and cultural performance.

ENDNOTES

for Alberto Sandoval-Sánchez' introduction

[i] See Tiffany Ana López. "Black Opium: An Interview with Migdalia Cruz." In Latinas on Stage." Alicia Arrizón and Lillian Manzor, eds. Berkeley: Third Women Press, 2000; 213.

[ii] "The Universal Dimension of Latino Theater." Review: Latin American Literature and Arts, 62 (2001-03): 12.

[iii] Analola Santana. Una máquina teatral: Sobre el teatro de Migdalia Cruz. Interview. Masters Thesis. Gainesville: University of Florida, 2003; 76.

[iv] The Glass Menagerie. New York: Signet, 1987; 27.

[v] "Artistic Statement." Contemporary Plays by Women of Color: An Anthology. Kathy E. Perkins and Roberta Uno, eds. London: Routledge, 1996; 107.

[vi] "The Universal Dimension;" 12.

[vii] "Sand." Telling Tales: New One-Act Plays. Eric Lane, ed. New York: Penguin, 1993; 1-2.

[viii] See López. "Black Opium;" 214.

[ix] Tiffany Ana López, chapter 23 "Writing Beyond Borders: A Survey of US Latina/o Drama." In A Companion to Twentieth-Century Drama. David Krasner, ed. Malden, MA: Blackwell Publishing, 2005; 381.

[x] Santana; 75.

[xi] See López. "Black Opium;" 209.

[xii] The Have Little, scene16. In Contemporary Plays by Women of Color; 124.

[xiii] "Theses on the Philosophy of History." In Illuminations. New York: Schocken, 1969; 257-258.

[xiv] "Out of the Fringe: In Defense of Beauty." Out of the fringe: Contemporary Latina/Latino Theatre and Performance. Caridad Svich and María Teresa Marrero, eds. New York: Theatre Communications group, 2000; xiii.

xv Kathleen Stewart. A Space on the Side of the Road: Cultural Poetics in an 'Other'America. New Jersey: Princeton University Press, 1996; 12.

xvi Lenora Inez Brown, interviewer. "Writing Religion: Is God a Character in your Plays?" American Theatre, 17, 9 (2000): 30.

xvii "Migdalia's Method: A Memory Playshop." Announcement for workshop in the Bay Area in 2006 circulated by NoPassport.

xviii Alexis Greene. "Migdalia Cruz." In Women Who Write Plays: Interviews with American Dramatists. Hanover: Smith and Kraus, 2001; 110.

xix TheatreForum, 13 (1998): 12.

xx Alexis Greene. "South Bronx Memoirs: Migdalia Cruz Explores her Urban Roots." American Theatre, June (1990): 58..

xxi Greene, Women Who; 115-116.

xxii Puerto Rican Obituary. New York: Monthly Review Press, 1973; 10.

xxiii Greene, Women Who; 120-121.